Snug Harbor Series

Book III

Fiddler's Green

F. L. H. Hudkins

This is a work of fiction. Names, characters, Places and Incidents are the product of the author's imagination or are used fictitiously, and any resemblance to actual persons, living or dead, businesses, companies, events, or locales is entirely coincidental.

:

DEDICATION

This book is dedicated to the men of the United States Navy who sailed destroyers built before the *Sprunce* class, small, fast ships that would roll on wet grass.

CONTENTS

ACKNOWLEDGMENTS

Julian H. Hudkins for his praise and critique after reading the rough draft of the first book in the Snug Harbor Series, *The Launching,* when he, too, was a sailor.

Wilson O. Hudkins Caceres who provided encouragement in publishing this book and for his gift of a new computer and manual on self-publishing.

Agueda Tonie Hudkins-Teague who provided valuable information in final preparation of this book.

Bill Leaseburg, *The Starving Artist*, who illustrated the cover of this book from nothing more than a rough idea from the author.

Other Snug Harbor Series Books:

Book I - *The Launching*

Book II - *The Cruise*

CHAPTER ONE

SAND CRAB

I'd positively lusted for a West Virginia spring morning during the three hundred plus mornings my Fast Patrol Boat muttered, sometimes roared, through mist-shrouded Vietnamese rivers. Vietnam wasn't the only place my lust had surfaced. Boyhood vision of breeze-soft mornings sometimes came to mind, regardless of endeavor: sailing the world's seas, showing the flag, pulling liberty in foreign ports, exercising at general quarters and a host of other times and places. The glory of spring in the mountains of West Virginia hovered even on the perimeter of pain killer in San Diego Naval Hospital after folks trying to break my stuff scored a bull's eye.

I had it all now, including the spring morning I'd longed for, but I wasn't no where near a satisfied kitty cat. I pondered on this strange dilemma at length while lounging in an old cane bottomed rocker on the porch of my farmhouse, watching wind blown clouds obscure the top of Berkeley's Knob, then lay racing shadows across the big meadow in front of the house.

I was cognizant of a sea bag full of reasons why I should have felt carefree as a young sailor in London with a thirty-day leave chit and a pocket full of Yankee Green Dollars. I was newly retired from the United States Navy. I could buy my family a pretty without straining my piggy bank when the mood came upon me. I was in no way rich, but I had enough stashed away that I wouldn't need to visit blood banks in the foreseeable future. I had freehold farms with both hillside and bottom land, which required no effort on my part to produce a profit. I had a gaggle of friends across the world I could count on for any sort of hook-up I might need. I had a crazy bulldog and a smart Persian cat. Best of all I had my wife, Patty and my son, Joe-Joe.

Legend has it that all good sailors go to Fiddler's Green when they die, a place of wine, women and song. Their journey entails bribing Charon to row them across the River Styx so they can enter the Land of the Dead in which Fiddler's Green is located. Getting to Fiddler's Green was not a concern of mine; I found my own Fiddler's Green right here on earth.

Still, I was not happy.

Acute mental discontent deemed it time for a little morale building. I heaved my carcass out of the chair, descended the age-worn, stone porch steps and ambled across the clipped orchard grass to where Patty and Joe-Joe were investigating forthcoming arrival of the Easter Bunny.

I grabbed Patty, swung her tiny body into the air and kissed on her until she kicked her heels behind her, squealed and blushed.

"Do me, Daddy! Do me!" Joe-Joe yelled, exhibiting the jealously of a near four-year old left out of a little mom and pop rubbing and purring. I complied by slowly swinging him through arm-length circles. When I had him wound up, I set him on the lawn and watched him reel rubber-legged across the soft grass. Patty and I laughed at his dizzy wanderings until he finally landed on his stern with a solid plop right at my feet.

"Hey, Joe-Joe, any sign of that old bunny yet?" I asked, pulling him upright and hugging him against my legs.

He made fast to my hand and took me under tow to a clump of Easter lilies growing beside an old, gnarled maple. "Look, Daddy. Mommy says he comed early so he can finded me Easter morning." Joe-Joe cried, pointing to a trail of rabbit pellets.

"He's been doing his recon alright." I agreed, grinning at Joe-Joe's misuse of verb tenses, something of which he was totally oblivious. Switching between English and Italian at a tender age had fouled him up, language wise.

"What is recon, Daddy?"

"Recon is short for reconnaissance,. The word means to look over an area to see what is going on. That's what the bunny did. That old rabbit sneaked around real quiet to make sure he can get in and out of our house on Easter Sunday. He did the very same thing at the very same tree when I was your age and that dumb bunny still can't remember how to get inside the house!"

"Easter bunny is not either dumb! He finded me here. My 'nother house is in Italia."

"That makes sense, Joe-Joe. I forgot he visited you in Italy last Easter, so he isn't dumb. He's smart to know you're now in West Virginia.

"Look, I appointed you chief master-at-arms so you'd keep Jarhead from going AWOL and tearing up the countryside. Don't you think it's about time you held muster on him? Check on Blue Suit too, although he is probably watching the morning news programs."

Our bulldog and cat were somewhat up in years and no longer too interested in raising hate and discontent as they had when we'd lived on the farm some years before. I figured Jarhead's advancing age caused anguish and heartbreak among dozens of adoring gyps that experienced loneliness during his lengthy stay in Europe. I didn't wish old Jarhead and his canine lady friends bad luck, but absence of an ever spiraling puppy population would stave off repeats of screaming and gnashing of teeth by neighbors, such as we experienced before we transferred first to Spain, then to Italy.

There was likely sighs of relief among males of various species when The Word circulated that The Terrors of Big Otter County had reached senior citizen status during their overseas sojourn. That freed male animals in the area from heavy intimidation and sheer violence, sometimes inflicted by both neighborhood scourges at the same time. Crossed Paws, one for all -- and all for one, was their motto.

With Joe-Joe out of the immediate vicinity, I took advantage of the situation and grappled onto Patty. Her lips were as soft and her tiny body as firm as the Sunday afternoon she'd first kissed me, a grand occurrence that happened a week after I met her. Her first kiss, that would have caused a monk to suit up and head for the nearest body exchange, wasn't totally gratis. Patty owed me Big Time for tricking me into accompanying her to church that morning and, later the same day, for engineering hostile discharge of my services by a perfectly good mistress.

"Clay-honey," Patty gasp, when I finally turned her loose. "You always make be think *Things*. I am thinking them now, but leaving Joe-Joe outside to play is not possible. He would soon realize we were engaging in something interesting and tear into our bedroom."

"Well, there's a sure-fire way around the little devil. We'll knock him out with a slug of wine at lunch."

"*Clay*!"

"That menace to our love life started pinching sips of wine in Italy and you know it. It never hurt him, just like it doesn't hurts European kids and they pour the stuff down -- every meal."

"I realize Europeans believe wine beneficial for children, Clay-honey, but I do not favor it. Joe-Joe is much too young for wine -- or beer."

"He doesn't think so. I caught him sucking the dregs out of my beer bottle last evening and that was probably not all he drank. I suspect he sneaked behind my chair and lashed himself firmly to the neck of the bottle, like every time I took a drink and set it back on the end table. He looked as happy as a possum in poke berry time."

"I suspect he was!" Patty threw up her hands. "Like father -- like son. Apples do not fall far from the tree, excreta, excreta."

"Well, maybe, but kids exposed to booze when they're little shavers are not likely to find it new and interesting when they're teenagers. Look at the Europeans. How many booze hounds did you see over there? Very few, compared to the United States where we try to keep booze far from kids. European kids get wine in their pacifiers. Makes 'em sleep good, so they say."

"It is a different culture, dearest.

"Speaking of sleeping, Clay-honey, you again tossed and turned all night. You mumbled in your sleep, which you do only when troubled. Is something bothering you?"

"Only that I can't talk you into putting your little boon-dockers under my bed, so I can get my paws on your teacups."

Patty reddened nicely. It was a continuing source of wonder that, after six plus years of enthusiastic lovemaking, she never failed to blush at the slightest sexual innuendo.

She leaned her wavy-curly, taffy haired head against my breast bone, -- as high as she could get without shifting into tippy-toe mode. "You are being foolish. You never *ever* have to persuade me. When we first . . . er, married I wanted you every darn time you smiled at me, or touched me. By damn-in-hell, I still do! Most women are not so blessed. Some are actually happy their husbands no longer desire them. I do not understand married women who do not enjoy making love, but I think --"

Patty's ability to explain her thoughts in a few sentences was non-existent. Detailed explaining, coupled with her usually speaking without contractions, was a trait that drove a lot of folks, including me, off-plumb. I learned, early in our relationship, how to knock that off smartly -- so I did.

"You better stop kissing me, Clay-honey, or I will have to take Joe-Joe to Mommy. She will start wondering if I do so too often."

"She never wondered why you spent entire weekends at folk festivals, fairs and such after we . . . er, got engaged."

"*Clay*!" Big blush that time. A big giggle too. "Oh, Mommy knew! She did not take me to task for our pre-marital escapades only because my total change of character confused her so badly she simply could not decide *what* to do. Daddy was the one who never suspected. Otherwise, dearest, you would have suffered the indignity of a black snake whipping, followed by an immediate shotgun wedding."

"Did you decide about letting Joe-Joe stay with your folks a couple of days per week? You know you'll have to surrender to them sooner or later."

"Their arguments are strong, but I dislike having him away. What do you think, dearest?"

"Let him go. I don't remember my own grandparents. He's not going to have his forever. He'll have a fine time and learn something too. Hanging with your dad, watching him mess with farm machinery and trade cattle and stuff can't hurt him. It'd be good for him to learn to dicker like your dad A good trader can always make a buck. Your mother will keep him well-fed. Let him stay with your folks from Saturday until Monday morning. We'll see him at church and dinner at your folks place, then come home and revert to our old, loose ways like we used to do on Sunday afternoons before he arrived on the scene."

That generated yet another big blush.

We wandered the yard arm-in-arm until we noticed Joe-Joe, Jarhead and Blue Suit had latched onto Mister Pollard, our farm manager, who was en route to salt the livestock in the pasture below us. We made our break and slipped through the white picket gate into the orchard.

"Clay-honey, something is *bothering* you." Patty persisted, as she always did when she angled for information. "Maybe you should not have retired from the Navy. Sorry, I meant entered the Fleet Reserve. That is correct, you know. One does not actually retire until one has a total of thirty years of active duty, or a combination of at least twenty years active and the remainder in the Fleet Reserve. One is subject to recall from the Fleet Reserve until reaching the thirty year anniversary at which time one is fully retired under a United States Code."

Shortly after we had gotten engaged, or whatever she had hooked me into doing, Patty ordered a sea bag full of books from the *Navy Institute* and boned up mightily on the Navy. Her ability to comprehend and retain volumes of information, seemingly without effort, amazed me. I chalked that up to her genius level IQ.

"It makes no difference. We get the same money whether it's called retainer or retired pay. I'm glad we have it, but it seems a lot for so little, considering how much the Navy gave me."

"Silly! You earned both your salary and retainer pay many times over. I get chills when I think you might have died from wounds before I even *met* you. Elizabeth says she experiences a similar sensation when she sees Gunny without clothing. She says he has been wounded so many times his body resembles a freckled blanket with puckers and zippers! So, tell me -- are you having reservations about leaving the Navy?"

I had known for a long while that Patty and Elizabeth, county sheriff and wife of Gunnery Sergeant Ronald D. Thorton, USMC, my best running mate from the time I was a young second class petty officer, were sisters in everything but fact. They apparently shared intimate secrets with ease, sometimes to the detriment of Gunny or me, or both.

I had learned another thing about Patty early-on. There was no way I could lie to her or fool her to get the bit out of her teeth when she wanted an answer. Once she puffed out her lower lip and went into her stubborn mode, it was time to furl my Flag. I chalked that up to her being a regulation schoolteacher before she chucked that job to run the world with me.

"It's not leaving the Navy. Yeah, I miss it like a newly homeless sooner dog misses biscuits, but it was time to go. It's not my Navy now. I'm not into the social engineering business."

"Something is bothering you. Clay-honey, do not close me out of your thinking, Please."

"I've been out of the Navy almost two weeks and, basically, I am going flat out of my skull! I can't stay interested in anything, even things I waited so long to do. I wake up thinking I ought to be doing something. I have to find something interesting to do!"

"You have lots to do! You could learn to manage our holdings. Mister Pollard is aging and will some day wish to retire as farm manager. He would welcome you doing that. Daddy will some day expect us to manage his holdings too. You in no way need a job. Think about it, Clay-honey. With our interest income, the farm profit, your retainer and other odds and ends, we will not need to touch our ever increasing principal.

'Dearest, I do not *want* you to have a job that would cause separation. We have been separated quite enough already! Being together is ever so much better than what we experienced in the Sixth Fleet, although we were not separated as much as most Navy couples. You should consider our being together during the day has benefits. For example, when Joe-Joe enters kindergarten, you could play with my tea cups at any time you wish!" Patty explained, turning the shade of a ripe cherry.

I folded her into my arms and kissed her sun-streaked hair, then her slightly pug nose. "I'm not a farmer, Kitten. I don't know beans about farming, nor do I care to learn. Mister Pollard is doing fine just as he has before I was born. I'd just get in his way. If he ever tells me he wants to retire, I intend to let him pick and train his relief.

"Patty, I feel useless without a job. I've got to find something that'll keep me interested. Damned quick too, or you'll have to check me into a room with soft, pink bulkheads and heavy locks on the hatches!

"I can't say I'm overjoyed at being something akin to a Sand Crab, which is, as you probably know, a Mark One - Mod Zero shipyard worker or government worker – and, loosely, a regulation civilian."

Patty giggled against my chest. "You're not fooling me. My big, bad master chief wants subordinates to boss around and some crippled kitty type people to care for. You will find the employment you seek. You can do lots!"

"Like there are civilian billets for people who know how to devise plans to break things lurking behind every tree in these hills." I grumbled. "I don't want anything in selling. I disliked that when I was on recruiting, trying to sell a lifestyle. The only good thing that happened in recruiting was I met you."

"Baloney! Clay-honey, think of the success you enjoyed and the friends you made during your recruiting tour. Your subordinates both liked and respected you. Your people were not only your recruiters, they were your friends!" She giggled again. "It must be your ability to influence unsuspecting beings to proceed exactly on the course you set and make them believe they enjoy doing it. You certainly did that to me. To use one of your lovely expressions, 'I fell from grace like a big dog!'"

"Liar, Liar -- pants on fire! I had no intention of marrying anybody, certainly not a girl twelve years younger. Not until you destroyed my love life in two states by lying to God-World about how I had to marry some young girl I got pregnant when I hadn't even so much as touched your interesting parts. After your college buddies spread that word around, I couldn't have bought a date! Then, when I was so confused I didn't know whether to dance or draw small stores, you seduced me and led me straight down the primrose path to formation steaming! You know this is A-number-one-ditty-bag true too."

"Patty turned a scorcher. It was not *quite* that way at all!"

"Close enough for government work, Kitten. Anyway, Monday morning, as the sun crosses Berkeley's Knob and lights that meadow right there, I go in search of gainful employment. Something independent so I can make it home before the kid gets sprung from school and can play with your tea cups and other parts that might interest me."

Shortly after I met Patty, I had drunkenly told my running mate, Gunny Thorton, that Patty's breasts appeared no larger than a shot glass or tea cup. Patty learned of this statement months later from Gunny's wife and started jokingly referring to her breasts as 'tea cups.' That was what we called them thereafter.

"Oh, you will surely find what you want, darling -- both at

home and in the world of civilian employment. Of that, I have no doubt. I am, of course, extremely biased. I do have *certain* concrete reasons for believing you are so wonderful."

Cute giggle that girl. Nice blush too.

"Yeah, sure . . . everyone is just dying to hire a dumb hill-billy sailor who knows how to devise communications needed to coordinate destroying huge areas of terrain."

"*Henry Clay Berkeley*! You are *infuriating*! I have repeatedly asked you not to refer to yourself in such a manner. You are the most intelligent man I know and the nicest one too! Admiral Grayson, himself, told me you were a fine planner and the best communicator in the fleet. He said it was a terrible shame you refused to accept a commission. So there!"

Patty never nagged and rarely complained, but she lost the bitter end every single time I made some off-handed remark concerning my lack of mental agilely. I chalked that up to some weird reaction to my being dumber than a nine pound rock, compared to her.

It mystified me why so many people considered me highly intelligent. Few other men were dumb enough to spend eleventy-eleven years racking up off-duty college credits that didn't mesh to anything, certainly not the history degree I'd aimed for. I finally had to settle for a cobbled together degree in Human Resources. I wouldn't have gotten that degree if Patty hadn't pushed me to take the boring courses I lacked: Tumble Bug Watching, Gravel Grading, Advanced Rope Platting, Newt Growing . . . whatever.

"Ah, forget the damned job for now. Let's discuss something really important. What time are you going to heave the Duty Rug Rat in bed for his nap?"

"Clay, I rarely attempt to advise you, but I am going to do so now. Sir, get your mind off my *cute* overbite and my *lovely* tea cups and turn your thoughts toward building a resume! I am certain an interesting position, other than in bed, is waiting for you!"

Little did she know how true that would turn out.

CHAPTER TWO

A STRANGE PROPOSITION

Easter Sunday dawned bright and clear with a stiff breeze swaying the forest on top of Berkeley's Knob. I'm not a deep thinker, but I did ponder why storms occur so often on Good Friday and Easter Sunday is almost always a pleasant day.

Joe-Joe and his two cohorts in crime jarred Patty and me out of a love-induced sleep, zero-dark-thirty, with yells, giggles, growls, hisses and snarls as they investigated their Easter baskets. Patty prepared baskets of goodies for Jarhead and Blue Suit on Easter, presents for Christmas and birthdays and took them trick and treating on Halloween. She had done so even before we adopted Joe-Joe. She believed the animals otherwise would feel left out.

The first thing I noticed when I crawled down the stairs to observe the festivities was the family room was shambles! Chocolate bunny containers, gold foil, candy wrappers, green strands of basket liner and goodies tasted and rejected littered the terrain -- all caused by Joe-Joe

Jarhead had likely gobbled his goodies as fast he could get them into his mouth. The fastidious Blue Suit no doubt picked daintily at his booty and ended stashing most of his stuff in hidden locations in event of famine. That cat's main occupation was

11

worrying!

At 0800, after requests, threats and firm rudder orders failed to produce the desired movement, we pried Joe-Joe loose from his basket of loot, suited him into the uniform of the day and lit out smartly for Patty's church in Big Otter. It was an effort comparable with the arrest of a bar full of drunken bikers.

The old preacher didn't dive hip and thigh into the hellfire and brimstone sermon he usually let fly on Sunday. He did a very creditable job of making us aware what God granted the world nearly two thousand years ago. Any grownup unable to understand that old man's Easter sermon, given in the plain, firm speech of mountaineers, would qualify as a near idiot -- or a member of the media.

We took dinner with Patty's folks, as was our custom since the first Sunday she'd sandbagged me into accompanying her to church. Missus Patterson had prepared nothing special for Easter, but it was, as always, a meal fit for a Mark One - Mod Zero chow hound: country fried spring chicken, home smoked ham, mashed spuds, candied yams, home-canned corn and peas and a dozen side dishes. We topped off with coffee and a slab of cobbler made of blackberries that had wintered in the freezer. No doubt in my military mind where Patty had learned to cook.

I reflected my status had improved mightily since my first meal with Patty's parents. Then, Missus Patterson stared at me like I was prone to committing obscene acts with sheep. Patty's dad treated me somewhat better -- about like I was the duty leper. My status improved to barely socially acceptable after I married Patty, thus saving her from the life of sin she so eagerly embarked upon after taking up with me, a one-man bad crowd. My low standing eventually improved to where I became the son the Patterson's never had. Mister Patterson had once taken me to task because I kept calling him 'Mister Patterson' and 'Sir.' He insisted I call him 'Pa.'

I offered to help with the after dinner clean-up, but the ladies shooed us out on the porch where Mister Patterson whipped a thick, greenish cigar on me. He started doing that the Sunday

Patty startled her folks with the news she had leveled her big guns and intended to drag me to the altar, something she had not bothered to tell me. He had since bestowed a cigar on me every Sunday we were together. Good cigars they were too. Patty didn't pout and lay disappointed looks on me when I smoked one of his cigars. She even seemed pleased when I smoked the occasional cigar at home, but she was pale death on cigarettes.

Mister Patterson clipped my cigar, handed it to me, then clipped his own and offered a lit kitchen match. He permitted no fumes from lighter fluid to spoil the taste of fine tobacco. When we were puffing contentedly, he leaned back in the swing and asked, "Which political party do you belong to, Clay'"

His question surprised me because he'd never before mentioned politics to me. I used an inspection of the burning tip as an excuse for silence while I formulated an answer.

"I'm not anything, really. I was never home to vote, but when I registered for absentee ballots I put down democrat, mainly, because that's how Mom and Dad registered. I changed to republican when the democrat party seen fit to nominate and elect folks I couldn't stand. I am more of an independent than anything, I suppose."

"Tell me, Clay. What do you think of politicians in general?'

"Not much. The Hatch Act prohibited my getting involved with politics while in the Navy. I paid little attention, except when some imbecile was trying to get me killed in some fool conflict he was pushing." I grinned at him, then said, "I believe politicians would claim rattlesnakes as blood kin, except the rattlers would resent that. Rattlesnakes have some sense of honor They give a warning before they sink in their fangs."

Mister Patterson let loose with a belly whopper, then gave me a long, piercing look. "You understand government, don't you? How it works, I mean?"

"I studied civics in high school and I took a course in government when Patty pushed me into completing my degree in

Advanced Pencil Sharpening. Yeah, I understand the process as well as the next man, I suppose."

"Clay, tomorrow, unless you got some firm plans, you and me oughta go to Clarksburg and see a man 'bout a job. Leave 'bout seven."

"Not so very fast, Buccaneer! Patty didn't bug you about getting me a job, did she? I'd be surprised if she did. She thinks the world of Elizabeth and Gunny, but she doesn't think it pusser that Elizabeth appointed Gunny as chief investigator for the county. She says it smacks of nepotism, even if Gunny is more than qualified. No hard feelings, Pa, but I'd like to find a job on my own and, if you are speaking of politics, I sure as hell don't want any of that!"

"Patty didn't talk to me 'bout you wantin' a job, Clay. She doesn't even know I'm a-talkin' 'bout anything like that. Better you don't tell her either. She doesn't approve of most politicians."

"You really think I could keep anything from her? Naw, you don't really believe that. You had Patty longer than me."

"You might say I got experience in that area! She can be one flat bear when she gets to wormin' something out of a man. That's exactly why I'm not a-goin' to say nothin' more. She can't find out what you don't know. Don't say nothin' at all, unless she suspects you're hidin' somethin'. Which she likely will!"

And sure enough, she did.

"What were you and Daddy discussing so avidly, Clay-honey?" Patty asked, after we'd bunked Joe-Joe down for the night and hit our own tree.

"Nothing important, Kitten." I replied, fingering the lace at the top of her gown.

"Clay?"

"He wants me to go to Clarksburg with him to see about a job."

Patty raised and positioned her lace-covered tea cups against my right arm. "What sort of job, Clay-honey?"

Patty's breasts really weren't too much larger than a big tea cup, a small cereal bowl at best, but they were damned sure distracting. They felt nice too, particularly after I slipped my hand inside her gown and stroked them a mite.

"Clay?"

"Kitten, my intentions are to jump your little bones until your ears ring."

"Oh, I like that idea! But what about the job?"

"I am totally in the dark about it, Kitten. I'm only going to make your dad happy. Now do you want to get your bones jumped or don't you? I'm losing interest."

Patty hooted, "You wouldn't lose interest even if Saint Peter was watching!"

"You're trouble, Kitten. Big Time Trouble. And you'll be trouble throughout eternity if they put us in married quarters!"

I had a great weakness for Patty flashing her slight overbite when she smiled her bright, broad-tooth smile. She was well aware of its strength and she laid it on me as she teasingly worked the straps off her shoulders and slipped the gown below her perky, little breasts. A few quick wiggles slid the gown below her hips and free of her body. She then flipped it into the air where the flimsy gown floated slowly downward.

"Poor, lonely nightgown . . . on the cold floor every night." She clutched me tightly and lowered her lips towards mine as she blushed and whispered. "I will tell you what real trouble is. Real trouble is the Cain this little girl will raise if Saint Peter fails to assign us married quarters so I can get my hands on you whenever I want!"

Patty Lane worked her wiles on her daddy when he held muster on me the next morning, but he escaped by stomping the gas pedal and awkwardly wheeling his wife's Gran Marquis down the gravel lane. He probably felt uncomfortable not driving his beloved, rust-red Ford pickup, so worn he didn't trust it on trips of more than a few country miles. He bought new farm pickup trucks every two or three years, but preferred to drive his old Ford that he had had since around the time of the Korean War.

"Clay, there ain't not one day passes since Patty married when I don't miss that little girl around the farm. I woke up nights a-thinkin' 'bout her when you two were overseas. But that doesn't stop me a-bein' glad you got full-time access to her stubborn streak 'stead of me. Lord-a-mighty! She used to puff out that lower lip and I knowed she'd weasel me outta what she wanted to know. That man that doesn't know Patty doesn't know stubborn!"

"Sounds to me like you've got a complete muster list and all the keys to the gear lockers. I realized, not long after I met her, that she's got Sir Winston Churchill beat all to shucks when it comes to being bullheaded!"

"Ought to know 'bout her!. I had her for nigh-on twenty-three years. Oh, she wuz sweet and respectful, but she could work me like a play toy."

"I know what you mean, Pa. Patty had my number from Day One. It doesn't strain her thinking machinery the slightest to figure out which way I intend to jump, then modify my course, speed and waypoints accordingly, usually without me knowing she did it!"

Mister Patterson laughed so hard he almost splattered a grass-fat woodchuck waddling in the road.

"Ain't that the Lord's truth! Me and my Virginia still get a good laugh when we think of Patty a-roundin' us up and a-sayin' she wuz a-goin' to marry Henry Clay Berkeley and she hoped we wouldn't fight her 'bout it. You never said nothin' to me 'bout marryin' my daughter, so I asked her when she planned to marry. Well, Sir, Patty said, just as sweet as cream, 'Why soon, Daddy. You and Mommy will be the second and third persons to know.'

"I asked her who wuz a-goin' to be the first to know. She said, real pert like, 'Why, who do you suppose, Daddy? Henry

Clay Berkeley, of course!'

"Clay, her a-schemin' to marry up with you weren't any real big shock to me and my Virginia, not the way she kept a-draggin' you all over creation. She never done that with any feller. Never seemed to go out with a feller more than a couple times. Never took nary a one to church with her. She worked real hard to bark your tree and I'll bet you never even knowed what she wuz a-fixin' to do."

"I finally realized the night we got engaged that she'd been maneuvering me into marriage like a tug controls a barge. It turned out from her point of view that we'd been engaged since our very first date!"

"Sounds 'bout right, Clay. Sounds 'bout right.

"Now Patty can be a real piece of goods when somebody slights her. You know that, or you two woulda had some real bad fallin' outs by now. Patty swears you two ain't had a real tussle yet. That says a lot 'bout what you think of each other. You keep a-treatin' her with the respect you been a-givin' her and she'll keep a-treatin' you like a new husband. So, don't you never let nothin' get in the way of her.

"I'm a-tellin' you this 'cause I'm a mite worried. If things work the way they might, you're a-goin' to be busier than a tomcat with a bad case of scoots! Lots of men get a big, important job and starts believin' the world can't turn without them. If that happens 'cause of today and you start a-puttin' Patty second I don't want even to be in the same with country her!"

"I might understand what you're talking about, Pa, if you'd tell me what you've got having fire."

"You'll find out directly, Son.

I was confused when we left I-79 at the Quiet Dell exit, turned away from Clarksburg and headed south on U.S. Route 20, then turned into a rutted, narrow, gravel road almost hidden by trees on the side of the road.

"Right there, Clay." Mister Patterson pointed at a two-story, water-stained, block building with rusted machinery parked around the perimeter. "The old man you're a-goin' to meet is right damned touchy, so keep quiet unless he asks something. No need to make him mad."

The interior of the building was little more than a huge, vacant, open bay with a landing jutting from the partial second floor. The room we entered on the second floor resembled a shabby night watchman's shack on a strip mine. The age-spotted man behind the cheap, wooden desk didn't stand, offer to shake hands, or even tell us to go to hell. He simply ordered us to sit in a harsh, dry voice.

"Jack, this is Clay Berkeley, my son-in-law."

"Know that, Charlie. I already looked him up in an old newspaper at the library from when he got the Silver Star. Let's start cutting the hog!

"If you're half-bright, Berkeley, I expect you are wondering why you're meeting with a near-corpse whose furniture looks like it come from a Goodwill Store." He waved a frail arm about him. "This stuff come from a secondhand store in Glen Elk. I suspect they'd call it an antique store now. Bought all this for three dollars and thirty-five cents when I got out of the Army, back when I was worse than poor. It hurt bad to pay that kind of money for a place to write, figure and set my ass!

"I was raised on a tenant farm on Brushy Fork. Went to digging coal in a starve-to-death, three-man coal pit at fourteen. I studied mining books long into the night. I picked garden truck off four acres of rented ground I worked with a colored man too. I done better than most in them hard times. I had eight hundred and two dollars and six cents when the Army called me to fight.

"I got back from France and worked and studied on what I could do. I had patches on my work pants and one coat I got in the Army. I had nothing else in the world, except a mite of money, a fist full of coal leases I owed money on and the four rented acres the colored man took care of while I was fighting overseas. I used what money I could scrape up to buy an old steam shovel and a

Studebaker dump truck that'd run about two out of three days. I went to digging coal!

"I still have that old shovel. It's the first machine that touches dirt in every mine or construction contract I start. Call me superstitious, but that old shovel made me a heap of money.

"Mister Lew, the colored man, never cheated me while I was in the war. He paid rent out of my share and took his share out of the pot. He banked the rest for me. Mister Lew had every penny accounted for. When I was able, I made sure he lived good until the day he died.

"I owe what I got to the Lord, plain hard work and the help of a colored man and a country that'd give a poor man a chance back then. It'd be hard to do what I done today, maybe impossible. There ain't much left for a man that works with his hands.

"I'm telling you this stuff so you understand where I came from and why I think like I do.

"Engineers keep saying there is no such thing as a problem that can't be solved, but I have a dozy that can't be solved with slide rules, or them computer things.

"This country is going to hell in a hand basket. There ain't hardly one damned politician that cares about nothing, except getting re-elected. All loves the power that goes with the job. Some claim to feel compassion. But when they talk about loving their fellow man, wanting to give him something for nothing, they're just grabbing power from folks who don't know better.

"I don't know as to where any of them old boys ever had a man killed to get re-elected. It wouldn't surprise me none, except they don't need to kill. Not so long as they can blackmail folks by using the newspapers and TV so people who wants to do right looks like pure damn fools. They're real good at tricking citizens that don't understand anything. The educated people are worse than uneducated folks for believing what the politicians say. I think, sometimes, that the more education folks have, the dumber they get!

"This country might end like the old Romans. It sure as

hell looks to be moving that way. We have a man in the White House who seems to think every citizen in this country is so stupid they can't do anything without government taking care of them. Neither him nor congress can see how business is moving out on us. That's a real bad thing. There's not going to be a job of work for a man before long. A man that has no job has no pride!

"People, even dirt poor folks, used to have a power of pride. Mister Lew was real poor, but you never seen a man with more dignity than Mister Lew. He worked into the night to feed his family and I never heard him cry about his life. He enjoyed his life, hard times aside. That old man understood pride. He passed that on to his kids who passed it along too. His kids and their kids and some of their kids who work for me are not much different from Mister Lew when it comes to hard work and pride. So, you see, Mister Lew's pride got handed down to at least three generations.

"You can't get pride from the government. They can't give it because they don't understand what it is. They don't understand a man has to have pride no matter what color they are, how down and out they are, how rich they are, or even how no 'count, low-down they are.

"I can't do much to solve this countries problems, but I am surely going to do one thing before I croak. I'm going to get rid of one carpetbagging, son-of-a-bitch congressman before I go. He's poor goods! He's so busy sucking up to that fool in the White House that he has no time to work to get business into West Virginia so folks can work. It purely does make my stomach crawl when I hear of him supporting some White House program that ain't worth a nit's ass, but costs a bunch of money out of poor folk's pockets.

"There was a fine woman gearing up to run for the house seat. She is honest and smart and she is good at talking to people and making them understand what she wants to do. She won the primary and started doing good in the polls against the incumbent, then it went straight to hell!

"She received word a newspaper was threatening to leak

dirt on her. She had an abortion in high school after she took with a smooth talking bastard and got herself knocked up. She was sixteen at the time, I believe. Folks tried to tell her if it did come out, it would get her three-quarters of the female vote and most all the male liberal vote too. She values her reputation and was so afraid of her friends and family learning about the abortion that she dropped out of the race. She was well aware too that the liberal press would tear her up because she's a republican. The media would have bragged on her abortion if she was a democrat.

"It's going to take a bit of doing, but you watch for your county's biggest newspaper to start having some bad financial trouble. I believe in payback and this dirty thing they did to that nice woman requires exactly that!"

The old man stopped talking for a few seconds, picked up a glass and stared right through me with his faded, blue eyes while slurping a liquid across toothless gums. I'm not a Nervous Ned, but his eyes like to give me a bad case of the shivers!

"So, how would you like to run for the United State House of Representatives, Berkeley?"

"I'll tell you in three sentences. I wouldn't. I couldn't. I won't"

"Folks did tell the God's truth about you. You're not a mealy mouth, beat around the bush sort of fellow."

"What folks?

"Folks you likely have forgotten. Folks that were interviewed about you."

"Mister, I don't know who you are and I don't much give a damn Whoever you are, and however rich you might be, didn't give you any right to interview *anybody* concerning me. You better tell me what is going on You've not seen mad until you see a mad Navy master chief!"

The old booger smiled for the first time since we'd arrived. "Praise the Lord! You speak right up! Maybe you really are worth two whoops in hell like they all said."

I was one befuddled sailor. All my halyards were wrapped around the back stay.

"Look, you old --"

"Shut up, Berkeley! You're not old enough to piss hard on the ground yet, let alone raise your voice to me! Opening your mouth like a mad poll parrot has always been one of your problems. Keep quiet and let me lay a little knowledge on you.

"I was in Washington a while back looking into some contracts and took time to visit with fellows I knew when I was contracting in Southeast Asia. We got to talking about how folks who work for a living are getting screwed by both the government and big business and how the military is treated these days. Military folks can't speak out like other citizens, but that don't mean they don't understand what is going on. They know one hell of a lot more than most so-called educated civilians. Military folks read and study a lot.

"Anyhow, I told them about losing that woman and said it was a damn pity that folks in West Virginia might have to again settle for the same piss poor politician. I said there wasn't many in congress with the guts to stick it out when a powerful lobby gets to waving threats and money under their nose and the one we had damn sure wasn't one of them.

"One fellow . . . he's a cagey old bird who'd be rich if he hadn't stayed in the Navy for so many years told me about you. He said you were about to get of the Navy and the republican party surely wouldn't go wrong by trying to get you to run for the seat. He said you were a hot runner, highly intelligent and so damned honest your head hurt. He said you could get people to do stuff without much effort. He said he didn't know whether you were a republican or a democrat and you might not want to be in politics and was, maybe, too outspoken to do good in that field. He said you were so hardheaded you almost got a court martial because you wouldn't back down when you thought you were right.

"Now, this ain't my first time hoeing a corn patch. I know people who likes a man don't usually know him as good as they might think. I feared he might be that way about you. You probably don't have the idea of a crawdad about civilian intelligence work, but some of the intelligence companies are so good they could get piss from the White House toilet and know who smoked dope yesterday. In your case, I almost know when you dirtied your first diaper!

"The Berkeley's was the first European folks to settle in your area back before there was a United States. They bought Indian land and made a life for themselves. The early generations made some money, but later men in your family threw lots of it away on booze, cards, horses and women. I suspect you don't know much about where the chunk of money you have now came from.

"Your mama's family wasn't much, not until your grandpa got himself elected sheriff of a backwoods, nothing county. He skimmed enough off the tax receipts to get your mama through teacher's college because she was the brainy one in the family. None of the rest of her kin ever amounted to much, but they had one strength that's worth more than gold. People *liked* the Preston folks.

"You daddy wasn't all that smart, but he was pretty fair at farming. He made enough to give his family a good living and he added a mite to the family pot. You probably believe he made his money trading cattle. Forget it, Berkeley! No way a man could make the money he left you by trading cattle in them hard times.

"Your grandpa Berkeley made most of the money you now have. He made it the same way old man Joe Kennedy made his first big pile. Your grandpa was land poor with lots of corn and grain. He didn't have much of a market for corn and grain, but he knew men who could still whiskey. He never made a fortune like Kennedy, but made enough to fix his family with a good lot of coin.

"The thing that keeps cropping up on both sides of your family from way, way back is shrewdness, hard work, guts and friends that count for something.

"You came a ways by yourself too. You went into the Navy and done good   There ain't many men who could have got bad shot up, then do what you do did. Your daddy did much the same sort of thing in World War Two, so guts runs in your family like I said.

"You have your share of faults. You can't keep your mouth shut. Except for fistfights, every time you've been in trouble was because of your mouth, like when you were fired from recruiting. You sure ain't a saint! You drank enough beer to float a D-8 Cat or two. You done your damnedest to crawl on top of every female on two legs before Charlie Patterson's girl got hold of you and straightened you out like a bent nail! But, knots and bruises aside, you are what I want to run for the office."

"Let's see if I have this straight . . .

"One of my grandfathers was a bootlegger and the other a thief. My Dad was a dumb hick. My mother was jumped up white trash. My ancestors were drunks, gamblers and womanizers who were dumber than homemade rocks -- and I'm a whore monger. Is that what you said?"

The old man's gruff laugh confused me. I wondered how many beers my barfly buddies, also aged and mean, would demand to slap him around.

"Your people were generally good folks. Your grandpa Preston only borrowed the money from the tax receipts. He might have lent it out on a short-term loan to make it grow into his own pocket. Whatever he did, he put it all back before anybody knew it was gone. Your grandpa Berkeley done what he had to do. It was hard in their times and they were strong folks who made their own way. Now you calm down and let's get to dickering on how to get you elected."

"I don't want elected. I'm not running!"

"Your State and your Country needs you, Boy. You give a damn about people. You are no left or right wing nut. You are nothing in the way of a politician, but I believe you have it in you to be a damned good congressman."

"Your own personal, jump-when-I-yell congressman. Right?"

24

The old man spit a goober in his trash can and sneered. "I wouldn't touch your sorry ass with a pole dipped in a dead skunk if I thought you'd do that. I never bought nary a one of the bastards. If I can buy a politician, so can another fellow who might want to do me dirt. What I want is a bright fellow with guts enough to get things done that need getting done. I'm not ever going to tell you how to do one damn thing while you're running – not even after you get elected, if you do. I never seen you today and I'll never see you again.

"I do want a few things. I want to us to feed and help folks who need it and are willing to work. I want a strong defense. I want the United States to stand up and tell other countries to go straight to hell when they try to tell us what to do. Big business has to be reined in somehow. Businesses must be stopped from moving overseas. The social security system must be fixed so we can balance our budget. We had to pay off the national debt.

"So tell me, Berkeley -- do you think you could work to do these things and maybe get some jobs into West Virginia too?"

"I have no idea how a politician can raise enough money to run on and not owe favors to the people who gives it. Your ideas of what needs fixed in this country are pretty close to mine, but it's a little late to get me nominated, considering I know mighty few people anywhere in West Virginia. I don't know where to start trying to get the nomination."

"There are politicians who raise money and ain't crooked. Talking to contributors ain't dirty if you don't let them influence you when they're wrong. You can't represent folks if you don't talk to them and find out what they are thinking.

"They're hells of available politicians and almost anybody is more qualified than you! But, Berkeley, I don't want those folks. Those who want to run are either crooked, or ain't got the brains of a woodchuck."

"I'm not running, but if I were I wouldn't use my own money. I'd be broke in about a month, probably less."

"I know how much money you have, Berkeley. You ain't

much better than well-off. Nobody expects you to use a dime of your own money.

"There is a campaign manager available who knows about getting folks elected. Most never heard of him, but he's good! Two presidents, one a democrat, owe their office partly to him. I don't expect either man is bright enough to know that. This man will raise the money and run your campaign. This late date makes it easy to get you on the ticket. There is not much time before the general election to hold a primary, so the republican committee will simply put you on the ticket. That's been done before, by both parties, in like situations Your job will be to stand on stumps and get elected!"

"You'll have to find yourself another boy because I am not running. Not even for dog catcher. I'm a sailor – not a party hack!"

"Charlie, you take this boy home. You call me if he gets sane."

"Who is that old man?" I asked Mister Patterson after several minutes of silent traveling on our way back to Big Otter.

"Clay, he's just a real old man who is mighty fearful for his country. He's secretive because he wants to be. He ain't the type to be in *Business Week*. I'm told he's got engineers and such who've never seen him. He runs things from afar, so I hear. I have no idea where he lives or where he works out of."

"Pa, you didn't just drag me to see him. You're involved in some way with this."

"I only met him the one time. What happened wuz a woman called and told me it wuz in the interest of my son-in-law for me to meet a man on the nineteenth of March. She wouldn't tell me who she wanted me to meet, or what they wanted. I agreed 'cause she got me interested.

"I went to that rundown building, seen that junkyard around the outside and I thought I wuz in the wrong place. There weren't nobody else around just like today. 'cept that old man a-waitin' for me outside the door.   There weren't one single soul inside the building either. Didn't look like anybody had been there for years. I don't know who owns it, but I'd lay money he does like he owns stuff all over the country. The world, maybe.

"I got 'bout the same welcome you did. I knew a mite 'bout him 'cause my Pa used to talk 'bout how they were in the war together and that tells you just how damned old he is!. He said some nice things 'bout my Daddy, then he told me that he wanted to talk to you. He didn't tell me nothin' else 'cept what he wanted you for. I wuz dumbfounded! I told him you didn't know anything 'bout politics and probably didn't give a damn. That didn't impress him. You know most everything I know 'bout him 'cept his name and he told me not to tell you that. Why, I don't know, but I'll respect his wishes 'cause him and my daddy wuz close at one time. Could you find out his name? I 'spect so, but it would take a sight of work, I believe."

"He's mad dog strange!   Is he some sort of Howard Hughes?"

"Not sure 'bout that, only that he keeps mighty close to the ground. I'd like to know more 'bout him. I'd surely do wonder why he picked you when there's scads of men and women ready to kiss his rear, the rest of him too, for that offer he made you. Clay, you might be only one of several men he's supportin' for office around the United States. I don't know. I don't even know what Patty is a-goin' to think 'bout me a-takin' you over there. That worries me a whole bunch more than him!"

"You're not going to jump slick, Pa. You're invited to the lunch we never had today. I'm going to tell her exactly what happened. I learned early-on that trying to gaff her off works about as well as a corn cutter in a gunfight."

"You looky here! I ain't a-eatin' no lunch in your house today. I'm a-goin' to do like you say at times and get the hell out of Dodge. She's *your* wife! I'm only her daddy."

CHAPTER THREE

RUDDER ORDERS

Patty came from the house as we turned into our lane. She walked towards the parking area, making way with her bobbing stride I liked watching. She was holding Joe-Joe by one hand and carrying a small 'AWOL' bag in the other -- a good sign and a bad sign. The fact that Joe-Joe was spending the night with his grandparents meant early to bed. That was good. It also mean Patty would pick my brain. That was bad.

Patty hugged me tightly and welcomed me home with a warm kiss. Joe-Joe protested mightily, "Stop, Mommy! I get to kissed Daddy first. Lifted me, Daddy. Kissed me bye-bye."

I picked him up and planted a big smooch on his cheek. "You owe me an extra kiss. I kissed you early this morning, but you don't remember because the sandman heaved a boat load of sand in your eyes last night."

"Mommy wouldn't taked me to our ship!"

"I don't have a ship anymore, Son. Maybe you'll have your own ship someday. I went to Clarksburg with your grandpa."

"I kicked Clarksburg!"

By the time Joe-Joe scaled up on my shoulders, Patty had

already kissed her daddy and was giving him firm rudder orders as to the care and feeding of one Joe-Joe Berkeley, after which she instructed him to hold Joe-Joe carefully when riding machinery.

"Honey, you were an awful tomboy growin' up. You done near everything I done and you never got hurt Don't you know me and your mama can take care of a little boy who ain't even half as nosy as you wuz?"

"I'm sorry, Daddy." Patty apologized, but she didn't look a tad bit sorry.

"Dearest, did you eat lunch?" Patty asked, as we walked away from the departing car. "No, of course you did not, considering Daddy's dislike of restaurant food."

"I'm not big on restaurants either, not since I got hooked up with a Patterson woman."

That got me a nice, warm look. "Clay-honey, what did you and Daddy do all morning?"

I'm no brighter than the average hillbilly, but I seen where that question would lead and I wasn't ready to spill my guts. I knew how to stop her queries, so I did. That action caused an instant bypass of the kitchen.

"Oh, the sun is setting! You must be starving!" Patty jumped from the bed, twisted a towel around her midships and padded towards the hatch. The towel hid little. I could see some of her interesting parts.

"Come back here, Woman! You're denying your husband his conjugal rights." I teased.

"I *never* deny you, Sailor!" she yelled over her shoulder. "You are going to eat -- a lot too, before you touch me again." She giggled, as she turned into the passageway. "When you finish eating, I will assist you in burning the calories I am about to feed you. I do not want a fat, lazy husband."

Patty sat cross-legged at the foot of the bed, sipping a beer while watching me eat. She apparently still believed the sea story I laid on her early in our romance about how beer is a strength restorer.

I chowed down on Great Northern beans cooked with ham hock, boiled potatoes in a herb sauce and meat loaf with fried, hot peppers. A Falls City beer washed it down nicely. A cigarette would have gone nicely too, but smoking a weed would have gotten me Disappointed Look One through Six from Patty. When I finished eating, I piled the plates on the night stand, pulled Patty to me and arranged her head on my shoulder. "How'd you like to be a congressman's wife?"

Patty nipped the flesh of my upper arm. "You silly! I would not exchange you to be the wife of a king." She pulled my head over and laid a lip lock on me. "You do *Things* to me!"

"Good."

"Good because you make me quiver out of my skin, or good because of something else?"

I told her about the mean old man and his strange proposition. I might have embellished my part of the story just a tad.

Patty raised herself up on an elbow and shoved her big, gray eyes into mine. "Oh, I could belong to *you* as a congressman? I did not initially understand that. That would be splendid!"

"You're joking?"

"I *am* not! You would be an outstanding congressman."

That statement caused a complete inventory of my sea bag and a check all my uniforms for proper stenciling. My lengthy silence caused Patty to pop off again

"You would too!"

"Good Lord, Patty Lane! I can barely spell congressman, let alone a hard word like politician. I couldn't hack the program."

"Yes, you could! You can do anything!"

I held a few more checks on my gear and counted the links

in my anchor chain.

"Kitten, I was paying that old man's pitch a lot of attention while he was running off at the mouth about what he wanted for our country. That old man has some fine ideas. Most parallel mine flat to a Tee. Yours too, I think, from what little we've discussed the state of our country.

"Remember I once told you why I took difficult billets in the Navy? I told you I wanted to be part of the men who counted. I didn't just want to turn the wheel, I wanted to control part of the speed and maybe even the course.

"If I had the background, which I don't, I'd give this congressman gig my best shot. But, Kitten, contrary to what you believe, I'm a Mark One - Mod Zero hillbilly sailor with no education to speak of. I have no social graces other than those my mother beat into my thick skull and what I picked up in the Navy, and from you. I don't like small talk. I don't suffer idiots lightly and the House of Representatives is filled with fools, idiots and morons. On top of that, I've got a hot temper.

"If that's not enough reasons, I've done things before I met you I'm not proud of. I've been knee-wobbling drunk across the world. I've been in brawls by the gross when I was a young sailor. Morals weren't something I thought about much until I met you. When the media and the opposition got done harping on those things, there wouldn't be enough left of me to feed a rat!"

Patty whipped another big, gray eye lock on me, then kissed me. "Dearest, you probably never noticed because you were too busy avoiding crazy Italian drivers, but I used to step on the balcony in Gaeta to watch you cross the street and walk down the hill on your way to the flagship. I would see the morning sun flash from your collar devices as you dashed across the street and I would say to myself: 'That is my husband and I am so lucky to have him. He's not just any man. He is a war hero and master chief of the entire Sixth Fleet. He can do almost anything he wants, and yet I have never heard of him being unfair or mean to anyone. A three-star admiral relies on my husband for reliable communications, the welfare of the sailors and a host of other things. He's directly involved in situations people read in the news and some so highly classified no one will ever learn of them.' I was *so* proud!

"But, Clay-honey, I could never help wondering what you might have achieved were it not for your hardheaded refusal to accept a commission because of your limited education. I believed, truly in my heart, that you would have commanded a fleet had you chosen that route.

"Dearest, I am not going to tell you what course to take with your professional life. As your wife, though, I believe I should tell you what is in my mind. I hope you *will* run for congress!"

We kicked it around for quite a while, with me losing every round. Finally, I broke out my big guns, trained in on her and opened fire with what I hoped would be the winning salvo.

"I'm aware many powerful men receive rudder orders from wives brighter than they are. Some of them wouldn't have accomplished anything in life if not for a shrewd wife. That's been going on since Eve, although she's really a bad example of what I'm trying to say. Eve and The Snake screwed it up for us all. I suspect all wives nudge at their old man, but many are smart enough to make their husbands believe it was his idea to begin with.

"The media knows that. They stay up nights trying to find fault with First Ladies. Look what the media did to Missus Johnson and Nixon. They savaged those nice women every time they got a chance because they hated their husbands. There were senators and congressmen whose wives the media savaged too.

"If I were to get elected, probably the national media would never notice me, not as a congressman from West Virginia -- a state that is rarely ever mentioned, even by the weather guessers on national TV! You must have noticed that weather guessers usually have their shoulder covering West Virginia on the map, even when they report storms in surrounding states that impact West Virginia. We're damned near invisible!

"If I did, somehow, get their attention by doing something good, or something bad, they'd go after me as will the local media if I run for office. The media detests conservatives. That would make me a target for the media right off, even if I refuse to talk to them, which I would. You'd get *your* share of it too. Do you want to put up with that?"

"Bother the media!!"

I'd have sworn I had a live round in the chamber when I fired . . .

"Clay-honey, I realize you have not yet made up your mind. Please do me a favor first thing tomorrow and look in a dictionary at the definitions of the words 'liberal' and 'conservative.'"

"Why?"

"Because most have forgotten what those words mean. The words are now used to demean, but there is nothing in their meaning to demean. Both are honorable. A person can be either and want the best for our country."

"And your point is?"

"You scorn liberals because you believe liberals treated servicemen badly when they returned from Vietnam. You believe protesting liberals prevented the war from ending after the Tet Offensive. I have read extensively on that subject since I met you. It was not true liberals who caused the war to drag on and on after the Tet Offensive."

"Just who in the hell were giving aid and comfort to the enemy? Bugs Bunny, or those two mean mice that terrorize that poor cat?"

"Clay-honey, do you remember explaining why the war went wrong when I interviewed you at the college the day we met?" She stifled a giggle. "You should recall *that* interview. Your remarks ultimately resulted in your termination from recruiting!

"You were correct when you said the government did not

understand the war and had no idea how to run it. You were not totally correct about those who protested the war and cursed the troops. Those were not true liberals. They were people with weak personalities who had never in their lives been respected or admired. They saw their chance to acquire recognition and exploited the fear of war to get it. They were led by radical rabble-rousers quick to take advantage of the discontent.

"Think about it, Clay-honey. Both liberals and conservatives want similar things. You may call them democrats and republicans if you like but that is not always correct. They do, however, want to acquire things differently. Some do, I admit, operate with an agenda that is not baseline to either liberal or conservative."

"Henry Kissenger would have trouble arguing with you, so I damned sure am not going to try! But, honey, it doesn't make one bit of difference what name you tack on them. Idiots in government and war protestors got a lot of us killed on both sides It's over and done with. That's not to say it couldn't happen again.

"It might too, what with people running the government who've never heard a shot fired in anger and not a glimmer what a battle is. Yeah, some of them have heavy degrees, but what they learned is what they were taught. They have no basis for knowing if they were taught right or wrong. I hope folks who understand war will get elected to office before Joe-Joe is old enough to fight. I don't want him, or anybody's kid, to fight in a war unless someone is trying to hurt us. Aw, hell -- there's nothing I can do about it except to try to figure out who understands foreign policy and vote for them."

Patty exhibited a peculiar smile. "There might one thing you could do in congress -- at least one.

"One of your strongest attributes in the Navy was your ability to recognize faults and influence people to correct those you could not, by yourself, correct. You accomplished that successfully many, many times. People *always* listened to you! You have a degree and additional college credits in a wide variety of subjects. You are very well read too."

I was checking her range and bearing in preparation to launch a counter-attack when Patty murmured, "Uh Oh!"

"What's wrong, Kitten?"

"My night gown. I cannot throw it towards the ceiling tonight!" she wailed.

"Why not?"

Patty turned the color of the rising sun. "Because, dearest, you stripped me bare hours ago between the front door and the staircase."

"You have a real cute birthday suit, Kitten. You'd never get dressed if I had my way, so I really don't see the problem."

"There is none, dearest. I just wanted you aware of the state of availability in which I find myself."

CHAPTER FOUR

UNDERWAY – SHIFT COLORS

With Patty alongside and Joe-Joe in her arms, I set sail into unknown waters. I could sense storms and rough seas ahead in our attempt to cruise to the hill on which stood our nation's capitol. I commenced my grab for my opponent's rice bowl from the steps of Big Otter's federal building. The three-story, red brick building, routinely referred to as "The Hog Trough" by local citizens, was no stranger to me. I spent two years visiting recruiting district head-quarters in that building while in the billet of recruiting zone super-visor for a portion of West Virginia and a tad of Kentucky.

Public speaking was not new to me. I'd spoken to large groups of military people awed by my rank and snazzy uniform with a cluster of fruit salad adorning my chest, but never to a plaza filled with civilian folks not impressed with my being. The turnout surprised me. Either there were a lot of curious hillbillies, or it was a mighty slow morning with no funerals and no trials at the court-house. I stood surveying the crowd for friendly faces until Patty squeezed my arm and whispered, "It is time, Clay-honey." I reached for the microphone.

"Get it *on*, Boot Camp! We'uns ain't got all damn day. Moe's bar is near t' open!" yelled Mister Rawles, my favorite barfly, right in front of God and everybody.

That was embarrassing, but it got a big laugh I hoped would shift the mood of the crowd in my favor. Damn the torpedoes -- full speed ahead!

"Good morning! Most politicians start their speeches with something like, 'My Friends,' 'My Fellow Americans,' or some such rot. I'm not a politician. I've never ran for an office. I'm just a common citizen. Most of you can't be my friends because I know mighty few of you. Some might be later. Others will cuss me like a yellow dog before my last round is fired. 'My Fellow Americans' is redundant. I couldn't run for congress if I wasn't an American and you couldn't vote if you were not Americans. Like me or hate me, I am one of you -- a West Virginia hillbilly.

"Now that I think about it, that wasn't such a bright statement, was it? Everyone knows there are no *real* hillbillies, except in West Virginia. Some of the wannabe states south of us claim to be regulation hillbillies, but we all know they're not! Listen! Some folks take offense at darned near anything. If any such folks are here and they believe 'Hillbilly' is offensive, I invite them to leave before I offend them further. I'm not politically correct."

Those comments brought a barrage of cheers, whistles, and hand clapping.

"I have a speech I was supposed to give, but I'm not going to give it. My wife, Patty, who many of you do know, helped me memorize that speech. It took me about a week. Maybe I ought not tell you this, but Patty knew it by heart in about two hours. If you're looking for a good speech giver, maybe you should elect Patty Lane.

"You will discover long before I finish that I'm not too competent in speaking the King's English -- American English either, although I can flat spill it out in plain, every day words.

"Patty, now, is pretty near a walking grammar book. She is so precise in her speech that she rarely used contractions. She is, though, guilty of using Navy slang, but only because associating with me corrupted her. If you decide my speaking ability suggests I should be doing something else, then you will have to blame me, not Patty. She gave it her best shot.

"I was told to play up to your better nature, tell you how great I am, what I'm going to do for you that no one else can, and give you eleventy-eleven reasons why your should vote for a nice, squeaky clean, West Virginian like me. I think that old nickname, 'Boot Camp' that Mister Rawles just whipped on me sort of ruined that!"

Another big laugh made me think I was either doing pretty well, or making a damn fool out of myself. I glanced at Patty. She as smiling. A good sign.

"I better tell you about that nickname . . .

"I'd never been married when I returned home a few years ago, for a tour in naval recruiting. I'd been known to drink beer, smoke the occasional cigarette and frequent bars. I didn't see any reason not to. I didn't have anybody at home, except a weird bulldog and a real smart cat. Good pets and companions, but they weren't much on oral communications back then. Come to think of it, they've not gotten much better at it yet. So, I hung out at various bars, Moe's Mote, mostly, after my usual twelve hours of work. Most of you know Mister Moses Mosley, who was once assessor for this district. He does, by the way, endorse me

"Some of you might know there is a fair sized group of smart as . . .er, smart-mouthed, retired men who hang out at Moe's. They're a right slick bunch of old men, which says something for age and experience. You have to get up really early in the morning and climb a tall tree to out fox them!

"All of them are veterans and when they learned I was one of the younger master chiefs in the Navy, they hung the nickname 'Boot Camp' on me. That was bad enough. Worse, they managed, regularly, to beat me out of beer. I figure I bought them enough beer to buy a good pickup! It was a great mystery to me why Pabst Blue Ribbon Brewery sold out when they did.

A roaring laugh told me the folks were still there.

"No telling what you will read in the newspapers and see on TV. Most all media folks are democrats as are most of you. I'm going to tell you enough about myself that you can fill in the bull . . . er, lies and such.

"I was born and raised on Berkeley's Knob. My long ago, whichever grand pappy left England in 1709, sailed to what is now the United States, somehow hooked up with my Irish grandmother on a dock in Norfolk, Virginia and they zipped into the Appalachian mountains and settled here. They were the first two Europeans in this area. It was years before enough folks showed up to populate and found the town of Big Otter. I'm not going to elaborate on my family tree because many of you have ancestors who settled in these parts long ago and you know the hardships involved.

"Good or bad, you know where I'm from. I don't believe any of my ancestors stole horses, not in this country, anyway. But I don't expect they were more squeaky clean than most. None of them put George Washington up for the night when he was surveying this country. None of them did anything major in the civil sense. All did well in war, from the Revolutionary War to the present era. They were just common folks trying to hew a living our of these hills.

"Some of you know my Mom and Dad were killed when the bridge across the Hemlock River collapsed. That put me at loose ends, so I joined the Navy, for what I thought would be a four year hitch. They kept me around for twenty-two years.

"I left the Navy as a master chief petty officer, the highest enlisted rank. I served a tour in Vietnam and I was wounded twice. I didn't kill any babies in Vietnam. I don't know anybody who did. Every dead civilian I seen there was killed by bombing, long-range gunfire, or by the VC. The VC often massacred their own people, just like we did in the Civil War.

"I have a campaign manager, Mister Robert Kyle Criss, from Washington. I don't know much about them, but folks who claim to know about elections tell me you have to have one each campaign manager to run for office. Kind of like having one each suit for church, weddings, funerals and such, I reckon.

"I don't yet know Bob Criss well, but they tell me he knows his business like a farmer knows his fields. He's probably going to go off-center because of the things I'll say this morning, so I'm going to try not to entirely ruin his day and discuss some of the things he thinks I should. It might be a little rough, considering I threw his speech away. You'll have to bear with me.

"I'm supposed to tell you this country is in terrible shape and that the democrats put us there. Well, there is no way they can weasel out. They held the muster lists and keys to all the gear lockers for many years, but they had republican help in fouling things up.

"When you see a politician on TV trying to push a program, or shoot one down, he's got a gunny sack full of charts to prove his point. I have no charts. I don't have to prove our country is not operating at its best. You know that. You can all read.

"Can I fix all of our problems if elected? Of course not. No single lawmaker could do that. Can I do better than the incumbent. Yes, I can. I couldn't do worse. He doesn't understand what regular folks want and need. His voting record proves that. He is a man who never had to root hog for a living, although I understand he is a hard worker . . . at whatever it that he does.

"I don't know him personally, but it does seem that he steams around with the sort of people who bunch together so they can tell one another how smart they are and how ignorant folks outside of their circle are. You know the type. Such people brag a lot and feed their egos off one another. Folks, his trips to Europe, the Caribbean and to Hollywood don't leave much time for West Virginia. You taxpayers are paying for his many trips within the United States and those abroad because he claims to be 'investigating' something or other.

"I personally wouldn't vote for him because he puts his party ahead of his state and his country. Every time there is a vote, he votes the party line. You can check this fact in the *Congressional Record*. Mister Criss looked long and hard and found not one vote against the party line. If the democrat party is for or against it, he's for or against it, regardless of West Virginia's needs. Did his votes ever hurt West Virginia? Damned straight some did, particularly those that were veiled anti-coal resolutions and those that raised various taxes. You're the folks for whom he works, but he doesn't listen to you, does he?

"You'll never hear me make wild, hairy as . . . er, accusations against the incumbent. If I claim it, I'll prove it, or show where I got the information. I *will* critique his performance or ideas and it won't be just static I'm radiating. If I don't believe it is true, I won't say it. I'm going to run a clean campaign. What he does is his business.

"I have a couple of strong points. I don't owe favors to anybody and I will not owe favors to anybody. I won't take money that obligates me. Yes, volunteers will be zipping around picking up Yankee Green Dollars for my campaign. If you want a change in congressional representation, then you ought to give them some. If you are satisfied with how things are now, then you give it to Congressman Burnside.

"Will I listen to power brokers. Yes, I will. They are citizens. I'd be obligated to listen to all citizens. Could they sell me on anything? Maybe yes -- maybe no. It would depends on if what they want is good for West Virginia and the United States.

"I'm told I'm good at getting people to work together. I'll try to do that. Call me what you like, but I never cared whether a person was a democrat or a republican. I tried to vote for the best person. I'll work with anyone who tries to make things better, regardless of party.

"I do not have a grand, glorious platform. I have only a few items I hope to accomplish.

"I intend to draft and sponsor a bill that keeps actual money out of the hands of welfare folks. I have nothing against helping folks who need it. There shouldn't be anyone in this country homeless, hungry or unclothed. What I don't like is money we own spent on drugs and booze. My wife thinks a credit card type system would work, a card that can be used only to buy nutritional food and clothing with all other items being rejected. Is that possible? I don't know just now, but I'm going to look into that because Patty is usually dead on. She's steered me on a straight course since I met her. She is not going to set policy for me, but men who are married know she's going to give me rudder orders."

Another big laugh, mostly males, it sounded like.

"I intend to work to keep our military strong because this world of ours is more dangerous than in recent years. We have enemies around the world and we might need to take an enemy to task at any time. We can't do that if we don't have the planes and ships to get there. We can't do that if we don't have troops trained to do whatever they have to do. We are lucky compared to many countries because we don't have people trying to blow us up inside our own country. But they are coming, folks – they are out there and they are coming! When are they coming? No idea, but they will!

"A host of unthinking, unqualified people harp about cutting the military budget. I agree the budget could stand some heavy tweaking. I intend to try and do that, but I'm not going to take money from the operating forces like some people want. We need troops in the field, planes in the air and ships at sea. What we don't need is hordes of staff people telling them what to do. I firmly believe we can cut many military personnel and civilians out of the Pentagon.

"I believe we can save billions by putting responsibility and accountability at the lowest level and shutting down as much bureaucracy as possible. We waste scads of money on procurement. We should purchase tools on the open market, such as Sears, rather than getting them through official channels. We would get them faster, cheaper and, in some cases, better tools. We need to do that.

"I want a foreign policy that puts the United States first! I'm tired of playing world policeman and letting wealthy nations off the hook that are able to take care of their own problems. I'm tried of seeing American blood on the ground. I'm tired of countries getting us into situations, then telling us how to act. Such countries want only our blood and our treasure.

"You might recall both Adams and Jefferson warned against foreign entanglements. I don't like war, but there will always be war. The Good Book says that, but it does not say we have to send our kids to fight them. I don't want my kid, or any kid, mangled in a war some fool started because of grudges that are centuries old.

"My belief is that if it doesn't harm us physically or economically, stay the hell out of it!

"Another thing that frosts my nu . . . er, makes me angry is big business moving their plants to other countries. I'll work to put a stop to that! I see no way to do that right now, but I'm going to study on it and enlist fellow lawmakers to assist if I get elected.

"If I can get the ship out of dry dock and make some progress on the items I've outlined I will finish my time in congress a satisfied man. I'll work with the other party. It makes no difference who gets credit for a program, not so long as it gets done -- **AND IT WORKS!**

"I expect to get tore up pretty bad in the media. They will support the incumbent. I hope enough of you will vote come November to get me elected, or at least enough to make it look like I gave the other fellow a good run -- which will make him worry enough about the next election that he will try harder to carry out your desires. I don't know if I'll even like the job, if I get it, but I'll give it my best shot. I will always remember what you sent me there to do and will try my best to do exactly what you want.

"Folks, it's hot out here in the sun. I've kept you long enough. You'll have other opportunities to hear me babble. I will expound on what I want to achieve as time goes on. I didn't get into detail today as time was moving pretty darned fast and we can't stay out here all day. More later.

"If you have questions, you can drop me a line or call me at home. Be advised I'll hang up on abusive calls faster than a raccoon can drown a hound. You want to argue with me fine, but I'm not going to be verbally abused by anybody.

"So long, Folks!"

I sure didn't make a John F. Kennedy speech, but people were still cheering, clapping and carrying on when I finally left the steps and went to my headquarters, a vacant five and dime store we'd rented on Magnolia Avenue. Bob Criss, who'd mustered on my door stoop the day after I agreed to run for office, was there ahead of me. He was red-faced and his hands were shaking. I took that to mean he was really ticked off!

"That's it for me, Buster! I quit! The folks who hired me neglected to say you're a moron. I blame myself though. I should have seen that coming. What a mess!"

"I take it you didn't like my speech?"

"**Like it**? It was the dumbest speech **ever**! Did I say *speech*? It wasn't a speech. A hillbilly ramble, that's what it was. I'm on the next ox cart out of these hills!"

"You know your business, Bob, but you don't know West Virginians. I admit I don't know how to give a good speech, but I do know about the people in these hills you keep bad mouthing. Patty knows a one hell of a lot more than either of us, having lived here her whole life.

"Most of them are plain, hard-working folks The younger ones, most of them, have a high school education, some have college. Most of the older ones had to drop out of school to work, but that does not mean they are ignorant or stupid. They're not! They are independent to a fault. They don't like to be told what to think and they don't like to be talked down to. That's what you set me up to do with the speech you wrote. Patty thinks so too. What you wrote would have gone over big in towns and cities where folks group-think and like to be led around by the nose Not in these mountains!. I told them the truth as I understand it and I gave them a heads up on some of the rocks the media is going to throw at us. Better me telling them than the media. It's difficult to pick at a person who admits his faults. Honesty works.

"West Virginians are ordinary kind of people who fought in every one of our wars -- from the very first to the last. Figures in the *Navy Times* showed West Virginia has lost more people in war, percentage-wise, than any other state. They go and do what they have to do, then come home. You might hate these mountains, but the people love them. They'll fight for them.

"I don't want this job so bad I lust after it. Don't let that fool you into believing I won't fight my best to get elected. I will!

"Bob, they sent you to get this campaign on the bricks. What I need and want from you is for you to find stumps I need to crawl on to talk to people. I can't give a speech worth beans, but I can talk to people and keep their attention. I also need you to raise what money we require and make A-number-one-ditty-bag certain we keep good accounts and submit correct paperwork so we don't end in the brig. That's all I know that I need from you. Patty will advise on the rest."

"I told you I quit!"

"Quit. But I'd recommend you tell the folks who hired you that people were still cheering in that hot parking lot for a good while after I stopped speaking. Fact is, Patty says some were still cheering after I left the steps. If you think we can't possibly win, and they agree, you should quit. I won't quit. I don't expect I've too much of a chance, even with you, but I have no chance without you. I know that, but I am going to be my own man here. In Washington too, if I win. I don't know what the folks who hired you promised. I don't care. They didn't buy me, so I am not going to let you, or anyone else, steer my boat. If I think it is good, I'll do it. If I don't, I won't. I'm not one of your hungry politicians."

Bob looked like he was watching California slide into the sea, but he finally sighed. "I'll stick around. I'll never get another job, not after this fiasco, but then I won't have to worry about that. I hear West Virginia has a real nice mental hospital: single rooms, good food, lots of art and crafts and stuff. Go freshen up, Congressman. You have to meet with the press."

"So sorry, Buccaneer! I guess you better load them to the water line with tea and crumpets if you want to stay in their good graces. I explained that to you before, quite a few times, in fact."

"You still hung up on *that*?"

"Do skunks stink? I'm not talking to a hostile press that won't listen because they're for the other man, or because I don't subscribe to their agenda. I always wondered why politicians put up with the media picking at them. It makes no sense.

"What I'm going to do is stash Joe-Joe with his grandparents, then I'm going with Patty to Moe's bar so I can wet my whistle and scuttlebutt with old shipmates. Patty Lane bragged on my speech, or whatever the hell it was, so I might buy her *two* beers and get her tipsy.

"They are not going to *believe* this in Washington." Bob groaned, flopping into a chair and grasping the sides of his head with both hands.

"Hang loose, Bob. When you get done pacifying the pre-pubescent know-it-all media folks, you tote one or two of the scum to Moe's, providing you can find any without rabies. I'll feed them a few beers, if I have money left after the barflies get done with me."

It was as though six years had never passed. Several of the people I'd supervised and steamed with when I was on recruiting duty were cuddled at the bar sucking up on beer. Some had retired from the Navy and some were still on recruiting as career recruiters. Most were regulation civilians who lived in Big Otter since Day One.

Naturally, the barflies were the first to latch on. All started talking at once, with my favorite 'fly yelling the loudest.

"Hey, Patty, yu still look like a kid, but yu sure done put age on ol' Boot Camp! Yu better watch hit, honey. Boot Camp's gettin' too ol' for thet foolin' 'round stuff yu whup on him."

The other 'flies got their licks in as oral abuse flew hot and heavy in my direction as if I had never been away. If their mission was to make Patty blush, they accomplished it. She shifted to the color of a ripe cranberry -- and giggled. Then she kissed each and every one of the nasty old men!

I didn't resent the abuse the old devils laid on me. It was their way of showing they liked me. I shook their hands, but didn't say anything. I was too choked up at seeing them again. They were so old when I'd last seen them that I expected most of them would have died. Not a single 'fly was missing. All were mustered at the bar, just like before.

"Stop tryin' t' make points with us, Boot Camp. Thet glad-hand stuff ain't goin' t' get yu no wheres. We'uns ain't a-goin' t' buy yu no beer. We'uns went t' yur damn speech. Vote fer yu too, if'n yu wuz to buy us 'nough beer." explained my favorite 'fly, a retired ship's cook -- vintage World War Two.

Gunny Thorton, realizing we were in the place, lumbered off his stool, grabbed Patty's upper arms just below her shoulders, lifted her straight into the air and kissed her on her forehead. He whirled in my direction with Patty still dangling off the floor at arm's length and let loose with his usual bellow, "Clay! Damn it, Clay! That was one hell of a good speech! I didn't know you had it in you!"

Gunny was my long-time best buddy, but I owned him far more than long-time friendship. He realized Patty's worth early on and gave it his best shot to convince me she was the girl I was waiting for. I resented it at the time because I was not waiting for *any* girl. But if it had not been for him pushing me, I might have managed to out-maneuver her efforts to pull me into formation steaming. Had that happened, I would have missed out of the best part of my life.

My ex-steaming buddies and ex-recruiters clustered around like bees in a sunny orchard. I didn't know what I'd ever done for them, but my getting elected to congress would have been easy as finding trouble in Naples, Italy if they had their way. They thought I ought to be president!

Angie Wallace, once my top recruiter, kissed Patty, then turned to me. "What I calls you now?" she asked, grabbing me around the neck, pulling my head down and hanging a lip lock on me.

"Just like before, Angie. Call me by my first name. Master

Chief." I joked.

"*Clay*!"

"Don't yell at him, Patty. It's better'n calling him God."

"Oh, that is so sacrilegious! Was that before I met him . . . or you fibbing?"

"He didn't makes no one calls him God, but I 'spect he damned well thought 'bout it!"

"Where's Charles, Angie." I questioned, thinking it was time for a sea change in the conversation, so I shifted it to the whereabouts of her husband, who I'd helped into the Merchant Marine.

"He be heading to a 'nother starving country in *Marine Princess* with a load of grain. Sudan this time. He be second mate now and be money hungry like a broke gambler. He do like them big bucks! I hardly got my hands on him since we be formation steaming!"

"Step on him Angie. You're a CPO. Exercise some practical leadership."

Angie, for reasons not understood by me, had no intention of ridding herself of semi-ghetto speech. I once told her that her non-standard speech would likely hamper her advancement into the top ranks, but she gaffed me off. She must have acquired her speech from friends and associates while growing up because her mother used good standard grammar. Angie had never mentioned a father. I suspected he was a secret buried in the past and make no effort to learn his whereabouts. His whereabouts was none of my business.

"Huh! I be a CPO with two kids to raise and feed with the fleet reserve breathing down my neck. It look like we ain't going to have no Merchant Marine long either, the way ships be re-flagging or laid up. We be trying to pay off a working farm before shipping quits."

"Hell, Angie, you're one of the top people in the Career Recruiting Force! The Navy will let you remain on active duty forever, even if you don't advance to senior chief."

"Advance like you, I suppose? That ain't likely. I ain't no hero. I gots no big medal. I ain't never been shot or blowed up. I never had no admirals writing evaluations that say I can stops water by looking mean. No, I be hanging up my anchor next two-three years. I gots to raise them two tough boys of ours, Master Chief."

"I was teasing about calling me master chief, Angie. I'm not in the Navy. I'm some sort of civilian, a sand crab, maybe, but not a regulation one."

"You be master chief to us recruiters long as we gots breath, but I prays to calls you congressperson. I don't knows what pull I gots with them other blacks 'round here, but I'm sure going to gives them a sea bag full of reasons why they *better* votes for you!"

Angie had been my mainstay on recruiting, once she accepted me as her boss. She was, almost every year, ranked as the top recruiter in an eleven state area. She was a real hard nose, but one of the best young leaders I'd had the pleasure to supervise. She had ran my largest recruiting station as recruiter-in-charge. She had since advanced to chief petty officer and now had my old job as zone supervisor, even though she was one or two pay grades junior to those who would normally fill that billet. She was an early supporter of Patty's attempts to maneuver me into formation steaming, although she had nothing good to say about any girlfriend prior to Patty.

"I appreciate the help, but most black folks would vote the democrat ticket if Simon Legree was the candidate. You know that. Say, how's Book, these days, or did his wife kill him?" I asked, referring to a recruiter who had bad clusters in his read-write disc. He acted as dumb as a door knob, but smart and sneaky at the same time. Book told the truth only once in his entire life, but lied his way out of it when he realized what he had done. His crazy antics like to drove me off pier head when he worked for me on recruiting.

"You remembers when she be mad and go home to Seattle?

She never come back! That let that fool Book keep doing exactly what he wanted with that high yellow woman, Linda."

"They still together?" I asked. The woman to whom Angie referred was a very light black woman with a doctorate degree and a drift factor almost as bad as that of Eugene 'Book' Arnet. They were a strange couple, her with a doctorate degree and Book a seventh or eighth grade dropout.

"*Together*? They be formation steaming! They be married three-four years now. Thank God, they gots no kids! Remember you said kids by them two would have the drift factor of the *Flying Dutchman*? They would too. Book is dumber than a sledge hammer and Linda's drift factor is worse since she started playing house with Book, if that be possible."

"For a man who can't say Black, he sure went off the rails with one."

"Ah, he still call us 'Coons, but he don't know no better and he don't mean nothing by it. It be crazy! Black folks like Book and he like us, her in a big way. He don't think 'bout much of nothin' 'cept her narrow waist, big butt and long legs! I likes her better'n I used to, Master Chief, but I be mess'n that woman up if she hurt Book. I don't 'spect she will. Linda be a plain fool about Book."

That was another thing that had not changed. Angie taking up for Book, just like before, no matter what wild, dumb stunt he pulled.

"Angie, a doctorate degree toting Black, married to an high school dropout redneck makes me all the more certain that The Big Admiral in the Sky doesn't exercise control over who jumps whose bones. What's Book doing since he retired from the Navy -- selling cemetery plots or living off her income as a professor?"

"Why, the fool wuz piped over the side and went right to work representing a company that sell farm machinery, tractors and stuff. He be a good salesman. He can talk BS to anybody. He be dumb and shrewd at the same time, Book is. Linda say they gives him lots of raises. The Lord do take care of His weak children!

"I sees you eyeballing the bar, Master Chief. Still, can't waits to suck a bottle, huh?"

"I only drink when I fall in with a bad crowd. Like today."

"You don't lie neither!

"Hey, Patty! Let's throws some drunks outta booth and plot against the master chief like when we be figuring on how to gets him married off to you. That wuz fun!"

After Angie and Patty hustled off to a booth, I crawled up on a bar stool beside Gunny, threw a fifty on the bar and told Moe to fill us up and feed the barflies some beer.

"You can't buy no beer in here today, Clay." Moe said. "It ain't every day I get some dumb ass in here that wants to be a congressman. I will take money for the 'flies though.

"Gunny, I watched Patty cash Boot Camp's whole pay check at a place called *Banco Andalusia* when I visited them in Spain, but I never seen her give none of it back to him. So where'd he get all the green? Knock some poor woman over the head and relieve her of her coin purse? Can't be much else. He lost his gigolo license when he married Patty."

Same old Moe. The more he liked someone, the more he worked to get under their skin. He must have been having a bad day. He missed bad mouthing me the instant I arrived and he didn't say anything to Patty to make her blush. I wondered if he was starting to feel his age.

After Moe hobbled down the bar to pacify the 'flies raucous demand for service, Gunny observed, "I see Patty is still locking them big, gray eyes on your beat up carcass, watching every move you make. Remember the night I told you she was doing that? You got to cussin' and sputterin' and I followed through and led you right down the primrose path. You almost had acute heart failure when I told you she was in love with you!"

"I thought you was a major stone-ass at the time, but I finally figured out I either had to marry her, or ship out to a distant land where she couldn't find me. Patty had all my halyards wrapped around the mast and you and Angie helped her tangle them tighter!

"Gunny, you never understood just how confused I was about her. You kept on me about how sweet Patty was and how I didn't realize she was head and shoulders above any women I'd ever known, including the blue-blood English gal, Mary I ran with when I was in the Mediterranean aboard *Forrestal*. You bugged me about how I thought Patty was only boarder-line cute, rather than ravishing like Mary. That was not true, Gunny. I never thought her plain, or anything like plain.

"Problem was Patty looked different at different times. One time she looked only cute, then she looked pretty, then she looked beautiful. It was flat confusing and weird!. I realized when she walked up the aisle that I was looking at the most beautiful woman I'd ever want to see. Another thing you didn't know, but I did. I liked her the day I met her and fell in love with her soon after that. I just didn't want to get married!

"You weren't keen on marriage either, as I recall. It took you even longer than me before Elizabeth beat you down to parade rest! Of course, I didn't push on you like you did to me."

"You didn't push on me, but you damn sure bad mouthed me about wimping out and not running the streets with you after I started taking Elizabeth out .

"It's good, Clay. Real good. We get along like two kittens in a basket. I'm still a little mad that you wasn't here to be my best man. Here I suited up in my full-dress uniform for your wedding and stood there watching you quake, all ready to catch you if you hit the deck. What'd you do? Hauled stern to Spain before I got married! I had to draft Sergeant Price as my best man."

"How's the baby?"

"She ain't no baby, you moron! Beth is almost three years old. You know, that's funny. I never expected to have kids. Hell, I never expected to get married. I sure never thought about having a baby girl!

"I don't know what it'll be like -- horsewhipping boys wild on the make when she's a teenager, but I expect I'll find out. She's terrible pretty, which will make it worse. Looks like she'll be a little, tiny doll like Patty when she grows up."

That was a relief. Gunny and Elizabeth shook the earth when they walked and neither was fat, just *big*! Then, again, if she turned out five foot-ten inches and one hundred-fifty pounds, Gunny would think her tiny.

"Elizabeth's son still around?"

"Yeah, he finishes college next year. He graduated high school early. He's going to law school next. It'll take most of the money me and Elizabeth and his dad can muster up, but he's a real good boy. He treats Little Beth like she was gold!"

"I wondered how you'd get along with her son. You didn't hardly know him when I left."

"I was kind of worried about getting along with her kid, but he's like my own son now. I get on good with Elizabeth's Ex too. I sometimes study on why their marriage didn't work, both are fine people Their divorce worked to my benefit though."

"He's probably afraid of your moose ass."

"You never seen him, did you? Guy Gene ain't no little fellow! Must be six-four."

We were deep in scuttlebutt, down about a beer and thinking on a second, when Bob had to ruin it by showing up with a skinny runt under tow.

"Clay, Gunny, this is Paul Rankin. His column is carried in over three hundred newspapers. He's also a sometimes Sunday morning talking head. He says you won't need rabies shots, not today."

We exercised our grips and grins, after which I introduced them to Moe and the 'flies at the bar. After handshakes all around, I asked Mister Rankin. "You a drinker of that French frog slime, or a wine sipper?"

"I don't much care for men who do not partake of the

occasional bottle of God's nectar. I'll have a long-necked PBR"

"You passed muster. Crawl up on this stood and we'll see what Moe can do about the Blue Ribbon beer."

"Speaking of PBR's . . . you commanded one in Vietnam, didn't you?"

"I commanded nothing. I went into the Riverine Advisory Group to square their communications away and somehow wound up riding herd on PBR's. At best, you could say I was an officer in charge. I say 'best' because a Vietnamese Navy lieutenant commander was in command of the flotilla in our neck of the woods. I ended in temporary charge after him and a bunch of PBR sailors got killed.

"He was a feisty fellow and a fine man with a nice family. He was nothing like what you journalists wrote about Vietnamese officers. He was fearless, loved his country and was honest. He never stole anything from his men. He looked out for their welfare twenty four-seven.

"I still hear from his wife now and then. She and their umpteen kids run a convenience store in La Vaca, Texas. They're making it okay, but they wouldn't have to run a store and sail a small shrimp boat if the commander had stolen all the money the media reported Vietnamese officers did."

"You needn't explain the media's actions in Vietnam, Clay. I know the product. I served two tours in the Highlands."

"The Highlands? That doesn't sound like you were an Al Gore, way behind the lines type military media person."

"Hardly . . . Al Gore wasn't a captain, or anything else in the Green Berets."

"**A real live baby killer!**" Gunny yelled. "The skinniest I ever seen."

"I've been called that." Paul smiled. "We weren't totally bad. We carried more Montag nard babies out of the Highlands on our backs than we burned."

"I was just joking. I worked some with the Green Grunts.

They were Straight Arrow troops. I never met any 'Nards, but I heard they are real bastards in a firefight."

"I hope never to fight another war, Gunny. If I do, I hope to have a troop or two of them."

"Nasty fighters, huh?"

"Real nasty. They had been pushed around by the Vietnamese for hundreds of years and didn't like either side. I never met one with education, most couldn't read and write, but they were smart. They realized they would experience a lot of hell if the North Vietnamese took over Vietnam, so they went with the South, more or less. They caught sheer hell when the war ended. You never read about that in the papers. It was not the party line. I think of the ones I worked with almost every day, wondering what happened to them. I intend to go there one day and see."

"Are you some sort of different media person, Paul?" I asked, wondering at his comments, which were quite unusual for a media midget as was his bitter remark about burning babies.

"I like to think I am the print version of Walter Cronkite, but that would be like saying a kitten is a tomcat. Cronkite was the best of the pack until he went off the rails about Vietnam. I never understood why he did that. But, like Cronkite did for most of his life, I take pride reporting both sides of a story, when there are two sides. Fellow members of the media swear I'm a conservative, but I'm not -- not when I write. My readers wouldn't like me taking sides."

"I don't know about that, but I do know one thing. I know I'll get drunk if I hang with you degenerates. My wife, Patty, can drink almost one beer. She's had that, plus one. A couple-three more for me and I'll be in no shape to sling her across my shoulder and tote her home. Then too, drinking and driving in West Virginia is not a real smart thing to do. State troopers take offense.

"Tell you what, Paul . . .I already asked Gunny and some other folks to our house tonight, seeing as how it's Friday and we've got a start on a good booze-up. If you're looking for a smoking gun, or hidden bodies, that'll be your best chance. Gunny and I served together three times, once in a ship, once in the same general area and once here. That woman with my wife in the far booth claims to know more about my escapades than the FBI who ran all my background investigations. She ratted me out the very first time I brought Patty here!"

"I suspect my wife would rather visit a private home than hang with me in the Foxfire Hotel bar. We'll accept the invitation, but that won't slant anything I might write about you."

"Don't expect it to. All I want is accurate reporting. If you think I'm a knucklehead, say so. If you think I might make a decent congressman, write that.

"I would, though, like to know one thing. Why would a big-time columnist come to a little burg like Big Otter to cover the kick-off speech of a backwoods candidate? West Virginia is too unimportant for a fellow to make much of a splash in congress, even if I am elected."

"The Word on the street is your knowledge of politics exceeds, slightly, that of a Himalayan monk. Stories making the loop of how you intend to run your campaign are difficult to believe. You may fade away in a matter of weeks, but writing about your kick-off will produce a column. If your campaign gets interesting, I'll have the jump on other columnists.

"I'm making something of an exception with you, Clay. My columns often concern politics, but I seldom write about individual politicians. Politicians are not unlike laughing hyenas. Some are larger than others, but all have the same spots and make the same sounds!"

CHAPTER FIVE

FEEDBACK

I sucked down more than a few Fall City beers Friday night, but woke with a clear head. Patty, Joe-Joe and I dug into our usual Saturday morning breakfast, which we all pitched in to prepare. Patty functioned as head chef. Joe-Joe and I, having no competence in culinary arts, served as mess cooks. Patty resisted my efforts to make coffee, which she said could be used to preserve lumber.

Paul drank about one-fourth of a case of my beer and his share of Spanish brandy at our Friday evening get-together. He obtained a sea bag full of information about me, but I had no idea what he might write in his column. I liked him as a man, but he *was* a card-carrying member of the sleazebag media. I could have lived nicely without some of the items my steaming buddies ratted to Paul, but I couldn't argue with none of it and thought it best to get all my good and bad points out in the open.

Angie made no bones about it. She said I could walk about two inches above the water and had cured the weak, the lame and the halt with a laying on of hands. She also said I was bad to chase trashy women before I married. Sluts was a word she used often. She maintained I was prone to use naughty language when mad.

Paul really got a load of information when Book and Linda showed up, looking like they had just crawled out of bed, which they probably had.

Linda, although suffering from a bad drift factor, was harmless.

Book was a Mark One-Mod Zero walking pet rock. He had the darnedest knack of saying the wrong thing. His sentences were apt to garble and his comments sometimes made no sense at all, not to people with a normal thought process. Book had bad clusters in his read-write disc.

Book was one of my favorite people.

When Book realized Paul was interested in talking about me, he went directly into Motor Mouth Mode. God would have had to zap him with The Big Finger to shut him up.

"Master Chief is right good t' work fer, 'cept he treats regular folks some kinda bad when he lets go with his awful bad temper. He's real bad t' get pissed fer not even one good reason. Ain't no one never chewed no human bein' out like thet master chief when he's pissed. Why, he done chewed me out like a boot seaman more times than I got hairs on my ass!

"I recollect one time all I done wuz carry some old men teachers to uh lap dancin' joint. Some way's thet got t' be my fault. It wuz right bad 'cause th' master chief done told me a-fore I taken 'em t' Orlando thet I wuz t' keep 'em happy. He done said, 'Book, yu escort 'em teachers on th' Educator Orientation Visit and yu keep 'em happy.' Thet's what he said and I done thet right good. And, when me and Linda, who wuz one 'em teachers I carried to Orlando, got back to Big Otter, he chewed on me fer maybe three-four hours. Why, he done chewed me out fer sayin' Linda wuz th' best looking 'Coon I ever done seed. Yu look at her and yu tell me if'n I ain't some kinda right! She's one fine 'Coon. Ain't nobody thet can't see that.

"I don't get what hit were I done wrong. He said 'Coons is furry kinda animals with black masks and he wuz a-goin t' drop me outta a helicopter if'n I called black folks 'Coons ever again. He can't be no place close right on thet. He don't seem t' know much 'bout colored folks, but I got me right smart uh thet sensitivity stuff. Why, when I done told him what my new woman, Linda, what I jes met in Orlando, said 'bout how I wuz th' most unlighted man she'd seed, he laughed and carried on like he went plumb nuts on me. Kinda like me bein' unlighted was funny."

Paul wasn't a weak link, but he acted a mite disconnected, as usually happened after one listened to Book for the first time.

Book would have been a disaster in any location, other than the one I had assigned him in Kentucky when he reported for duty as a recruiter. How he had gotten himself shifted from the naval reserves to active duty as a recruiter was a mystery I never solved. Fortunately, he fit perfectly with the natives in that area and was a great success as a recruiter. He apparently still fit in, from what Angie said about his success as a farm equipment salesman.

Gunny got under sail and told Paul I was the only anchor clanker he admitted to knowing. Unfortunately, he'd had a drop or two of Kentucky bourbon and told Paul about fighting his way out of a Palma bar loaded to the gunwales with Royal Marines. He claimed to have done that while dragging me behind him. It might have happened that way. All I remember was a Royal calling American Marines 'Fairy Bum Suckers' after which the wrath of God descended about my head and shoulders and it got dark. Gunny mentioned a couple of other falls from grace too

Several other of my old steaming buddies and recruiters got their licks in too.

I could hardly wait to see Paul's literary effort.

Late in the evening, Patty and Grace Rankin had pranced, arm-in-arm, into the den from the library where they'd stashed themselves to do their chatting, gossiping, trading husband control techniques, whatever.

Grace was a tall, chic blonde with a hint of good breeding and old money in her bearing. Patty was a tiny, taffy haired woman with the air of a fresh, perky country girl. Although outwardly nothing alike, they were acting like long-cruise shipmates. I'd seen Patty hit the bar for only two small glasses of Bristol Cream Sherry, but they must have slopped down more than that.

Patty went into a dissertation that made my ears redder than a possum's rump in poke berry time.

"Paul, you have probably evaluated Clay as something of a diamond in the rough He is that, as are many men in West Virginia, including my Father. Clay is no saint, but he is a man with deep convictions. He does not much care what a person thinks, no matter how important one might be, once he is satisfied with his decision.

"Praise embarrasses and confuses Clay, so he will dislike me saying this, but he is as honorable as he is brave. Dating me was the only time when he was honorable, but not brave. He was frightened to death of me!

"I was frightened to death of Clay too -- before I met him!

"My cousin, then acting recruiting public affairs officer, asked me to conduct an interview with Clay for my college newspaper, of which I was editor. He briefed me about Clay. He said Clay was mean, a heavy drinker, a bar fighter and a woman-izer who didn't have a girl in every port -- he had two or three! My cousin didn't just fib. He lied! Well. . . not about the women . . .

"I had no real experience with men. My girl friends, if I might use the term loosely, took advantage of my inexperience and frightened me even more than my cousin. One of them was the girlfriend of my cousin who I later learned had disliked me for years and years. They told tales of the two-fisted, hard-drinking, womanizing Henry Clay Berkeley, much as my cousin had done. They caused me to expect a Popeye type sailor to appear for the interview!

"Clay was nothing like what I had been led to believe. He was not a rooster-brained, muscle bound sailor at all. He was tall, slender, very erect and looked positively splendid in his dress blue uniform, which blazed with colorful ribbons and devices! He was a perfect gentleman who had me totally at ease just minutes after we met.

"Near the end of the interview, I managed to obtain a date with Clay. I maneuvered a date with Clay because my girlfriends argued I could not do so, no matter what I did. I later discovered, to my horror, that my girlfriends had tricked me into attempting to obtain a date in order to embarrass me when he declined. Well, Sir, they expended a lot of effort for nothing! I knew I wanted a date with Clay before the first hour passed, a real date. Not one I arranged solely to prove something.

"The more I thought about it, the more I realized I had to tell Clay what I had done. Otherwise, you see, any relationship that developed, and I was, by then, determined one would, would deteriorate once he discovered and believed I had dated him only to prove a point. So, the evening of the not-real date, I told him.

"He knew what I was doing the entire time! The girlfriend who disliked me had asked him to assist them in playing a trick on me. The fact that he neither mentioned it, nor told me he had refused to assist them, made me aware he was a kind, under-standing man who would not take advantage of anyone. He did not then know I really *did* want to be with him!

"I had a wonderful time the Sunday of our first real date, which could not really be classified as a date either because all we did was go to church, which I trapped him into doing, planted a yellow rose bush and went to Moe's bar. It was the beginning of my life! Clay acted as though I was the sole woman in the world, but he did not make a pass at me. That was terrible disappointing. I was already in love with him, you see, and I wanted him interested -- Big Time interested. He even tried to shake hands with me when he took me home . I was so hurt! Well, Sir, pass or no pass, I showed him a girl could be inexperienced and still execute a kiss!

"I thought kissing him would make him . . . er, interested, but he spent nearly the next four months trying to escape from me. It was strange. One minute he would act as if making love was the sole idea in his mind. The next he ignored me as though I suffered from plague! He generally treated me as an innocent child. I could have screamed! I *was* innocent, but I *knew* what I wanted. I kept dropping hints and he kept fending me off. It did not do him one bit of good to ignore my efforts. He never had the slightest chance of escaping marriage with *me,* not from the very first day!

"Clay later explained he was attracted to me from our first meeting in my office, but he believed he was too old and too jaded for a young, inexperienced girl. The dummy! He is only twelve years older.

"What he did not understand, unfortunately, was I did not want a saint and he being older was not a concern. I wanted a flesh and blood, mature male who would love and protect me. A man I could love and respect forever.

"I am telling you this because you have no doubt heard considerable concerning Clay's drinking and womanizing. I made it a point to meet every one of his women that I could. Talk about obvious females! I do not believe he ever took advantage of a woman who did not wish to be taken advantage of. He certainly would not take advantage of *me*, although I did everything except sit up, wag my tail and beg!

"When I first ran with Clay, he and Gunny drank beer like they were trying to support a brewery! Yet, I never seen him wild, unruly or uncouth. Gunny either. Neither of them used foul language . . . well, not very foul.

"Regardless of what you might hear, Clay now barely drinks. I keep beer in the refrigerator, but a case of Clay's favorite beer, Fall City, lasts for days and days. Today was the first occasion he drank more than two bottles of beer at one setting since his retirement party in Gaeta, Italy.

"Grace told me you strive for accuracy in your columns. I ask only that you look at what Clay actually is, instead of what you might have heard. Clay has enemies in this area, my cousin and the publisher of the county newspaper who hates all military men. Neither are to be trusted!"

The Big Otter Fire Department could not have extinguished the glow on Patty's face when she finally finished, but she had her lower lip puffed out and she was loaded for bear if Paul said the wrong thing.

"Patty, I will do my absolute best, as always, to ensure accuracy. I will, however, need to make judgment calls. I have had only one day of exposure to Clay. I never heard of him until five days ago. Whether you approve of what I write, I cannot even guess."

After a few hundred additional words from Patty concerning my worthy being, Paul and I slipped away to the farm office, which remained furnished with my great-grandfather's uncomfortable, horse hair stuffed chairs.

Paul didn't ask many questions, but he had lots to say. He argued mostly about how I should cooperate with the media if I wanted my name in front of people. I listened to his pitch, but it didn't change the course I planned to steer.

"Paul, I expect you've been studying politicians for a good while. You've likely seen all sorts. Well, stick around and you'll see a different sort. Maybe not better, but different. I might make a damn fool out of myself, or I *might* manage to keep the media off my back. Oh, I'll talk with them at times, but on my own terms.

"I'm running as a republican, so I couldn't impress the media if I took suction on them six ways from hell. They will also believe, without checking, that I have the infamous military mind-set and that I raped, looted and pillaged my way across Vietnam.

"They won't like me not cuddling up with their happy band of whimpering pseudo-intellectuals who believe the citizens of this country are ignorant clods who need them to interpret the news. They'll treat me like I'm a dumb hillbilly, jumped above his station who wants to steal the rice bowl of a perfectly good, liberal congressperson, who is a card-carrying member of their mutual admiration society.

"They might level their guns on me, but you can bet your stern I'll fire back! They have bigger guns, but maybe I can make up in accuracy what I lack in firepower."

Paul looked at me for a long time before commenting, "I'm

going to do some research, but I don't believe anybody ever tried freezing the media out of their campaign. Looking at it your way, it makes sense. Looking at it from my direction, it makes for stupid!

"Clay, I wish I could give you morale support, but I really don't believe your plan will work. The media will report what they want, regardless of how you massage them, or don't massage them. It will be interesting to watch you run and I'll likely get columns out of it. I don't give you much chance of gaining the seat -- one in a big number. I'll do something for you after the election. If you stick with your current plan and fail to gain the seat, I'll write a column to the effect you went down with your flag flying, your guns firing, that you scored a number of direct hits and didn't surrender until water sloshed over your sea boots!"

"That's the only way I know to operate, Paul. Salute the colors and ride hell bent for election (no pun intended) into the jaws of hell!"

After we cleared up our breakfast mess, Patty invited us shopping I instantly begged off. Patty Lane could spend hours prowling stores and buy nothing. I didn't enjoy inspecting bras and panties without Patty inside them.

I grabbed Joe-Joe from his animal partners in crime and made a speed run to an electronics store where I purchased an answering machine with the largest recording capacity available. I expected to get a lot of nasty telephone calls that I wouldn't bother to return. When Joe-Joe and I had it installed and operating, I took him and Jarhead for a walk. I invited Blue Suit, but he wouldn't go. He feared a sudden downpour, which is known to cause sniffles in cats.

I showed Joe-Joe an aged, moss-speckled cherry tree and explained the fun a neighbor girl and I once had playing house under that tree. I pointed out the depressions in exposed roots we'd used as dishes for the berries and fruit we gleaned from the orchard. Joe-Joe scrambled through the cherry grove, asking questions and demanding answers, like mother -- like son. I told him of the games we'd played from the age of four until we aged and lost interest in such things I didn't tell him we'd held detailed physical examinations while playing doctor. He'd learn about the pleasures of such things soon enough. He had the cherry grove. All he need was the little girl.

I also didn't tell him this was the place I'd seen my first female breast when the little girl later wanted to prove something was happening to her body that was not happening to mine. I was quite taken by her just developing breasts. Unfortunately, when we go old enough to make use of them, her brother caught us in their barn and we had to knock it off. I had big time designs on her, but she discovered when we entered junior high school that there were boys available who did not live just down the road where her brother could keep an eye open for ill-intentions toward her. Her discovery knocked me flat smack out of the running.

All of that lay ahead of Joe-Joe.

"I seen a bear right there, Joe-Joe, when I was a little boy like you, maybe a bit older."

"A bear? A big bear?"

"He looked big to me!"

"Did he eated you up?"

"No, it was funny how it happened.

"Mom, your grandmother, went to pick peas and stuff from the garden and dragged me along. I was fooling around near a hay feeder that used to stand over by those shag bark hickories when I heard a grunting noise. I ran to Mom and told her I heard a bear. She said there were no bears in this part of West Virginia and that I must have heard pigs grunting on a neighbor's farm.

"Well, Joe-Joe, I'd never even seen a bear, let alone heard one grunt, but I had made up my mind that it *was* a bear and kept pestering Mom about it. Mom rarely spanked me, but I think she was about to take a switch to me when she suddenly cried, "Run to the house Clay. Now!"

"I took off like a striped as . . . er, ape! I looked back when

I got to the gas well, that same little shed right down the hill -- and it was a bear!"

Joe-Joe's eyes were as big as Patty's homemade cookies. "Did the bear eated you up?"

"No, he didn't pay us any attention. I suppose he was just passing through the country. He kept going and Mom kept picking peas. My Father later ate her as . . . er, bawled her out for staying there when a bear was in the area."

"Why didn't she runned?"

"I remember her telling my Dad that there wasn't any moth-eaten bear going to keep her from picking her peas when their sugar was up! She was a brave woman."

"Real brave?"

"I'll say! Your grandma Berkeley was a brave woman."

"Is brave good?"

"Yes, it is. Being brave can be a lot of different things. I'll tell you more about it when you're older. For now, let's just say that a person who does what he thinks is right when everybody is against him is a brave person. A man who goes along with the crowd when he knows what they're doing is wrong is more than likely a coward. You'll get into that kind of situation in school before long. Kids will try to get you to do things Mommy and I have told you not to do. If you're brave, you won't do it. Knowing you're right and sticking to your guns is the bravest thing I can think of."

"I'm brave."

"I'm sure you are, Joe-Joe."

"Is Jarhead brave?"

"Jarhead is really brave, but he doesn't know right from wrong. Well, he does, sometimes, but he acts like he doesn't understand so he can get away with doing something bad."

"Like eated Missus Post's flowers?"

"Yeah -- that's one example."

"Is Blue Suit brave?"

"Not unless he eats a lot of catnip. You know how he likes to watch the news on TV? Well, he's very bright and seems to worry about things that makes him afraid, except when he's into catnip. Eating catnip makes him so brave he once beat up a tough, mean, old tomcat that was bigger even than him."

"Will catnip maked me brave?"

"No, but some other stuff will. It's a false bravery though. It's not real. You want to stay away from anything like that. I'll tell you about that stuff some day when you're a mite older.

"There comes Mommy's car up the lane. Let's go see what she brought me." I teased.

"She didn't broughted you nothing. She broughted me something!"

"She didn't either! She brought me something."

"She didn't!"

I was reasonably certain she did, but I didn't expect to get it until bedtime

The old preacher was in fine form Sunday morning. He lit into the sinners, which certainly included me, like it was his final chance for success. He whipped up on The Snake and the rest of us, for most everything bad that happened in the world during the past week. He seemed to be looking right at me. When his harangue of sinners crawled to a halt, he spread his bony arms and said. "We've got one more prayer to say before we go.

"Folks, Henry Clay Berkeley has enlisted to fight the Philistines in Washington. Now, I know the degree of sin in all of you, but Henry Clay hasn't been home enough for me to get a handle on *his* actions. I do know, though, that Patty Lane wouldn't have married him if he was no 'count. Yes, he's a sinner. Some say a black sinner and some of you might not pray for him. You don't have to, but I tell you if you pray against him, it's a sin. It's a sin to ask God for any person to fail. Let's have at it!

"Lord, we're asking You to bless Henry Clay and keep Patty Lane and him and their little boy from harm. We ask You to let people praise his good and understand his bad. You know his heart, Lord, and You know he's a sinner like the rest, but only You know if he will do Your work.

"Lord, you know there's hard and terrible sin in our country. There's filth on the newsstands, in the movie houses, on TV, on the streets, even in some churches. Filth is all around us, Lord. Young women with lips only a few years dry of their mother's milk are birthing children out of wedlock.

"There are a host of people using money intended to do good to buy drugs. It has made them crazy, Lord. They are starving and beating and even burning their children with cigarettes and the like.

"We know there were a lot of old kings in the Bible that didn't follow what you ordered. You cast them kings out. You smote them hip and thigh. You destroyed them until the third and fourth generation. That sounds cruel in this modern world, God, but we suspect you were ending bad blood lines so the mean ideas of those folks would die away with their seed. Maybe that is what You have planned for us, Lord, if we don't clean ourselves up.

"Most folks in this country tries to do right, but we are weak vessels, Lord.

"Some say Henry Clay is a man who tries to do good. He almost got himself killed doing what he thought was good in a terrible war. We see the scars on his face. That makes him look hard and cruel like Bible pictures of the avenging angels. He's not hard and cruel, Lord. You know that because you know his heart. He is soft in his heart, but he is not a fearful man. That make us think You saved him for something. Maybe he will fight the good fight in Washington, if he can understand what it is You want.

"It's sad not a one of us have the ability to hear You directly. We are of a feeble nature and can only feel what you want, and then, only at times.

"Now, I hear Henry Clay reads the Bible 'most every day, but other things I hear makes me think he doesn't have a lot of experience talking to You. Patty Lane has. She's a praying woman. She's followed your way since she was a girl near young as her son. Lord, if You tell Henry Clay something and he does not heed, I believe You can send the message through Patty Lane. She will hear You as well as a human is able.

"I'm not trying to tell you anything, Lord. There's never been anyone able to do that, not even Abraham, Isaac or Jacob, all who could talk directly to You.

"I'm not going to ask You to get him elected, Lord. You might not even *care* what goes on in Washington. Maybe not even in the whole United States of America, which You once chose to bless. There is not one of us enlightened enough to know Your way, even though some TV preachers claim they do.

"We thank you, Lord. Bless all us sinners. Help us to see the Light. In your name, we pray. Amen.

"OK, folks, go forth and eat your dinner. I don't want to hear tell of sinning all next week, particularly from you young folks who are walking out together!"

Mister Patterson mustered me up after we escaped and dragged me under the cherry tree. I never understood their way of doing things after church services. There seemed a taboo against men and women hanging together after church. The men always mustered by the old cherry tree while the women clustered under the wide branches of an old oak tree. The kids went wherever they damn well pleased.

Several men said they would vote for me -- Mister Patterson's loafing buddies, probably. There were more than a few, however, who looked at me like I'd crawled out from under a flat rock. Democrats, probably. A number of women grabbed me when we were edging towards our car and said nice things about my running for congress. Republicans, probably. Still, there seemed more women on my side than men. Patty didn't seem to appreciate their support. She glared at each and every one forward enough to sidle up and pat me on the arm or shoulder. I thought she was taking their actions a little to personal. At least none of them was such a staunch democrat that she looked at me like I engaged in debauchery with sows.

After dinner with the Patterson's, I made a touch and go at Heck's Drugs and Sundries to check out their supply of newspapers. The shop had only one out-of-state newspaper.

Back home, I changed into my Sunday grubbies, then went to the porch and stretched comfortably on the padded swing with my newspapers. I hoped to find the occasional mention of my name, but I also hoped the media wouldn't break me on a wheel spiked with barbed words.

I found a few blurbs that mentioned the kicking off of my campaign, stuck deep inside the papers between such interesting subjects as the rice crop in Bangladesh and the common market happenings. Most of the articles were along the lines that an unknown, of the last water hillbilly had crawled out of his swamp, didn't have a prayer, knew it, but wanted to cause problems for the fine, liberal incumbent who boasted of a lengthy record of support for his party. Those that mentioned my naval service seemed to equate that with an ass the KKK had cast out! Then I found it in a Wheeling paper. Paul Rankin must have stayed up all Friday night to write the article in time to get it in the Sunday papers.

"Hey, Patty -- will you come out here, Please?"

Patty closed the screen door behind her, pushed her reading glasses to the top of her wavy-curly hair, laid her book on the wicker table, and smiled. "Yes, it is Sunday. No we cannot do anything. You know what the preacher said about sinning.

"Sinning? We're formation steaming legal like, so anything we do can't be sinning."

"It might if Joe-Joe wakes up and catches us engaging in . . . you *Know*!"

"I'm sure open to conducting body exchange drills, but that is not why I called you. Read this to me, please. This article has me so befuddled I don't know port from starboard."

Patty took the paper and settled her fine stern on my lap. I guess my sheer charm go to her, because we got a little side tracked until Joe-Joe pounded through the door and tore across the yard. with Jarhead and Blue Suit in hot pursuit."

"The King is up from his nap."

"Yes, dearest," Patty smoothed the now crumpled newspaper and folded it over. "I told you that would happen. There goes the debauchery!"

"I sure love that kid, but Sunday afternoons sure aren't like they used to be when you paraded your birthday suit, laying your wiles all over my innocent carcass." I grumbled.

Patty turned red. "**Hush**! Let me read.

Rankin's Rambles

Brilliance or Buffoonery

I had the occasion Friday last to hear the kick-off speech of a very different campaigner. I won't refer to him as a politician. He is not one.

Henry Clay Berkeley, of Big Otter, West Virginia, launched his campaign from the steps of the Big Otter federal building and set his course towards the United States House of Representatives on the republican ticket. His folksy presentation contained none of the usual emphatic declarations and promises heard in political speech. It was well laced with words and phrases common to Appalachia and the sea, rather than those usually heard from a politician's podium. He appeared totally at ease, as if discussing the price of cattle over the rails of a stockyard pen.

His campaign, if successful, will be quite an accomplishment in West Virginia where the majority of voters are democrat. He is not concerned that he is totally new on the political scene, or about his chances of winning the congressional seat. He says, should he fail, his showing will be strong enough to scare the incumbent into voting the desires of constituents, rather than casting every vote with his party as Mr. Berkeley contends he does. Mr. Berkeley feels, strongly, that the wishes of constituents should take precedence over the dictates of a lawmaker's party. He does not intend to heap blanket criticism upon his opponent He set the tone of battle by saying the incumbent is a hard worker, then joked that he wasn't certain what the man worked at. He promised to provide, upon request, the source of all future criticism he might level against his opponent.

He informed the surprisingly large crowd that he had a limited program. He cautioned he could not fix all problems, but promised to work on those he considered major: welfare, defense, international relations and job flow from the United States.

He has unique ideas on fixing welfare. He intends to introduce legislation to issue welfare recipients a form of a high tech credit card useable only for material needs: food, clothing and housing. One measure of his strength became evident when he gave credit for this idea to his wife, Patricia, commonly known as Patty

He is no isolationist, but believes the United States should chart her own course without direction from other countries. He believes many countries want only our wealth and the blood of our young. He is firm against involvement in wars of others, unless the United States is, itself, threatened economically or militarily. If elected, he will be one of a tiny minority of congressmen who know war first hand.

Orphaned at sixteen, he joined the Navy at seventeen and remained there twenty-two years. He rose to the rank of master chief petty officer, a rank held by less than one percent of the total force. He was twice wounded in Vietnam. His naval service earned him several decorations: Silver Star, two Purple hearts, Meritorious Service Medal, commendation and achievement medals, unit awards and an even dozen: 'Hey! Me too! I wuz there!' medals and ribbons.

I would not have known of his medals had not his wife showed them to my wife, during which time his wife expounded at length concerning his bravery, his fairness, his kindness and his deep concern for others. Few wives have such high regard for their husbands as Patricia Lane (Patterson) Berkeley -- a strong force in her own right.

Those with whom I spoke agree his anger is terrible to behold. He demonstrates this trait when disparaging statements are made of troops who fought in Vietnam. He is quick to take offense at suggestions anyone he knew burned babies, or raped, looted and pillaged. He is, however, in no way reluctant to broach this subject when he wishes to taunt those who accept the Vietnam party line. Those who mentioned his quick temper maintain he is equally quick to forgive.

It is difficult to believe a man, not a high ranking officer, accomplished the things friends and associates insist he did, but their claims were confirmed with other sources. High ranking naval officers view him as a man able to plan, organize and manage at any level. He is known for working behind the scenes to obtain what he wants to accomplish. He was, among other things, the prime C3 (Command, Control and Communications) planner for every major evolution conducted by the Sixth Fleet during his tour of duty.

He has no trust in the media's ability to accurately report the news. He believes the media is hostile to anybody not a liberal politician. He maintains he will neither brief, nor take questions from media persons who attempt to advance an agenda. He asks neither praise nor approval. Honest, fair reporting is what he wants from the media.

Mr. Berkeley is a unique individual who projects total candor. He was once a registered democrat, but he cares little whether a person is a democrat, a republican or an independent, which will surely put him at odds with both democrats and republicans.

His Appalachian origin is readily detectable in his speech, despite a basic competency in Spanish and Vietnamese. Regardless of accent, many people will listen. He may not win, but he will surely cause his opponent sleepless nights!

"Paul's article is quite good! Clay-honey, it is more than we hoped for."

"It is pretty good It's different too. It doesn't look much like an American wrote it. It's sort of like the articles you find in Limey newspapers – personal like, instead of reading like something cranked out by a machine."

"I read his columns regularly, or I did before we transferred to Europe. He writes to his readers, not to impress contemporaries. He is known for directing his columns towards the average person. Dearest, I believe he is on your side!"

"You're usually right, Kitten, but if he is, he'll be the only one in the media that is."

"Possibly not. People do listen and believe you. Why should the media be different?"

"Because they're a bunch of stone-as . . . er, forget it. Most media folks would report Jesus Christ bobbed three times before He got his balance, then failed to walk exactly flat on the water. "

"*Clay*! Don't say such things!"

"Sorry, Patty, but you've got to admit that Jesus didn't get a fair shake from whoever was reporting the news for the Jews and Romans. That goes to show you nothing much has changed with the media since forever!".

CHAPTER SIX

FEEDING FRENZY

Suddenly I, or rather we, were everywhere: on billboards, barn walls, tree trunks -- even on the side of a little house at the end of a path, a two holler, I think,

Blue Suit had trouble with our TV spots. That cat was some kind of confused. He'd see us appear on TV, jerk his head around to ensure we actually were present, then turn back and study the screen with great concentration. He'd figure it out eventually. Blue Suit was one intelligent cat. He seemed to have the entire program schedule in his head and could tell the difference between news, which he preferred, and other programs

When it was time for the morning and evening newscasts, he would scramble to the top of the wide-backed couch and stretch out. If the TV was not on, he'd make cat-type noises until somebody energized it. When the newscast finished, he left his perch and went about his business. He'd even watched the news in Italy and Spain, which made me wonder if we had a multilingual cat on our hands. He seemed to need the news, probably because he was a Mark One - Mod Zero worrier and wanted to keep abreast of hail, rainstorms, pestilence, disaster, whatever. He did, sometimes, watch shows that featured animals. He particularly seemed to enjoy *All Creatures Great and Small.*

Bob Criss spent a lot of time muttering to himself after I gave a speech, but I couldn't fault his ability to raise money or find stumps for me to crawl on. Rumors of secretive men and women flitting about the terrain querying my background were regular fare at our briefings. Bob said it was a common campaign tactic, but we needn't worry because, unlike other candidates, I had no 'paper trail' for them to dig through. Bob was already bad shaky, so I didn't tell him they didn't need a paper trail. The barflies at Moe's could help them out. Then, again, probably not. The barflies considered me fair game, but were not likely to tolerate an outsider trying to put hooks into me. Outsiders stood a good chance of getting whipped into a state of extreme ill health by the aged, but tough 'flies.

My opponent blanketed the TV airwaves with slick, professionally produced commercials. One panned across our beautiful state showing playful children and happily working men and women. Another showed a man praising the virtues of my opponent while the man trout fished a clear, swift stream. None of my opponent's commercials mentioned anything he'd actually accomplished for West Virginia, but they hinted at much. Healing the sick and advanced water walking were, apparently, among his lesser achievements.

Fancy commercials aside, he was in the same fix as his party. He didn't know anything about me and hadn't found anything to use against me that I had not already reported by spilling my guts in speeches. I had not yet cast stones, which put him in the position of not wanting to be the first to run negative ads. He stumped the district, calling my platform unworkable at every bend and dent in the road. He cited my lack of experience as proof I couldn't accomplish anything in Washington if, through some weird twisting of voter's minds, I was elected   Bob's polls indicated my opponent's support decreased with every speech he made, although my own numbers hardly increased at all. There had to be a host of 'Undecided' running loose. My opponent stopped stumping, regrouped, and demanded a debate.

After a lengthy argument with Bob, we blanked the

airwaves ourselves.

"Hello, Folks. I'm Clay Berkeley, the republican candidate for the U.S. House of Representatives. You've heard my opponent state I'm afraid to debate him. That is true, so far as it goes. He's spent his life in politics and has likely taken courses in public speaking, and debating. I have not done so – there are no such courses at sea where I have spent most of my life. What he wants me to do reminds me of what an old coal miner told me when I was a young sprout. He said, 'Any man can be made a fool of, but that doesn't make him a fool. He is only a fool when he makes a fool out himself.' 'nough said'"

My refusal to grant interviews or hold press conferences caused a strange thing to happen. I was sought after! The more I refused, the more the media chased Bob trying to get me to say something to them. They were not unlike a host of male castaways pursing the sole female.

Bob was coming apart like a wooden ship with a bad case of sea worms He seen my tactics work, seen that I was getting publicity, seen the polls rise slightly, but refused to believe it. He tore his hair and rent his garments trying to convince me to cooperate with the media.

Finally, after a discussion with Patty, I agreed to do one press conference with the print media. Bob was so happy he went out and got wasted on Old Stump Blower. It took him one day to get mobile, two days to get completely sober and a few more days before he was four-oh and fighting fit.

Although establishments were available with large meeting rooms, I insisted Bob rent a rather uncomfortable conference room in the Foxfire Hotel. The media squealed like stuck hogs when they discovered the room's size restricted them to twenty people seated in four rows of hard, folding chairs. I'd beaten them down in numbers, but suspected they'd come up with a press pool loaded to the gunwales with mad dog media type persons.

I didn't want Patty to attend the bloodletting, but she puffed our her lower lip and went stubborn on me.

I knew exactly how a Moor felt when dragged before the Spanish inquisition when I stepped in front of the podium. The media looked a mean bunch. Strong lights in the rear of the room made it impossible to determine their reason, but I suspected somebody had sneaked in TV cameras. I glanced at Patty, standing to my right, and got a wide, broad-toothed smile. I cast off and let her rip.

"I'd normally say good morning, but I don't expect it will be -- not for me.

"Most members of the media who have dissected my speeches and my commercials called me everything from a near idiot to a rabid, right wing lunatic. A tiny few published fairly accurate accounts and called me nothing worse than a rock-bound conservative. I am none of these, but that made no difference to the media. What I say today will made no difference.

"I want you to understand I agreed to this interview only because my campaign manager, Mister Bob Criss, a pretty nice fellow, threatened to steal a Civil War sword from my house and fall on it if I refused this conference.

"Just between us, Mister Criss didn't exhibit the slightest sense of political correctness. He said he was going to fall on the cavalry sword Mother's great-granddaddy, Arch Preston, used to cut through Yankee troops when he rode with Stonewall Jackson, instead of great-granddaddy Mason Berkeley's Union infantry sword. Now, Bob knows the rebel position was politically incorrect and he should not have even considered doing himself in with a sword that belonged to a man who fought on the wrong side. Why, that would cause a hissy fit in the media!

"You all have an idea I'm hostile to the media? Good grasp, Folks! I damned sure am!

"It appears the media chucks rocks better when they don't actually look into things, or pay attention to what a person says or does. I can understand that. It's easier to get on the telephone and check as to what party line is currently in vogue, then bang out a few dozen words along that line. That technique provides more time to hang in fern bars, or whatever it is media folks do for recreation – stick pins through tumblebugs, maybe.

"One newspaper reported I don't believe in a free press. I've visited countries where the government controls the press and I've talked with citizens of such countries. They believe nothing broadcast or printed.

"We are guaranteed a free press in the United States. Do we have one? Free, yes. Fair, no. The majority of the media is staffed with people who subscribe to the same political and social ideology. They spent their time debunking ideas of folks who think differently.

"You don't believe me? I challenge you to sit down with me and a pile of newspapers. I will show you dozens of sly remarks in articles that appear to be totally above board, but are actually revealing the author's true beliefs. I can do the same with TV newscasts. I stand ready to prove this, but I will not get the opportunity. None of you have the guts.

"How many citizens in this country believe what you write and broadcast? Only the weak, the dull, the halt and fellow travelers who subscribe to your school of thought. Look at your poll numbers. You should be ashamed! Only child molesters and members of congress rank below the media. Actually, congress and the media alternate for the next to worst ranking, depending on when the poll is taken.

"What I just said will undoubtedly re-enforce the media's idea that I'm a dog-bit conservative who hates liberals. I do dislike people who lash themselves firmly to one train of thought. Both conservatives and liberals do that, but liberals are far more inflexible in their beliefs. Don't believe that? Watch the peace creeps, the tree huggers and other liberal groups in action. No slack for anyone who believes differently. None at all.

"I am not speaking of true liberals, of which few exist. You'll have to check the dictionary to learn what the word liberal really means. It is far too broadly used today. My wife, Patty, explained that to me.

"Liberals are okay, if one remembers what old Tolstoy

wrote in *Anna Karenina*. I might not have this totally correct, but he wrote something like, '. . . thus liberalism has become a habit with Oblonsky. He enjoyed his newspaper (you could substitute TV) as he did his after-dinner cigar, for the slight haze it produced in his brain.'

"You should realize you cannot survive without people like me to feed on, unless you want to write feature stories and want ads. You have a problem. I can survive nicely *without* you. I don't *need* you!

"I am going to open the floor for questions with a couple rules. Call it muzzling the press if you like. The first amendment protects you, but does not say I have to feed you! The main rule is that I will not answer anybody who hits me between the running lights with a leading question, or works a twist into my answer before I even utter it. You ain't seen ignore until you try that!

"I'll also ignore those who try to argue with an answer. You're reporters. That means you should report exactly what you hear -- not what you want to hear. You are not the most intelligent people on earth -- far from it. You do not, contrary to what you might believe, know ever so much more than average folks. I can hear more common sense from a bunch of aged barfly veterans in one night than I can from media spouting throughout a week of Sundays!

"I'll start at the left, rear row. Have at it."

"Mister Berkeley, does your dislike of the media have anything to do with the reporting during the Vietnam era?"

"Do hogs wallow? Along with what I said about skewed articles and lock-stepped thinking you acquired when your college professors shoveled globs of American-hating, left-wing manure into your receptive skulls. Next question."

"You say you never seen atrocities in Vietnam? How can that possibly be -- if you had the combat experience indicated in Paul Rankin's column?"

"You came real close to my ignore mode, Buddy. I'll answer anyway, just for drill."

"I didn't see atrocities in Vietnam, except that war itself is an atrocity. Look at the guys and gals who visit the Vietnam Wall. Ask one of the guys without arms or legs. Go to Saigon -- or whatever it is called now. You will see the same sort of guys begging in the streets. Want to talk about innocent civilian casualties? Go to England or Germany and ask old folks about bombs raining down on them in World War Two. Next question."

"You sound anti-war. How? You did, after all, spend years in the Navy."

"Fellow -- that's also close to what I said would cause cut off. If you want to report my twenty-two years in the Navy, do it."

"I am anti-war. I don't know anyone in the military who is *not* anti-war. Oh, I've heard of a couple-three who might have been warmongers, but I never met one. I will say being anti-war doesn't mean war is never necessary. You'll likely see another in your lifetime, if we don't figure how to keep weapons from fanatics who seem to be crawling from their slime all over the world.

"Yes, I spent a good while in the Navy. And I loved it -- mostly. I stayed in the Navy because I felt I was doing something useful and I liked the camaraderie. I also liked the sense of responsibility, both in my occupational field and to the sailors who worked for me. Naval service is not easy, but it is exciting and satisfying.

"Men and woman are doing 'volunteer' service so lily-liveried, narrowly educated young men don't get dragged from their mama's breast, kicking and screaming every step of the way. I believe every man and woman who served in the military, whether they liked it or not, prevented conflicts. That goes for those who will serve in the future.

"Military folks give up a lot to defend you and also to keep people free in lots of places. Sadly, the only time the media pays attention to them is when they stumble and fall. It might not trip your trigger, but it is almost impossible to obtain great success without a few failures along the way. Some touchy-feel people want to turn the military into a weird sort of social testing ground.

That is not the job of the military. Their job is to overcome the opposition by killing the opposition and breaking things. Sound dirty? War is dirty!

"Why do men and women volunteer? It surely is not because they couldn't survive nicely in civilian life, contrary to typical media belief!

"Those of you with children had better start looking at the world as it really is. Otherwise, there is a really good chance your children will bleed out in a foreign land where we had no business to begin with. I say 'children' because women could be drafted in future wars. Next question."

"How can you say you will accomplish more than the incumbent when you have no experience in politics?"

"True. I have no experience in politics. I've never even been to Washington. I avoided that place like acute leprosy when I was in the Navy. I'll have difficulty steering a good course up and down the passageways of the capitol building.

"That said . . . what has my opponent, Mister Burnside, accomplished? I see a lot of people out of work, so he hasn't brought business into our area of West Virginia. I've asked around, mainly to democrats, to try to determine what he has accomplished in his many years in Washington. No one could provide anything, except ribbon cuttings, grips and grins and such things. It is more than likely that he solved problems for individual constituents, but I have no way of determining that. I'll give him credit for that anyway. Now, I have never met the man. I have nothing against him. He's probably a pretty good fellow. But, his voting record tells me he's a shill for his party. I'll do better. Next question."

"You state in nearly every speech you intend to work with the other party. How can you do that and maintain good relations with the republican party?"

"I don't owe my party loyalty if what they want goes against my grain. I don't much care which party a person belongs to, not if they put constituents first -- after the United States, that is.

"I've met but few people I couldn't deal with. I have a record of being able to get people to work together and get things done. Don't take my word for it, there are people in the Navy who will tell you that. A few live around here. Next question!"

"I'm not faulting either your speeches, or your advertising, but they are quite different. Do you really believe your tactics will result in your getting elected?"

"I hope they do, but I won't don sackcloth and ashes if they don't. I don't need the job to stay out of blood bank lines. I guess my campaign does look strange. Maybe it is strange, but it is mine. Patty's too.

"The Hatch Act prohibited active participation in politics while in the Navy and my travels kept me from keeping tabs on it anyway. Like most folks in the military, I tried to keep an eye cocked on Washington nuts who wanted us involved in every conflict going, not that there was anything I could do about it -- except write letters that church-going folks wouldn't like. Now that I can legally do about anything I want, except campaign in my uniform, I find politics interesting.

"I enjoy the talking head shows. They amaze me! I wonder why anybody, particularly a republican, put up with the abuse laid upon them just so they can get their face and voice on the airwaves.

"A thing I notice about many running for office -- those already elected too, is they believe we're all a bunch of thick-headed numbskulls! Do they really think we believe them when they change position constantly, or try to smooth over their screw ups with a lot of babble that means nothing when you dissect their words? I simply cannot understand why politicians don't tell the truth and have it done with, People will usually side with a person who is honest about a foul up,. Foul up -- 'fess up, like in the Navy!"

I figured I was in big time trouble when the next media person raised her hand. Her appearance indicated she had flown directly from Pointy Head University -- pasty skin, beads, granny glasses, long dress, sandals -- the whole package.

"My question is for Missus Berkeley. You stated in TV spots you were once a teacher. Why did you sacrifice your career for marriage?"

Patty seen that snake in the grass.

"I did not give up teaching because I married. I taught school until my husband transferred to Spain. I enjoyed teaching, but certainly not more than the opportunity to live in Spain with my *new* husband.

"I intended to continue teaching in the on-base school in Santa Cruz, Spain, but I suffered a miscarriage soon after we arrived. My immediate interest was not then directed towards teaching. I was offered a position when we transferred to Italy, but teaching full-time would have prevented my traveling the Mediterranean to meet Clay at his ports of call. Spending time with my husband and visiting foreign cities was much more important to me than a career.

"I consider a career to be every woman's right -- providing she wants to pursue one. I do not. I have a great career. My career is taking care of my husband and my son. I consider being a mother, housewife and helpmate to my husband a full-time career, one that takes more ability, knowledge and effort than some careers that require a college degree. It provides all the satisfaction and feeling of accomplishment I need.

"My goal is to support my husband to the extent needed. I encourage him. I encouraged him to run for congress. He will be a great congressman, although some will hate him for following paths he deems proper, rather than the politically correct, or the popular. Will I influence him in making difficult decisions? I certainly will! But I will not *tell* him what to do. Pillow talk? Yes, it is. Every person needs an anchor. I want to be there when Clay needs me. We are partners, but I consider him the senior partner. If he succeeds, I succeed. If he fails, I fail. He has never failed

"Does that answer your question?"

"I suppose it does, but you just told me you believe women should be camp followers, rather than their own person."

Patty puffed out her lower lip. I girded my loins for a Patty-type explosion, but she just signed and said, "I should invoke Clay's rule, but I won't. I sympathize with angry, frustrated women, such as yourself, who dislike men. I feel sorrow for women who claim not to enjoy a man's company. Such women react to an agenda instead of their own feelings and desires.

"I am doing *exactly* what I want. I know *exactly* where my life is going and I am savoring every minute of it. I do not need a job to feel important and useful. I am important. Useful too. I am part-time dietician, part-time cook, part-time farm manager, part-time accountant, part-time teacher, part-time taxi driver. Oh, I could go on and on as to my part-time expertise, as can any housewife. I would, however, rather be known as the *wife* of Henry Clay Berkeley than anything else.

"Camp following? You must admit that camp following is not restricted to following men. It is broader than that and widely practiced. How many times have *you* transferred to further *your* career? I consider following advancement the same as following something else for personal gain or pleasure.

"I love Berkeley's Knob, which is our home farm near Big Otter. I have no desire ever to leave there, but I am going to follow Clay to Washington -- and to wherever else he might go in the future. I do not intend to be separated from him ever again. Camp following? Maybe, but it certainly beats sleeping in a cold, lonely bed! If you do not understand that I feel extremely sorry for you and your husband . . . something you probably do not have . . . or no longer have."

The Poster Child of Pointed-headed People twitched like a mule struck by lightening. Her chin sagged, her mouth worked, but no words emitted. Finally she plopped rather heavily into her chair.

Patty done good!

"Fire 'em at us -- either of us." I said. "This might be your last chance."

A small, well-groomed woman stood, "I'd like to direct a question at your wife, if I may.

"Missus Berkeley -- what you just said will do wonders for the egos of women satisfied with keeping house, but who are criticized for doing so. One Question: What do you believe to be the major attribute of your husband?"

Patty flashed her wide-toothed smile as she turned a bright pink. "I trust you are asking what I consider his major attribute for congress. Clay has many, many attributes that will enable him to do a grand job in congress. I speak of kindness, courage, fortitude, intelligence, and an ability to plumb the depths of complex issues others try to mire. I can think of long-term tasks that require less time and effort than trying to fool Henry Clay Berkeley!

"Clay-honey, please resume the podium. This is your press conference, not mine."

A tall, ragged looking man with long, stringy hair raised his hand. I feared the worst.

"I'd like to say something to you both.

"I've heard speeches where you credited Missus Berkeley for some of your ideas. I've seen your TV ads too. I believed you were playing the 'Loving Family' game, for political purposes. I thought so until today.

"No actress could flash her eyes as Missus Berkeley just did and speak so eloquently with no prepared script without truly meaning it. You might be Chairman-of-the-Board in your family, Mister Berkeley, but you have a strong, supportive, and obviously loving CEO I'm not married, but when I do, I hope to have a wife like yours!

"My question is this: You frequently expound at length on the necessity of keeping 'Yankee Green Dollars' out of the hands of people on welfare to prevent the money being spent of alcohol and drugs. Do you really believe your plan -- or rather your wife's plan, will work?"

"I don't know, but I hope so. A lot of folks drawing public money -- money from your own pockets, ends up shoving money into the pockets of liquor store owners and dope dealers. It makes good sense to restrict that as much as possible. Stopping it totally will never be possible. Close one loophole and another will surely crop up. Crooked people are not always intelligent, but all are sneaky-smart.

"Another thing I've been toying with, and before you ask, this is my own idea, is submitting a bill for a program similar to the WPA that President Franklin Roosevelt devised to alleviate the number of unemployed during the Great Depression.

"Oh, union bosses will weep, wail and gnash their teeth about stealing jobs from working people. They will not mention their own fat pockets. If the construction industry and unions are so stupid and greedy they can't understand such a program would accomplish only work that cannot be funded, let them yell and cuss all they want. You can believe this or not as you choose, but there are people in this country who would not take a lick at a snake unless forced to do so. Some simply do not want to work!

"The president is big on a word I cringe when I hear. "'*Investment*' usually relates to throwing money at a problem instead of solving the root cause, but I am going to use it now. I really believe a WPA type program would be an investment.' There are dams, bridges, roads and other infrastructure that needs work. We don't have the money to do the work! We should utilize unemployed people to accomplish such construction. They would earn a living wage and learn a trade at the same time. We can use military engineers and military personnel to plan and supervise the work at the same salary we're already paying them."

"Your wife is known as a strong religious supporter. What are your views on separation of church and state?"

"What my wife believes -- or does not believe is none of your business! Far as I'm concerned religion is, in general, a glorious thing that ought to be practiced. We had one hell of a lot less serious crime when it was. I'm not going to criticize any religion, but I believe some read stuff into the Good Book that is not there. Stands to reason. Judges read stuff into the Constitution that is not there and it's only a couple hundred years old. The scriptures are thousands of years old . . . the stories, not the writing. Monks and scribes surely wrote their own agenda into it on the midnight watch when no one was watching. Next question."

"Isn't your putting the United States first nothing more than isolation?"

"Maybe -- to some extent. Think of how many times we've helped another country only to have them sneer and kick us in the teeth. We've given our wealth away. We're still doing that even though we are strapped for cash ourselves. Some foreign aid, particularly food, will always be needed. I have no problem with feeding hungry people.

"It makes me want to barf when the United States is taken to task by a foreigner who knows little or nothing about us, wailing about what we do in the United States. Pick up almost any international edition of the *New York Times* and read the letters telling us how to conduct our affairs. The comments make your hair curl – or should.

"It's time we steer our own course. Our descendants will have to live with our decisions -- right or wrong. We can't force any country to act like we think they should. How they act it's not usually our business. What we need to do is expend our efforts in squaring our own country away -- and do it as we see fit.

"Well, you've had me nailed to the cross for a good while and I need a cold drink, beer, preferably. One last question, then I'm turning you loose so you can return to your offices and study your thesaurus for new nasty words to call me. If you can't find any, you can always fall back on the word 'fascist' -- no one has yet called me that.

"You, in the orange dress in the front row. What's your question."

"I expected somebody would have asked this question early in the interview, but none did. My question is, do you intend to ignore the media even if elected?"

"Yes."

CHAPTER SEVEN

FROM THE PAST

I don't know if it was my interview with the media that caused the sea change, but media reporters slacked up on me a mite. Their news articles did not anoint me with oil, but were, for the most part, fair and reported pretty much what I had actually said. The editorials remained hang dog mean and flat nasty, particularly those in the *Star-Journal*.

Mister Criss scheduled speeches at every town, village, hamlet and dent in the crossroads across the congressional district. Consequently, I had little time at home. Patty did not like this, so she stashed Joe-Joe with her folks and went on the road with me during most overnight stays.

Patty was popular with the media and often chatted with reporters and such on an informal basis. This came to a head when the host of a leading TV morning show requested an interview. Patty, who *enjoyed* exchanging darts with the media, was quite willing to participate in the interview, provided she did not have to travel to New York.

Mister Criss, although fearful when either of us had contact with the media, was overjoyed at the prospect of Popular Patty scratching up votes from women folks who would watch the show.

The producer informed Mister Criss that the talking head *never* interviewed anyone external to the studio, except once in the White House.

When Mister Criss' best efforts failed to produce the results Patty wanted, she somehow contacted the producer herself, puffed out her lower lip and beat the poor woman down to parade rest. The results was an interview taping scheduled at our house a week from the following Saturday.

Mister Criss was in a near total garble state when he called just after I'd walked out of under the shower. He was difficult to understand, but the gist of his conversation was that one of the periodicals that sold from racks near checkout stands at super-markets was about to publish a front page article concerning some woman I'd gotten pregnant and abandon!"

"That's old news, Bob. Patty started that fib when she was trying to lash me down into marriage. It was never true -- just a thing she engineered to chase my lady friends away."

"Not Patty. Mary!"

"Mary *who*?"

"God, don't you *know*? An English girl, according to my source."

"Oh, that Mary!"

"You *admit* it?"

"No, I do not! I'll be in headquarters in a little while, Bob." I told him, hanging up the telephone before he could go off on me.

I turned to Big Eared Patty who had heard only my end of the conversation, but was totally at sea as to what was discussed. "Get dressed, Patty. We have to go to headquarters. I'll tell you about it on the way."

It was too late for a Mark One - Mod Zero panic, so we stopped for a donut and a cup of java en route to my headquarters. Bob was livid when we arrived.

"Why'd you bring Patty?" he queried, nastily. "So I could tell her of your shameful past instead of you doing it? Where in the hell have you been? I called over an hour ago!"

"Bob, I told Patty all about Mary when we went to Europe, in case we run into her, or one of her friends, in some city on the Mediterranean coast. If it doesn't bother her, it sure ought to not bother you!"

"She *approves* of you jilting that woman?"

"I never jilted anybody!"

"You weren't engaged to her, didn't impregnate her, and didn't send her on her way like some castoff?"

"Not hardly."

Bob made a flutter of 'give it to me' with his hands.

"We met in Cannes at a reception aboard the battle group flagship and I ran with her, off and on, during the two cruises I made to the Mediterranean in *Forrestal*. The last time I seen her was after she sent a radiogram to the ship just days before we were to meet in Mallorca. The radiogram said she thought she was pregnant. I sent a wire back saying if she were pregnant, we'd talk marriage, if that was what she wanted.

"She met me on the dock when the liberty boat pulled in -- smiling and cheerful. We went to a bar, The Atrium, where she told me she was not pregnant after all. She then said, since we'd already decided the issue, which we had *not*, some type of government wheel in Gibraltar, to whom she was related, was prepared to issue a quickie marriage licenses.

"I informed her I couldn't marry a foreign national without the Navy's permission because I had a high-level security clearance. I told her it'd take an investigation of her background, a gunny sack of paperwork and six months, or more, to obtain approval. She chucked her lighter and stuff in her purse and stalked out of the bar.

"I waited an hour for her to come to her senses and return. When she didn't, I went to her hotel and found she'd just checked out. I telephoned her folk's place in England that night, and a couple of other times before the ship sailed. She was there, according to the fellow who answered the phone, but she wouldn't accept my calls. She didn't answer my letter either.

"I don't believe she really wanted to marry me. I was just somebody to play around with. She knew I was dirt poor compared to her. Her family would have screamed and torn their hair if she had even mentioned marrying a common sailor. That's about it, Bob. I was *never* engaged to her! She was *never* pregnant by me. I *never* jilted her."

Bob hung his head in his hands. "You would have to pick up a member of royalty to get crosswise with. Good God!"

"She's not a Royal. She's a blue blood. There's a difference, somehow."

"She's a Royal now! Or isn't the wife of an English Lord a Royal?"

"Well . . . I never did understand British royalty rankings, but that would make her a Royal. No idea what her title would be. Regardless of what she is, she isn't going to like the article any better than me. Her husband is not going to like it at all!"

"Listen, Clay -- this is big news! You and Mary are going to see your faces on every trashy paper there is, to say nothing of TV programs that specialize in trash. The local TV stations and the *Star-Journal* will nail you to the cross! I don't feel one bit sorry for you, but I do hate it because of Patty. She doesn't deserve this."

"No, she damned sure doesn't. Do you have one of those papers?"

"The article won't be published until a couple of weeks. They're still digging dirt on you two."

"How did you know about it?"

"I saved a sleaze's butt once who was about to get sued for slander. He works for that paper and, owing me like he does, he called to tip me off. Oh, his paper ain't much by itself, a few thousand subscription copies and a few thousand in racks. It's a recent spin off of a London tabloid that puts topless women on page three. Size of his paper won't make a difference. Everyone in creation will pick up on the story the day it hits the streets, mainly because of who she is.".

"I wonder why she told? She hates paparazzi. I've heard her cuss them and she used really bad words doing it. I would think she hates newspapers that print trash about the rich and famous too."

"What makes you think she told? You just said she's not going to like the article either."

"She had to tell. There isn't but three-four people knows about it. Mary, Gunny, Patty, and me. There are others, but all they know is that I run with an English girl. My running mates, and I had only a couple-three real buddies in *Forrestal*, likely thought she was a wild Brit. girl running with a sailor to get her kicks No one knew who she was, so far as I know. Gunny only knows because he was in the Med aboard the cruiser *Springfield* and his ship and mine ended up in the same port a couple of times. So he knows her and knows about her."

"Clay, I wish I knew how much this'll hurt. It's no *Monkey Business* boat type story that ruined Senator Hart's shot at the White House, but it'll hurt.

"I think we better write today off. I'll see what else I can run down on it. Maybe the little jerk don't have it straight. He did know about it though and those kind of papers are worse than a bulldog hanging onto a big bone when it comes to hanging on to a hot, trashy story. I expect we're down the tubes, particularly with most of the female vote."

I should have been tore up worse than a tin can that collided with a bird farm, but I wasn't, not really. I'd learned early on in the Navy that getting ulcers over something that couldn't be corrected was a non-starter. Patty was what I felt bad about. She had done nothing to deserve the hurt she'd feel when the media started pounding nails into my palms.

Moe had not yet opened, but we got in by banging on the door. That fact that Moe and Missus Moore, his wife in everything but law, visited us in Spain for a week, and again in Italy, didn't mean he was going to let us off the hook with his caustic wit.

"You look all tuckered out, Boot Camp. Patty, you should have married a younger man like we told you when you went after Boot Camp. There's got to be a defect in your make-up some-wheres that attracts you to men with no class. You want I should fix you up with one of them young Kennedy fellows? They got less class and more vim and vigor than your husband!"

Patty had long since given up on trying to best a Moesim, so she giggled and said, "That is how I like him, Moe. Tuckered out and home with me!"

"Ain't no accountin' for taste . . . nice girl like you too." He gimped it down the bar, popped a Fall City for me, poured a coffee for Patty and returned. "It's the great mystery of Big Otter - - Patty and Boot Camp."

"Yeah, Moe, it's a great mystery to me too." I threw a couple of twenties on the bar. "Patty and I are going over to a booth for a discussion. You keep the barflies off my back when they show up. I've no patience for them today."

"I sure won't let them know that! They'll be breathing bad breath all over you if they figure you'll buy them beer to keep them away!"

After we'd taken a few sips of our drinks, I reached across the table and rumpled Patty's wavy-curly, sun-streaked, taffy hair. "Honey, I probably haven't told you that I love you more than five-six times total. It's hard for me to say that, somehow. But, Kitten, I hope you know what you mean to me. There is nothing in this world with your value."

Patty smiled, stood on her tippy toes, stretched across the table and gave me a big kiss. "Your actions speak much louder than mere words."

"Stop that, Patty! I've been telling you since you started chasing Boot Camp that this ain't no quickie motel! Don't you get enough of him at home?"

Patty reddened at Moe's jibe. "No, Moe. I do *not*."

She looked at me with her big, gray eyes and questioned softly, "Why did you tell me what you just now did, dearest?"

"I never had another wife, but I believe any other woman would shout old Billy Hell, heave my carcass flat out into the lane, and chuck my sea bag after me."

"Why? Your past escapades are of no concern to me, except I might not now be able to see you as a congressman. Oh, I did want that for you!"

"Well, I am in the deep, dark kimchee because of a woman."

"Yes, but I see no reason to fault you. You were thirty-four years old when we met." Patty's face flickered. "Just because I was an twenty-two year old virgin is no reason to be angry because you were not chaste. Clay-dearest, you married *me*! That means all of the other ones -- this Mary, for instance, meant nothing to you. Angry? Why should I be angry? You needed women. Who would want a man who did not?"

My kissing on Patty resulted in another barrage from Moe and a couple of early 'flies too.

We kicked the situation around for a while, then Patty asked, "Dearest, how much money do you have with you?"

"A couple-three hundred, maybe, and change."

"Please give it to me. All of it. This may take a while. Do not leave!"

I asked where she was going, but she just smiled and charged out the door.

Two beers later and a sea bag of war stories from the barflies concerning The Big One -- WW II, Patty returned and motioned me to the booth. I hurried to her, wondering where she'd went and what she was going to whip on me this time. She refused to tell me anything until I bought her a beer and she'd gulped a couple of inches from it, a lot for Patty who was a beer sipper.

"The story will never appear in that tabloid. Neither you nor Bob need worry further."

"Huh? I mean how? You can't stop a newspaper from publishing something like that. Not with a few hundred dollars!"

"I did *not* bribe them, Clay-honey. I did not even speak with them."

"What in the hell did you do?"

"Our bank president called Barclay's Bank in London and acquired Mary's telephone number. I then called her, which cost a bundle."

'You did **Whaaat?**"

"Telephoned Mary."

"**UGAAAH!**"

"*Hush*! Mary knew absolutely nothing of that filthy story. She said, immediately, she has never been pregnant in her entire life and nothing you did constituted jilting her.

"Dearest, they have strict libel laws in Great Britain. She is, as we speak, en route with her barrister to accost the publisher of the parent tabloid in London. She intends to sue them to the heavens should they insist on publishing that story."

"But . . .but . . . how did you call her? You don't know her married name."

"Oh, but I do -- her maiden name, which you told me -- and her married name too."

That clanked my anchor. "May I know how?'

"I do read!"

"Read what?"

"Oh, newspapers, magazines, tabloids and the like."

"Mary was in one of them?'

"Constantly! She is a jet setter. When I was in Monaco awaiting your ship's arrival I noticed a magazine photograph of a British aristocrat who had just arrived aboard her yacht. After reading the article, I knew it was Mary. Her maiden name is affixed to her married name, she moved in the resort-casino-yachting circle and she matched the description I pestered out of you when you warned I might one day meet her.

"I followed her movements through gossip papers and magazines for the remainder of our tour in Europe. Clay-honey – she appears quite the round-heel!"

"I never thought I was the only dog in her kennel, honey. Why did you never tell me?"

Patty sort of hung her head.

"Well?"

"Insecurity, dearest." Patty said, very softly.

"*You*? Insecure? Honey, you've never had a moment of insecurity in your entire life, except maybe on our first date. Shyness, yes -- insecurity, no."

"I was, Clay-honey -- really insecure. Oh, she is so wealthy and so tall and so beautiful! Just looking at her photograph made me aware of my shortcomings and I . . . Oh, damn-in-hell, she was anchored in Monaco and I feared we'd meet and you would still want her!"

"Kitten, I never heard you say the slightest stupid thing until now, but that statement ranks right up there with big time dumb. Book has a better thought process than that!"

"Women feel that way about their husband's past lovers!" Patty wailed. "Besides, I overheard something that badly worried me not long before."

"What?"

"Er, nothing, really . . ."

I whipped my best master chief glare right into her big,

gray eyes.

"It is of no importance, Clay-honey."

"Speak!"

Patty did something I'd not seen since our first date when she was as nervous as a nun in a cathouse. She jerked her little hanky from her purse and commenced twisting it.

"Dearest, the day I heard the comment was much the same as any Saturday mornings when your ship was in Gaeta. You would go to the ship to read your messages, then go to Art's Beef and Ale and drink beer with your shipmates until I finished shopping. I would meet you and we would have lunch.

"Betty Lloyd and I finished shopping that Saturday. Betty needed a restroom, so we stopped in Vic's bar. I was sitting in a window booth waiting for Batty to return, sipping my soda pop and looking at the flagship and the cruiser tried alongside her when I heard your name mentioned. I eve-dropped on the conversation, only to hear a man I had never before seen, probably ship's company of the cruiser outboard the flagship, tell a chief from your staff that he did not understand why your married me. The chief said, "Well, she's cute, lots younger than him and built like a little brick . . .I'm not going to say *that* word!

"Clay-honey, that man then said I was the plainest woman he'd ever seen you with. He could see nothing outstanding about me. He said you would deep six me when a prettier woman came along, unless you had married for money. He said other things too, but I really didn't hear them because his statements made me almost sick to my stomach.

"I felt just terrible for days! I kept remembering that man's statements. I could scarcely eat. I could not keep my thoughts focused. It got worse when I seen that magazine and realized just how gorgeous Mary is. Nothing about me could *ever* compete with *her*!"

"Kitten, any man who thinks you're plain has got real bad eyesight! Oh, I realize your face is unique and it does confuse people. It did me too, for a while. I puzzled whether you were cute, pretty, beautiful, just what category you did fit into until I got accustomed to you looking somehow different every time I looked at you. Finally, I decided you are the most beautiful woman on earth. I first thought that when you came walking up the aisle when we married. I still think so. Always will."

"Only my husband would think me beautiful, but I love you saying so -- even if it is a monstrous fib!"

"Even if I didn't think you're beautiful, I'd have to say that beautiful ain't got it all, Kitten. Maybe none of it, really. A woman can be damned beautiful and can't hold a man. You have it all! You're always interesting. You make me laugh more than any person I ever met. You're great in bed. You support me until hell won't have it. You make me proud just to be seen with you. You're a great mother. You're smarter than Einstein. Maybe the best thing about you is that you make me aware every day how much you love me. I lived in a cold world until I met you. That world is now warm."

Patty sniffed a little, then snapped her hanky back into her purse. "Dearest, I will always remember what you just said. Another thing I will never forget is you did not at once realize this morning of whom Bob was speaking!"

"Hmmm, I never though of that, but you're right. I haven't thought of Mary for years. Probably not since Gunny bugged me about her that first Sunday afternoon you and I went to Moe's. Angie dragged you over to a booth to give you the low-down on me, then Gunny started in about what a fine piece of work you are and how much class you have. He said something like 'As much class as that posh English witch had, Patty's got more.' That was likely the last time I thought about Mary, except maybe in passing when Gunny popped off about her. Gunny *really* didn't like her!"

"Oh, I know! I know!" Patty jumped up and down in her seat. "I really know!"

"You needn't get so excited about it! Gunny has been a big Patty booster since Day One."

"I am excited -- no, I am ecstatic. I know *who* caused this problem!"

"No, you don't, Buccaneer. I called Gunny while you were gone. That's one thing, maybe the only thing, he never told Elizabeth about. That's what I thought happened. That he told Elizabeth and she spread it all over like she does and someone who doesn't like my running for congress slipped it to that rag."

"Elizabeth does not spread gossip. She is no gossip. You believe that because she told me things when we were dating. Anyway, it was Curtis."

"Curtis? It can't be Curtis. I'd never tell that clod anything! I don't even speak to him on the street. Just seeing him makes me want to start whipping him about his head and shoulders. It'd take four of him to make one decent human being!"

"It was too, Curtis! He and Joan were sitting at a table near the bar, directly behind you and Gunny that afternoon. I remember perfectly because I was listening to Angie and watching you. Oh, I'll get him this time! He caused your firing from recruiting. This is worse. Yes! I'll have Daddy shoot him!"

The more I thought about it, the more I thought Patty might be right. Curtis has retired from the Navy at first opportunity after my recruiters, more than a little angry because he'd caused my firing from recruiting, engineered his transfer to an aircraft carrier in Yokosuka, Japan. (See Snug Harbor Book I, *The Launching*.)

Curtis, being an retired Navy chief journalist and a current card-carrying member of the media somehow learned the names and location of shipmates I ran with on *Forrestal* and one of them had, in fact, knew who Mary was and what she was. That really surprised me because I thought nobody knew anything at all about her. I'd never told anybody who she was. I couldn't recall seeing a shipmate in any of the high-class bars and restaurants she insisted we frequent. I wondered which shipmate it was and where he might now be serving, but came up blank.

Curtis would certainly know how to get such dirt into the media, just like he used my interview with Patty for her college newspaper to get me fired from recruiting. I realized that Curtis, now a reporter for the *Star-Journal,* was one probable reason why that paper was so rabid against me. I had had no contact with him since returning home and knew only what I had heard. He was not somebody with whom I wanted to have contact. I couldn't totally avoid him though. He was not only my enemy -- he was Patty's first cousin!

"Patty, let me sic Bob on it and try to determine if that's how they got the story. If Curtis did it, your daddy won't have to shoot him. I'll smite him hip and thigh, as your preacher says."

"Please do not, Clay-honey. That situation with the interview might not have happened had you not thumped him in the bathroom at our wedding reception."

Great John Paul Jones!. She even knew about that!

Patty let loose with her rich, whooping laugh.

"You are going to be the death of me!" she cried, throwing her pretty head against the back of the booth. "Oh, the look of sheer horror on your face just now! Oh, you are so . . . Oh, Goodness!" She continued laughing until she finally wound down with every 'fly in the bar looking at her and wondering what in the hell I was doing to her. They were a tough, knowing bunch of old men, but they had never gotten accustomed to Patty's outbursts of laughter, or a girl of her shy nature grabbing onto me in front of God and everybody.

"I abhor violence, Clay-honey, except when necessary for protection, but I would have loved to have seen you thump Curtis." she said, between spurts of laughter and giggles. "Oh, the idea of you knocking Curtis cuckoo, then stuffing the toilet with a towel, flushing the commode and leaving him with cold water running across his body could come only from your devious mind! I am so pleased you did that. It was time someone took Curtis to task for his meanness. I, myself, thumped him with a stick two or three times because he was terrible to me when I was growing up. I tried my best, but he was a lot older than I was and able to prevent me from doing him damage as I intended!"

"Honey, what Curtis said had to hurt your feelings. Why do you think it's funny?"

"*You* are funny! You get the strangest look on your face when I tell you of something you hid from me. What he said about me was funny, in a way. Curtis no doubt truly believed you *would* have to rape me on our wedding night. I did, after all, have the reputation of being untouchable, an 'ice box' as Curtis told you. He had no way of knowing we made love many, many times before we . . . er, actually said our formal vows. He would not have believed that possible!"

"Finish your beer, dearest. Mommy will be bringing Joe-Joe home later. We will have a couple of hours before that to do . . . as we wish."

Bob lost it again the following Wednesday when a three page, anti-Berkeley pamphlet hit mailboxes all over the voting district. Its cover page indicated the distributor was a religious organization no one had ever heard of: *God's Believers for a Moral Government.*

It accused me of being, among other things: a drunk who hung with degenerates who hated God; a seducer of innocent, young women; a jailbird; a harsh taskmaster who abused his employees; a Bible quoting Satan lover. It maintained I had the mark '666' on my forehead -- but only God's chosen few, them, I suppose, could see it. It also mentioned my tendency to associate with women of low character in houses of disorder.

"Clay, this is terrible! I've never seen anything like this in thirty years of politics. I'm paid to help you, but I have no idea how to fight a bunch of religious loonies!"

"It's not so bad, Bob. Their intelligence isn't all that good. It doesn't say anything about me being a wife beater, child molester, drug addict or hired killer. Hell, it didn't even mention I belong to the White Knights and the Black Panthers, or even the John Birch Society and the American Communist Party."

"Get serious! We've got to issue a statement rebutting this.

Otherwise, people will believe it, if for no other reason than the nuts who spread it all over the district claim to be Christians."

"No, Bob. We're better off ignoring it. Most of it is stern wash."

"*Some* of it's *true*?"

"Depends on how you look at it."

Bob got so excited I didn't know if he was going to faint, have a heart attack, or just fold his tent and sneak off into the night. When he stopped screaming and beating his in and out baskets to smithereens with the telephone, I grabbed him by the arm, dragged him to a joint across the street and threatened to pour a pitcher of beer on him if he didn't shut up.

"Bob, you know more about political campaigns than anyone in the whole country, but I come from these hills and I tell you that you can hear Bible-thumpers like these on the radio every single day of the week. People send them money, so folks do listen to them. Most listeners are very religious – not so many of the radio preachers who are in it only for the money.

"These kinda preachers are experts at taking a minor issue and blowing it up like Hiroshima. No one ever sues them because it would give them a forum. If sued for slander, they'd make it look like the trial of Jesus Christ! You've got to understand that they have a Bible and a pulpit to hide behind. The good thing is main-stream Christians pay very little attention to them."

"I know one who will. Gladly too. Your opponent! You're almost even in the polls. He'll grab this like a snake grabs a toad. (Oh, my God, I'm starting to speak like a hillbilly!) Forget the gentlemanly campaign you've forced him to run. He's got a big club now and he'll beat you like a cop on a mean drunk."

"I forgot about that. But we'll still be better off laying low. Let him say what he wants."

"You're acting strange about this -- like you might be guilty. I've got to know if you did any of this."

"I told you, it depends on how you look at it. Wait! Don't

go off-center on me again. Drink your booze and I'll tell you why I say that."

While Bob alternately drank and sloshed his drink all over his shirt front, I laid The Word on him. "Let's take those they could use to make a case. Forget that stuff about being a Satan lover and the number on my forehead, that's stern wash.

"Take the claim I hang with degenerates. You've heard of the barflies at Moe's. I suspect the 'flies are who they're referring to. They are half-drunk most of the time, but they really aren't barflies in the sense of the word. All are retired on pension and most of them own property. Some own a lot of property. Every one of them is a veteran and some are war hero's. They're lonely, Bob, so they hang together at Moe's. They're not degenerates and they don't hate God.

"The only woman I've hung with who was a lot younger than me is Patty. I didn't seduce her, or anything like that. Not that I didn't think about seducing her. I'm squeaky clean on that one. I tried like a big dog to get away from her for months before she got me cornered.

"I'm a jailbird, only in the broadest sense. I was arrested by the shore patrol in Casablanca for being in an off-limits establishment -- to wit: a cathouse, along with most of the crew of our ship. I was then eighteen or nineteen years old. I spent about half the night locked in a wire cage until the executive officer came and signed for our sorry asses. I guess they called him when they discovered our captain was one of those they hauled in. You can take it to the bank that none of us ever went to Captain's Mast!

"I was apprehended another time in Barcelona, Spain. I was accused of assaulting a German tourist. I did too. I smote him mightily, but they arrested him and turned me loose after they learned he'd tried to knock my brains out with a wine bottle over a pretty senorita we both wanted to escort home.

"I also spent three days in the brig on piss and punk . . . er, that's Navy talk for bread and water, Bob. That was for blessing out an officer way back when I was a seaman, eighteen years old. My captain understood that officer was a stone ass, so he tore the proceedings and sentence out of my record after I served my time. He had to heave me in the brig. He couldn't have a junior cussing out a senior, even if the senior was an imbecile.

"I've never had employees, not unless you count Mister Pollard and his crew who work on my farms. I damn sure am not harsh to Mister Pollard! He was working for my parents when I was born. He's more than an employee and a friend and I'd be lost without him. That aside, I don't know enough about farming to issue him any sort of rudder orders.

"The bit about my having a tendency to associate with women of low character in houses of disorder could only refer to my frequenting *Pink Place* and *Pearl's Topless*, the only titty bars around here. The woman I once run with from those places might have flashed her tools every night, but she was not of low character. That woman has more character than many who weep and wail at revival meetings! Except for showing her tools in a titty bar, her morals are damned high.

"As much as Claire, the topless dancer, liked me, she wouldn't sleep with me after Patty put her friends up to lying to God-World about how I got married because I'd knocked up some young girl. It was a total lie because no girl I'd messed with was pregnant and I then had no intention of marrying Patty or anyone else! I was right friendly with several other women around here too, until Patty chased them all off with the same story. All fabrication! She worked it so she was the only woman in Kentucky and West Virginia that'd have anything to do with me.

"I've not seen Claire in years, but Gunny told me a fellow who owned a trucking line came along and recognized her worth and carried her off to Ohio. She's living there with a good husband and a couple of kids. I'm thankful for that. She's a real fine woman.

"There are people who crossed my bow and who think I'm one mean bastard! I can think of two or three of them right around here who might think that.

"There are sailors who will tell you I can be meaner than a cat with an earache and a bad case of fleas, but they also believe

I'm fair and can cure the weak, the lame, the halt with a laying on of hands.

"You've met Angie. She's one of my biggest supporters, but I chewed her terribly bad for getting herself in position to possibly get raped by a bunch of tobacco-chewing, dope-smoking Klansmen. She couldn't set her stern down for a week after I finished with her.

"Book Arnet, who you've met, is the only sailor around here who never understood why I chewed on him when I had to do it -- every week or so. No sweat there. He's another who thinks I walk about two feet above water.

"Wait! Come to think of it, a lazy, useless secretary I had on recruiting, belongs to one of those churches that drinks lye, picks up live rattlesnakes and beats each other over the head with pissed off wildcats. She might know something about this pamphlet. I'll have to study on Marcie. I'll let you know what I come up with.

"That's it, Bob, the sum total of my sins and misdemeanors those people wrote me up for. What'd you think?"

"I don't see much there, but I still don't know how to fight against it. If we could pull them out in the open and expose what you really did, and not what they infer you did, we might recover ground. We can't do that though. We don't know who they are."

Bob nervously rubbed his bald spot, which covered most of his head. "I'll call your opponent's headquarters and tell them that pamphlet is loaded with lies and that they're opening themselves up to looking foolish, but I don't expect much. They're about to the position where they ain't got much to lose by getting caught in misrepresentation."

"I can work up a rebuttal in a speech and hope the media picks it up and reports what I say, the way I say it."

"That won't work. You must be the first candidate in the history of the United States who don't have a few friendly columnists and/or reporters in your hip pocket. You have one, maybe. Paul Rankin."

"'. . . and with flags unfurled, into the valley of death rode the six hundred.'" I grinned. "In our case, it'd be nice to have even six swinging swords. Horses would be nice too, if we have to leave town in a hurry to keep from getting tar and feathered."

Bob gave a deep groan and dropped his forehead right into a puddle of booze.

"Buck up, Mate! Patty told me Monday who probably set me up with that jilt rap. It was her own damned cousin, Curtis Longly. You need to call around and see if you can get proof. He's a real piece of work who tried time after time to slip a knife between my ribs, and did manage to knife me once. I wanted to smite him, but Patty talked me out of that by promising her family would handle it. Well, her family either hasn't talked to him or he didn't listen because I strongly suspect he's got something to do with the pamphlet. I hate to give him credit, but he's a good writer and he's employed on our local rag. No matter. I don't think he'll be real interested in sandbagging anybody else once I show him The Light."

"What are you going to do?"

"Like the old hillbillies used to say . . . I'm going to 'Read him outta The Book.'"

"After what you promised Patty?"

"It's sort of like skinning a catfish, Bob. You have to do it right. You get your hands all punctured and cut up if you don't use vice grips."

"Let me ask another dumb question, Clay. Do you hillbillies ever use the law to settle your differences? Like suing somebody instead of maiming them, shooting them, or some such."

"If God had intended right thinking folks to use lawyers, He wouldn't have invented rocks, fists, knives, dried kitty cats, jawbones of asses and guns. Would he now?"

A strong moan from Bob told me he had not yet adapted to mountain living

CHAPTER EIGHT

SAINTS AND SINNERS

Bob wasn't the only one who'd saved a man's stern. The guy for whom I went toe-to-toe with our CO in his defense would have received brig time and maybe a bad conduct discharge for a Navy crime, for which he was innocent of the charge. I had originally thought Giuseppe nothing more than a New York hoodlum striker with movie star looks. I ultimately discovered his father had suffered deportation for income tax evasion the year Giuseppe was born. Giuseppe's father had then shifted abode from a plush, New York high rise to a villa on top of a hill above the Bay of Naples, right next door to the later residence of Lucky Luciano. I also discovered Giuseppe had enlisted in the Navy about one-half step ahead of the draft and that his father had his son's career in the gambling world all napped out after he finished his hitch in The Big Canoe Club.

Gooey, as *Mount McKinley's* radio gang nicknamed him, wasn't one to take a favor lightly. He never forget what I did for him, despite the fact that it was my duty to defend him of a charge he had not committed. He made every effort to clear the books of his debt up to and including the present era. I received a bottle of top-of-the-line cognac every Christmas and a box of Cuban cigars at random times, and an occasional telephone call.

He always seemed to know where I was in the world and what I was doing. I received a telephone call, followed closely by a huge basket of fruit and a gigantic bouquet of flowers that arrived while I was recovering in Balboa Naval Hospital in San Diego from wounds received in Vietnam. Expensive Cartier wrist-watches for Patty and me arrived by bonded courier at our wedding reception, which made me feel guilty because I hadn't sent him an invitation.   He even called me the morning of my retirement ceremony aboard the Sixth Fleet flagship, which was no mean task -- mighty few civilian calls are routed via satellite shot from the Pentagon. He wanted to know, among other things, if I needed a job. He said he had 'legit' radio and TV stations in Nevada and other Western states crying loudly for a firm hand.

I'd watched for years for Gooey's arrest picture or a front page obituary notice in newspapers, but none appeared. I did, however, see pictures of him at film premiers, charity balls, casino openings in Vegas, Jersey and the like. I finally realized that Gooey would never make the news for any of the reasons his predecessors did. Gooey was one of The New Breed who under-stood business didn't require him to personally bump folks off and success meant remaining squeaky clean on his taxes so he could keep his gambling licenses I wasn't naive enough to believe Gooey's organization didn't participate in unsavory practices. Gooey had told too many stories on quiet mid watches at sea, for me to believe that. Unsavory practices was where expendable, low-ranking soldiers trying to advance to 'Made Man' came in.

He realized, quite clearly, the value of what I'd done for him. A Bad Conduct Discharge would have prevented his ever acquiring a gambling license. He kept that thought locked firmly in his mind and frequently reminded me he'd be there if I ever needed him. This was the time. I needed him like a tumble bug needs a fresh cow patty. I dialed the telephone.

"Clay! Great to hear from you! About time too. Hey, sorry it took so long for my secretary to switch your call. I'm not in Jersey. I'm in Palm Springs soaking up some S and S -- suds and sun. I've got an soon-to-be-ex-wife with me, so I can't soak up the other S and S -- Sex and Sin. Hey, I heard about you running for congress. You need a few K? I've got some long green laying loose that needs a home. How many thou do you want?"

It was the same old Gooey -- loud, excitable and generous. "No, Gooey, campaign money is not my problem. I couldn't take your money, even if I needed it. That wouldn't look good if my opposition learned I'd taken money from a gambler."

"What kind of bilge is that? I'm as clean as new snow. Legit all the way!"

"*Sure* you are, Buccaneer! Look, I have to ask you something, Gooey -- something I don't like to ask. Is your phone safe?"

"Lay it on me, Shipmate. I still use landline with bug sweepers on top of bug sweepers. See, some guys in my business like to monitor other guy's calls."

"I want you to understand exactly what I need, Gooey. I have a fellow I need scared really bad, but I don't want him roughed up. I *do not* want him roughed up! Understand, Gooey?"

"Yeah, sure. You want him to dirty his pants, but not because he just died."

"Pretty close, but no brass ring. I don't want him thumped, not even a little bit. He needs getting beat down to parade rest, but that can't happen because he's a close relative of my wife. Neither of us can stand the prick, which doesn't make us unique. Most folks can't stand the sneaky bastard.

"Anyway, my wife made me promise not to whack on him because it might make him worse, like it did the last time I laid a couple of rounds alongside his skull. I wouldn't need you, if she'd go along with the program. I'd smite him hip and thigh, or give it one hell of a try!

"He done me some dirt a few years ago that got me fired from recruiting, not that leaving twelve-fourteen hour workdays and transferring to sunny Spain with my new bride pissed me off. This time, I think he hooked up with some holy-rollers and wrote stuff about me that is not going to help my campaign. I can't attack the religious group, no matter if they are twitchy as a rabbit in heat. My hands are tied, Gooey. My ship is in irons."

"You want a hook-up, Shipmate, you got a hook-up. I've been waiting to make an installment payment on my debt to you."

"You do not owe me anything! You never did. You were innocent that time.

"I'll let you know the date when I get it set up. Basically, I have to get him in a place where your people won't be bothered. That'll take a day or two, if I can arrange it at all. If nothing works out, I'll call so you can turn it off.

"I want him scared out of his skivvies! I want him scared so bad he agrees to call every newspaper and radio and TV station within range of this voting district and confess the pamphlet was produced out of spite. I also want him to write a letter denouncing the pamphlet and saying something to the effect that what it said wasn't true. I want the letter to have the same title he used for the pamphlet. He's to distribute copies of the letter to everybody they mailed or dropped off copies of the original pamphlet."

"Nothing hard about that, Clay. You sure that's all you want? No bones broke? No teeth removed? No fingernails pulled?"

"That's all I want! Scare him 'till his knees knock Nothing more. I don't need my wife's family embarrassed, so if he can get the newspapers and radio and TV stations to report it as false without using his name, that's okay. How he clears it with the religious nuts is his business. Remember, I don't want him marked up!"

"Wilco! I'll muster up (Hey -- notice how I can still use the old Navy lingo?) a couple of my associates and have them standing tall until I get your call giving me a go, or no go and more information on the fellow. You'll want them somewhere around that hick place you live? Is that a Charlie?"

"Charlie! Gooey, I'm sure your associates are competent, or they'd be . . . gone. You made it clear enough when we were aboard *Mount Mac* exactly what lower-level employment with your organization entails – or did during your forefather's era. I realize you're squeaky clean, but that don't mean your associates are. It oughta follow that I can't have any contact with them. None at all. They have to get into West Virginia without using the local airport, bus or train station; everybody watches those places. They have to keep a damned low profile while they're here. I don't want to know who they are, let alone see them."

"Hey, I *know* about members of congress. You think I've not done favors for any of them? You'd be very damned surprised!"

The next, and most important stage, proved harder. That took the cooperation of my lawyer. As the main character in a movie about Gooey's professional forefathers, said: 'I made him an offer he couldn't refuse.'

I stretched my legs across the expensive carpet. "So, we understand what we want to do, don't we?"

The lawyer didn't look well -- a sickly sort of fellow, I suppose, bobbed his head that did, in fact, understand.

"You're doing right good, so far. Keep doing that."

"Clay, let up on the guy. He's going to go along." Bob Criss begged.

"He should. He's been legally looting my estate since I was sixteen years old. Don't look so pious, Law Dog. You've charged maga-bucks to settle my folk's estate and you tried your best to bleed me dry every time I needed legal work done while I was off in the far reaches of the world. Now, when I try to launch you into an acting career and borrow your office for maybe an hour, I find you belong to the same lye drinking bunch that's trying to deep six me!

"I'm mad, Bob. The more I learn, the madder I get. Every rock I turn over has a maggot under it, but I never guessed old Swivel-head here was one of them, not until he started moaning about how he wanted to handle the churches. He's going to do it my way, Bob. If you can't stand the carnage, get out."

Bob flopped his head against the leather couch back and moaned. Our 'good cop - bad cop' routine was a bit stronger than Bob suspected. He seemed to have difficulty understanding how hillbillies conduct such business.

"He's going to do what I want and he's going to keep his mouth shut tight as a married Muslim hooker in a mosque full of mullahs. If I tell him to chuck 'n jive in front of the courthouse at high noon, he's going to do it.

"You seen how upset he got, and the smoke screen he threw up when I hit him with my request to borrow his office for a bit. Do I have a legal case against him? I don't need one.

"If I spread what he's done around the county, he won't have a major client left. Nary a one. All I have to do is whisper in the ear of folks I know in law enforcement, tell the barflies, and let a couple-three other folks know about it -- Patty's dad, her preacher, Mister Pollard, a couple of judges. I've got him by the gonads and I'm going to squeeze as hard as I like. All this little piss ant is going to say is: 'What? When? How High?' You understand the need for cooperation, don't you, Shyster?"

"I had little to do with that pamphlet! Why can't you believe me? " the lawyer wailed.

"Because you're a liar! You can deny it until the hubs of hell freeze, but I know you types hang together tighter than barnacles on a ship. I expect it's because none of you want to miss out on the casting of stones and such. I didn't know, for certain, who any of you folks were until now. I suspected Marcie was one and your reluctance to help me trap her flat let the cat loose. Why, I'd bet you're high up in one of those churches, a preacher, maybe. Hell, you might even be a deacon or a cardinal, or some such! You play ball and don't foul this up and maybe I won't tell your church members who gave me their names and what rattlesnake abusing churches were involved."

"I can't give you names! That would be a terrible breach of trust!"

"I'll overlook that 'breach of trust' bit. You can't spell trust. You'll draft the list while you're waiting for me to finish with Marcie. Patty asked me not to whale the demons out of the prime fellow I want, but she didn't prohibit me from whaling on anybody else."

The lawyer hauled stern into his private head, gagging every the step of the way.

"Bob, I want to talk to Marcie by myself. I'll see you at headquarters in an hour or two."

I bucked up my lawyer until I heard his paralegal announce the arrival of Marcie Niles, my CETA secretary when I was on recruiting duty. I then went into the adjoining conference room, switched on my end of the intercom system and listened.

"Ah, Marcie -- it's so good of you to rush right over." The lawyer's greeting simply oozed sincerity.

"I was reading the Bible when you called."

"You're a good Christian woman, Marcie. Everybody is talking about your superb contribution to our effort. We could not have accomplished anything like the end product without your input."

"It was my Christian duty, Deacon."

He was a deacon! And a pretty fair actor too.

"Yes, it was. You did just fine. As I told you on the telephone, we want to prepare another surprise for *Candidate* Berkeley. We have managed to acquire a few rather insignificant tidbits, but we need a big punch for our next pamphlet. You worked very closely, or rather near to him for quite a while. We are counting on you, Marcie."

"I *do* know other things he done. That prissy wife of his too. No one knew for certain, but what with her clothing messed and her lipstick smeared . . . *Well*! It doesn't take much imagination to understand what went on in his office when *she* visited. They were not married then. That makes her a *fornicator* too!"

"Er, possibly. We're not after Missus Berkeley. What can you tell me about him?"

"Lots more than fifty dollars worth!"

"Marcie! You know we haven't got much money to fight against his election. Fifty dollars is a lot of money for information needed to do the Lord's work."

"Remember, Deacon -- 'bread cast upon the waters.' Ben ain't worked lately. His bad back and all. His unemployment ran out months ago. I don't make much cleaning the mall at night. I don't know what we'd do if it wasn't for welfare and food stamps."

"Would seventy-five help, Sister?"

"A hundred would help more, Deacon."

I heard the lawyer sigh. He didn't like to see money going into any pocket, except his.

"Let me turn on this recorder, Marcie. That will be much easier than you writing it down as you did before."

Marcie gave it her best shot. She rambled for a good forty minutes about how I took the Lord's name in vain. How she smelled alcohol on my breath when I returned from lunch. How I tried to 'smooth talk' every woman who visited my office. My lewd telephone conversations with women. How I placed a mean, black woman in charge of my biggest office over white people. She also discussed a young, innocent girl I'd taken advantage, then married because she was pregnant.

When she ran out of fuel and the pressure dropped in her boilers to an occasional hiss, the lawyer snapped off the tape recorder and said, "That was very good, Marcie. If you'll wait, I'll get your money."

When I heard the door to the outer office slam, I quietly opened the conference room door and walked into the room.

"Why hello, Marcie. It's been a long time, hasn't it?"

I wouldn't have thought her pasty face could have gotten

whiter, but it did. She let out a scream that could have been heard across the street and bolted out of her chair, pretty deft for a woman of her bulk.

"You keep away from me, Master Chief!"

"Now, calm down, Marcie. I don't intend to hurt you. Sue you. Put you in jail, maybe, but not physically harm you."

Marcie lurched drunkenly across the room, fumbled with the doorknob, then collapsed in a pudgy bundle on a leather couch beside the door when the knob wouldn't turn. I could actually see sweat streaking her face powder.

"He's going to rape me!"

"Rape you? No. That's not what I'm going to do, although I suspect you've thought of sex many times when you eve-dropped on intimate telephone conversations with my lady friends. Did you enjoy those fantasies, Marcie?"

"Rape!"

"Shut up, Marcie. No one is listening. I *own* you!"

I'd never before seen terror and lust together in a woman's eyes, but I seen it then.

"Marcie, I know a few things about you. I know you are married to a worthless man that quit working and hasn't hit a lick at a snake since you inherited your folk's house. You own a nice Chevy pickup you bought with money the government intended for your children. You've got a few bucks in a bank under your maiden name. No fortune, but a few bucks. Your husband doesn't know about that money, does he? I'm going to own your house, Marcie. Your pickup and your bank account too, after the judge gives them to me. In fact, I'll be a fair-sized landlord after I am finished with your Christian brothers and sisters who helped you lie about me."

"You can't sue us for telling the truth!"

"You told what you *believed* to be the truth. That's different, Marcie. What you told and what your group circulated can't be proven, even if it were true. What you did is slander.

Maybe even criminal mischief. You can go to jail for that."

That broke the dam. She cut loose like a banshee.

"Save the crying for the judge, Marcia. It might help."

"No, please. Don't put me in jail, Master Chief. Please don't. It would ruin me."

"Seems fair. You tried to ruin me."

'But you're evil. You want to make laws to murder babies and put Christians in prison. I fought the good fight to keep you out of office like the Bible tells us to fight evil." she cried, alternately dabbing at her eyes and nose while sniffing like a hound dog with a bad cold.

"I might be evil. I'm sure no saint. You're not either, Girl. Jesus Christ, himself, said let the one free of sin cast the first stone. You don't understand that part of The Book, Marcie. I'm a sinner. So are you and your snake molesting running mates. Everybody is a sinner."

"I am not a sinner!"

"Yes, you are, Marcie. You spread falsehoods. The Good Book says that is a sin."

That comment caused a big break in her dam.

"Marcie, I never liked you . . . mainly because you were totally useless in most everything you did for me. That aside, I think you try to be a good woman. You just let hate get in your way. You hate everyone who has something you don't. I guess you hated me because I worked hard and got things done, totally unlike the man you married. You hated Angie because she's got a lot on the ball and people did what she said. Her being black may, or may not, have had anything to do with your hate for her.

"I can't think of one single sailor you seemed to like and you wouldn't let any of us like you. You bad-mouthed our life-style, our salty language and our drinking at Moe's. You acted like your problems were our fault. I can understand hard luck and being down and out, but your poor lifestyle is mainly your own fault, Marcie. You let Ben lay around claiming a bad back. It can't bother him too much when he hunts or fishes nearly every day, can it?"

Marcie shook her head and sobbed.

"Marcie, there's a way out for you, but you've got to do everything I tell you to do."

"You won't take my house?"

"I won't take anything. I don't want to hurt you, even if you did try to destroy me."

"What do I have to do?"

"Not much. I want you and your deacon to get Curtis Longly to your church Thursday night at nine o'clock. You can tell him anything you want, so long as he shows up and he doesn't know I'm involved. I also want a letter signed by you and the church leaders that says your group promulgated that pamphlet, not knowing the information to be false. I don't want your group, not really. Curtis is the one I want!"

"I don't hold with killing!"

"I'm not going to lay a hand on him. I'm going to make a Christian out of Curtis."

"A *Christian*? He *revels* in filth! He's a *liar* and a *blasphemer* and a *mocker* of Christ!"

"Many who claim to be Christians are some of those things. That makes them sinners, just like the rest of us. That has nothing to do with Curtis though. What Curtis did was sell you folks a bill of goods.

"The second thing is that you have to keep the congregation away from your church Thursday night. Totally and far away. You and your deacon work that anyway you want. I don't want anybody within a mile of there, except Curtis."

"But, but . . . you said I had to get Curtis there?"

"I didn't say anything about you meeting him. I don't want you anywhere near that church. Understand?"

"Yes, I understand. Who is going to meet him?"

"Forget who's going to meet him. You better forget you ever had this meeting too. I can always press charges. I have the tape recording where you spilled your guts. This is your only chance, Marcie."

She didn't like her playhouse crashing around her head. Working me over in print was probably her first time ever of experiencing the feeling of power, other than when she was whacking on sinners with the rest of her congregation. It took her a lot of soul searching before she agreed to do it. There was no doubt in my military mind there was considerable backbone under her fat.

"Good girl, Marcie." I handed her a hundred dollar bill.

"You are giving me *money*?'

"You did what your deacon asked. It's owed to you

"Marcie, I don't like you personally, but I admire your strength. I also like the way you hid some of your money from your lay-about husband, who I'm sure would like a new gun, a new fishing rod, or maybe even the occasional nip of the devil's brew." I hit pay dirt with that comment, the way she broke into sobs. I'd done what I had to do, but I didn't feel good about it.

"You make Ben get a job, Marcie. It's not right for you to do all the work and live poor like you're doing because Ben ain't worth zip. He's never going to be any good, not unless you push him to get a job of work.

"Look, if he tells you he can't find a job, I have one. My farm manager is getting to where he can't see too good, particularly when he drives. He has to make several trips each week, pick up supplies, take livestock to the stockyards and a bunch of other stuff. He can't very well take his other helpers away from jobs they have to do every day to drive him around. He can use some more help in other areas too. I'll give Ben a chance, but I'll smite him hip and thigh if Mister Pollard has to fire his useless butt. You tell him that!"

Marcie's face petrified as though a demon had crawled

from a crack in the earth and offered to jump her bones. "I don't understand. Why are you helping me?"

"Let's say I'm a sinner who reads the Lord's Word. I've always read the Good Book, but not as often as I should have until I was encouraged to do so by my wife, the girl you bad-mouthed. The difference between you and me is I do try to understand what God wants. Not that I always do it, which you well know. But I'm real good at turning the other cheek, provided they don't do it again."

"The Lord does move in mysterious ways when a person prays for help." Marcie's neck fat quivered as she stared at the ceiling tiles like she expected to see them open to display a vision. "Who'd have thought He would pick *him* as his tool!"

You win some -- you lose some.

After I got my nervous lawyer, The Leader of His Flock, calmed down, I laid it on him. "You screw this up and you'd better make certain Saint Peter knows he's supposed to collect your soul 'cause your stern belongs to me!"

"I'll make it work. You'll never hear from my group ever again!"

"No, I don't want exactly that. Next Saturday afternoon, when I've nothing better to do, I intend to speak to all six congregations and I will speak to them in only one of the churches. I want them to see that I'm not what they seem to believe I am. I don't want to starve kids, kill babies, burn Christians or loot the poor box.

"I'm not going to put up with a lot of guff, but I'll try to answer questions asked in a civil manner. You set it up. Remember, I can cause the churches involved a lot of grief. I'm vindictive enough to keep the lot of you in court for years."

"OK! OK!"

"All that remains now is for you not to screw up. Contrary to what you might think, I'm not going to fire you. For all your crooked, conniving ways, you're the best lawyer in this county. Not much of a shepherd, but a good lawyer. You keep stroking my holdings, but you make damned sure you charge only the going rate for legal work and keep your sticky paws out of my coin purse. You do that and we'll get along fine."

He looked like he was going to puff up and get righteous on me, but he thought better of that and just babbled a few versions of I thank you, my wife thanks you, my kids thanks you, my dog thanks you, and you will be rewarded greatly for your compassion to those who fell by the wayside.

Pompous ass!

CHAPTER NINE

CHURCH CALL

Gooey came through like Admiral Arleigh Burke's Little Beaver Destroyer Squadron running The Slot in the Pacific during World War Two. Snips of news concerning repudiation of the pamphlet began appearing on local radio stations late Friday morning and dominated the TV local news by Monday afternoon.

It wasn't total vindication. The local talk media questioned the validity of the person who telephoned the stations. That patter pretty much ceased when a letter issued by *God's Believers for a Moral Government* apologized for the pamphlet, saying the accusations made were found to be false. Most of the media accurately summarized the telephone call and published at least a portion of the letter, usually with little comment. Still, some media insinuated my election headquarters was the actual source of both the telephone calls and the letter.

An editorial in the *Star-Journal*, reiterated the media's allegation that both the telephone calls and the letter of retraction were fake. That, and the 'maybe he did, maybe he didn't' retraction letter Curtis drafted made me wish I'd been less lenient with him. I wished I had asked Gooey to instruct his associates to convince Curtis to provide his name when calling the media and for him to sign his name to the letter too.

Patty was so busy preparing for her interview with the talking head that she didn't pick up on what I had done. She cached Joe-Joe with her folks, then shut herself in the library with about eleventy-eleven issues of various woman's magazines. Far be it for *any* talking head to catch Patty out!

I didn't tell Bob of my planned meeting with the snake handlers. It would have excited him and he was already in Sweat-Panic Mode Eight over Patty's impending interview. I simply told him I didn't want to be present during her interview and that I was clearing out of Dodge. That caused him considerable relief. Bob believed either Berkeley talking to the media required the degree of control of a White House press conference. I could have done without the cheering.

The crowd in the parking lot of the tiny church my lawyer picked for the meeting looked like the banks of the Red Sea when the Children of Israel were twitching and panting for Moses to part the waters. No doubt the dozens of people felt much the same about my arrival as the Israeli's did about the Egyptian army closing ranks behind them.

I met first with the preachers and elders of the six tiny churches who had produced the pamphlet. They assured me all who had participated in the effort were present and that each church had sent as many of their flock as possible to the meeting. Curtis was not present. No one mentioned him. I hoped they had cast him into the rattlesnake holding pit -- or the lye vat.

None of the assembled people inside the packed church looked like fanatics or nuts. All looked what they were: plain, hardworking folks who believed fervently in their religion and who had been sucked into The Wayward Way by Curtis.

"Folks, I didn't ask for your presence here to threaten or chew on you, for what you did to me. I came here so you could get a look at me and realize I'm not much different than you all.

"But I am different in some ways.

"I've traveled the world and seen things that, I suspect, none of you have seen. Oh, some of you fought overseas and traveled some, but I had twenty-two years of it. I've seen the joys of this world. I've seen the horrors of the world. Some of the starvation and cruelty caused by religious beliefs would make a hardened person cry. We know about terrorists and see reports of massacres on TV, but how much do we know about the religious prosecutions in Africa, the Middle East, India and a host of other places. Not much, we don't.

"What is now The United States of America was founded, in part, because of a desire for religious freedom. Folks came here to worship God in their own way. That didn't exactly pan out. Remember the whippings inflicted on Quakers in some New England States and Maryland? Those are examples of people being terrorized because of their religious beliefs or practices. Folks, that was not the religious freedom guaranteed in the Constitution!

"Some of us call Him God. Jehovah Witnesses call Him Jehovah. Muslims call Him Allah. Every religion calls Him something. It doesn't make much different what He is called. He's mostly the same God. Most religious people are good folks looking to follow His decrees as best they can. Where it goes to pieces is that some religions believe they are the only ones who understand what He wants to be called, what He wants them to do, how He wants them to act -- and all other religions are a bunch of flakes. That causes people to believe they have to take others to task for how they search for God. It causes people to torture, mutilate, and kill.

"I'm telling you this because what others believe, what I believe, what you believe are different. What we have in common is we are all trying to go to the same place. I suppose there might have been a human in the long history of this world who didn't stumble and fall. I doubt it though. If anyone thinks they are squeaky clean, they ought to read The Book some more and search their hearts. God, Himself, said: 'No man is free of sin, not one.'

"I've read considerable, mainly because I had time at sea to do that. I don't expect most of you folks read a lot. It's not something you probably want to do after you sweated all day in a hot field, a coal mine, a sawmill, a steamy kitchen, whatever.

"Conventional wisdom is the more a person reads, the more their understanding improves. Well, I 'm here to tell you the more I read the Bible, the more I find things I don't understand. I suspect that's a problem we all have.

"I didn't come here today to apologize for anything, but I will tell you I've done things in my life of which I'm not proud. Anyone who says they didn't is a liar or they are ignorant of what constitutes right and wrong. I'm not making excuses, but I was single for a lot of years and I was lonely. I'll leave it up to you to decide what I mean by that. The Bible says it's better to marry than it is to burn. It doesn't explain whether that refers to burning in hell or burning with passion. It also doesn't tell us what we are to do if we don't meet a person we want to marry. That's one of the many things that confuses me. I did, finally, meet and marry a woman that any man would be happy to share a life, but I still don't understand what I should have done in the mean time

"I'm telling this so you'll sorta understand a lot of the things I am accused of -- some of which I did, were natural. Such things have happened to some of you too, though I don't expect most would admit it. Not even to yourselves in the quiet of the night when a person remembers sins.

"I hope you folks will give some thought to what Jesus said about chucking the first rock before you go off and attack somebody else. Old Paul, I think it was, wrote in one of his letters that a person should get three chances before casting him out of the church. Keep the rocks piled and give folks a chance to find their way. You have to think about the possibility that the way they find to God might be better for them than the one you want them to follow.

"I'm going to open the floor to questions, but I don't want everyone yelling at me at once. That is why I told your preachers and elders to ask questions for all of you. Have at it, Padres."

"Mister Berkeley --you speak right out and don't try to hide your sins. It takes a right big man to do that, or one that has no shame. We don't know which you are, Mister Berkeley. I can't argue with most of what you say, but why shouldn't we fight against things we believe are wrong? The Bible tells us to do that. What are we supposed to do about that?" asked a stooped, elderly man

"I think you should continue to protest issues you believe are wrong, but you should do it using strong argument and common sense. Yelling, screaming and making blanket accusations isn't the way to go. That causes people to think the religious right folks are a bunch of lock-stepped kooks instead of the caring, worried folks most are. I think quiet, well-behaved demonstrations go further than all the screaming you could get out of a host of people. Use economic sanctions when you deem it appropriate. Next!"

"How do you stand on abortion?"

"I'm against it, but I can also see where it might be necessary for health reasons. I've heard arguments on both sides and I still don't know which way I'll jump if it comes to a vote if I get to congress. My wife, Patty, is dead set against abortion, unless the mother's health is such that she could die. She doesn't like to see children born out of wedlock either, but she likes that scads better than abortion. We've had discussions concerning abortion and she's beat me about the head and shoulders with words, for my wishy-washy position. She thinks most babies would be adopted if the laws are changed.

"We need to look hard at the reluctance to let a couple adopt a baby of a different race. What difference does it make, so long as a baby has a loving, stable home? If a couple wants to adopt a baby, they should be allowed to take what is available. I don't believe keeping kids in group homes or with foster parents is better than them being part of a good family, regardless of who is what color. Next question."

"What about prayers in school?"

"We had prayers in school when I was a kid and it sure didn't hurt any of us. No arguments were heard at that time, probably because we all were Christians of one type or another and

I doubt any of us had even heard of an atheist. The argument is, though, what sort of prayers should we have. Christian prayers? Jewish prayers? Hindu Prayers" That is a tough question. Heck, we have different prayers within different sects of the same religious doctrine. I think we should allow prayers directed towards a Supreme Being, which most everyone worships Atheists are so far out of the loop that they can go bite sticks and howl at the moon so far as I am concerned.

"There are a couple of old fellows I read once in a while who pretty much sum up what I think about school prayer and organized religion in this country.

"A man named Chesterton said, 'When people cease to believe in God, they end up believing in nothing at all. Rather, they believe in anything -- however bogus.' You don't have to look far to see what he meant. Look at the Hollywood crowd. One day they are worshiping blue crystals, the next pink crystals, then, maybe, green tumble bugs with orange racing stripes. Well, it's a free country and they have the right to do that, even though sane people suspect their bizarre beliefs are caused by something they smoke or sniff up their noses.

"An old Russian, Solzhenitsyn, said, 'Man has forgotten God. That is why all this has happened.' He might be correct. Something sure has changed things for the worse."

"What about gun rights, Mister Berkeley?"

"I'm a strong believer in the Second Amendment. I had a single shot twenty-two by the time I was, maybe ten years old. I moved up to an old thirty-forty Krag and a Winchester thirty-thirty when I was about thirteen and could hunt deer by myself. Most kids of my background had similar experiences. I no longer hunt for a couple of reasons. I'm no longer a kid eager to kill game and I surely don't need to kill an animal for food. I don't expect to hunt again, but I have nothing against people who do.

"People around here hunt mostly for food. Any pleasure they get from the sporting aspects of hunting is aside to needing the animal for food. A couple deer, or a bear, goes a long way to feeding hungry kids in the winter when work and money are short.

I believe animals were put here for our use. The Good Book says so. I've read where the Indians apologized to animals they killed. That was a nice thing to do -- show respect for the life of an animal they had to kill for food.

"I'll vote against any law that tries to restrict or register guns. We might need them some day. Anyone who doesn't believe that should read the history of US citizens rounding up privately-owned guns, any sort of gun -- rusted, beat-up, outdated, or in good condition, to ship to England during World War Two. The reason was that England had very restrictive gun laws and when they needed guns for home defense, they didn't have any. Sadly, they didn't learn their lesson. They still have very restrictive gun laws. Next question."

"Taxes is in the news a lot. Some of us have been on welfare and know some tax money is used for good. What hurts is they take so much out of us when we're working that we ain't left with none to put away for hard times. Where do you stand on taxes?"

"I like the flat tax. Some say it is unfair to the poor, but that's mostly whining. All taxes are unfair to the poor, but every citizen should pay taxes -- even if it is only one dollar a year. I haven't studied flat tax much, but I hear the high end is around nineteen percent. That would probably make the low end less than now. I'll have to look at various tax systems before I decide which horse I want to ride. We have to change the tax laws though. That's a given!"

It was past country suppertime when they finally let me go. Even then, they trapped me before I got to my truck and hit me with more questions.

I received one nosy question. Why did I drive an ancient Dodge Power Wagon when I was thought to be well off. I explained the truck had belonged to my Dad and I was attached to it for that reason. I further told them there was nothing wrong with the material condition or the way the truck ran. I also said I didn't feel the need to drive around in a brand-splinter new pickup to impress folks.

They seemed pleased that someone considered them important enough to visit and let them ask question. These folks, except my lawyer and maybe a couple others in their group, didn't rank high in the community. That was a pity because they were, for the most part, good hearted, well-meaning people willing to share what little they had. Most were excellent citizens in all respects.

CHAPTER TEN

INTERROGATION

Camera pointers, production weenies and general rock packers were loading gear into a van when I pulled into the parking area near our barn. I'd heard rougher language, but it took a whaleboat load of drunken sailors to muster up so much of it.

The female TV talking head was not in sight. I wondered if she was still in the house, which was quite unlikely. Talking heads seldom ride in Detroit wagons or rice burners and there wasn't a limousine in sight. That meant she'd already packed her wigs in her sea bag and made her creep. Another possibility was that Patty had driven her over the brink with a barrage of words, she committed suicide and her carcass was toted off by a third party.

On the outside chance the talking head was still around, I slipped through the front door and stepped into the foyer where log walls from the original two-room log cabin were visible. Although the sprawling, two-story house now boasted fourteen odd-shaped rooms, various generations who drafted expansion plans took care to ensure the age-darkened chestnut logs remained visible as two side walls of the foyer. The old walls often caused me to wonder about the thoughts of my ancestors as they laboriously mixed caulking of clay with burnt limestone to chink the gaps between the logs they'd cut, trimmed, notched and laid. I sneaked across the colorful rug, hand braided by a whatever grandmother, and laid course directly towards the stairs.

I almost made it.

"Clay-honey!" Patty called as she dashed from the living room, jumped into my arms and wrapped both legs around me as she hung a massive lip lock on me.

Kissing Patty was in no way arduous, but my arms finally wore out, so I slid her to the deck, still squeezed tightly against me

"How'd it go, Kitten?"

"Bob just left looking like a storm cloud churning above Berkeley's Knob! I do not understand why. Other than a few sneaky questions, the taping went quite well. We even chatted a bit over a sherry after finishing, but little in the way of girl talk. That was impossible with Bob hovering about. I really did want to speak with her about a few items. Why the media is so mean to you, for example."

"It'll be that way until the Second Coming, unless I win election, then it'll probably get worse. You going to tell me what she asked, or do I have to tickle it out of you?"

"Yes!"

"Yes what?"

"You must tickle it out of me." Patty whispered, working on my necktie with one hand and shirt buttons with the other.

"Not a problem, Kitten." I said, scooping her tiny body in my arms and heading for the somewhat crooked, always squeaking, walnut staircase.

"Civilian life must be weakening, dearest. Before you entered the Fleet Reserve, you were able to carry me with one hand and remove my clothing with the other!"

Minx!

Some time later, Patty beered me, gave me a stogie she

likely misappropriated from her dad, settled herself inside my arm and rested her back and head against a pile of pillows she had thumped into place before settling into her nest. She took a sip of my beer and gave a happy, little sigh.

"Things going pretty well, Kitten?"

"Oh, yes!"

"Make my day and tell me about your interview. I'm breathless to hear how you destroyed the talking head's mind."

"Yes, you are breathless, or you were a few minutes ago, for the same reason I was breathless. But I am not going to tell you about the interview."

"Why the hell not? I tell you everything."

"You do *not*!"

"Uh . . . what, specifically, didn't I tell you?" I queried, knowing she'd laid a noose, snare, pit, trap, whatever, for me to step in. It wasn't the first time. She was scads brighter than I was.

"*You* did not tell me how you arranged retraction of those falsehoods promulgated by that church group."

"What makes you think I did?"

That caused a puffed out lower lip. There were thing worse than Patty going stubborn on me: flogging through the fleet; keelhauling; heaved in a cargo net and hung over the side of a ship far at sea with only a loaf of bread, a pint jug of Mad Dog Twenty-Twenty and a sharp knife; leprosy with complications of advanced gleep.

"Who else, dearest?"

I couldn't think of anybody, so I told her about my session with Marcie and the lawyer and the meeting with the church group. I thought I covered the happenings very well.

I was wrong.

"Now, please tell me why you thumped Curtis when you promised you would not do so."

"I *didn't* thump Curtis. I have not *talked* with Curtis. I have not *seen* Curtis!"

"Since the last time you thumped him?"

I wasn't real sure how to answer that, but I gave it my best shot "Yeah, I guess you could say that . . . sorta."

Patty clapped her hands and exclaimed. "Oh, goody! Now that we have determined you did thump Curtis, tell me when."

"The day we married."

"You are saying you last thumped Curtis at our wedding reception? When he called me an 'ice box' and said you'd have to rape me on our wedding night? Really?"

"Yep. That's what I'm saying." I said smugly, thinking I'd weaseled my out of that one, which would have been a first.

"Did you have Gunny thump him?"

"Nope."

"Then, dearest, can you please explain why Curtis came home last week shaking so badly he had difficulty composing the letter of retraction?"

It took a while before I answered that one. It ain't easy to re-stow your sea bag and inventory a gear locker at the same time.

"Who told you that?"

"Missus Post."

"Missus Post? Where did she hear that?"

Missus Post was chairwoman, president, general manager, facilitator, whatever, of a multi-county quilting circle and gossip network that knew no bounds. Their ability to collect, digest and disseminate intelligence was the envy of the CIA and the KGB.

"His wife told someone. Someone told Missus Post. You understand how that works?"

"I'd be a moron if I didn't. Missus Post ministered me body and soul after my folks drown, but a closed mouth is not one of her better attributes. I probably told you before, but the night I was dressing for our first date, she called to complain about Jarhead eating her mums. She was in Talk Mode One, so I told her I had to run to an appointment. She said I didn't have an appointment, but that I was 'courting 'that nice little Patterson girl.' How she derived that bit of info is beyond my comprehension.

"What did Curtis' fat wife say, anyway?"

"Joan is not fat, really. She never lost weight after their last child."

"Speaking of which, who do you suppose is the father?"

"*Clay*!"

"Who, or what, is the father of the other two?"

"You are being *mean*!"

"Why are you taking up for her? She did you dirt since you two were in grade school. Look how she helped Curtis get me fired from recruiting. She did that mainly to get back at you. I believe we once agreed on that, didn't we?"

"Yes, but I believe she is faithful to Curtis, despite his evil nature."

"Joan was so round heeled during the two years I was in Big Otter on recruiting duty that she could pivot, flat-footed, through four full circles! She never attended ballerina classes that I know of. Her engaging in body exchange drills with Curtis didn't slow her down as you well know, having attended high school and college with her. She was build like a slender brick . . . er, well built and now she's fatter than Rosanne. Probably eats all the time. What else she can do with Curtis as her husband? The milkman only comes once a day."

When Patty finished her rich, whooping laugh, she gasp, "Clay, you are sometimes so mean! I feel sorry for Joan."

"You have a bigger heart than I do. But I have to agree. I'd feel sorry for Hanoi Jane if she formation steamed with Curtis."

"You would not! You agree with Angie who believes the government should have stood her against a wall and shot her for treason."

"I don't believe in the death penalty. but there are those who should be cast away on a devil's island sort of place, for the good of society."

"Changing the subject, you did not thump Curtis. Gunny did not thump Curtis. Who did?"

"Patty, I don't believe anybody whipped up on Curtis."

"Somebody did! What did you do? Hire a hit man?"

Patty's question wasn't a joke or a guess. She had just entered her mind-reading mode. When outta ammo, outta ideas, and retreat denied, there is only one logical course. Surrender under the best terms obtainable. I furled my Flag and told Patty about Gooey's associates.

Patty threw her hand over her mouth before I got well underway with my story. I took the route of the brave and continued, letting it all go.

Patty was quiet for a while after I finished, so I asked her why she was so concerned about Curtis, a person she detested.

"I am not concerned about Curtis. I am concerned about *you*!"

"Me? Nothing happened to me."

"It will, if an enemy discovers you have friends in the Mafia. Congressmen do *not* associate with members of the Mafia!"

"Gooey says they do. Anyway, he's The New Breed. He gets invited to all the fancy shindigs around the world. The man in the White House invited him to some function a while back, but Gooey didn't go. He's got more class than hang with that crowd."

"Clay-honey," Patty said, in a tone of voice that told me logic was about to be laid upon me. "You did not invite him to our wedding, so you know perfectly well that associating with him is wrong. Dearest, you should not have requested his help."

"It's *your* doing. *You* said I couldn't smite Curtis."

Patty, for once, was so confused she didn't know whether to dance a hornpipe or draw small stores. She hemmed and hawed for nearly a minute before she got her guns reloaded. "Had I known you were going to hire a hit man, or whatever is the proper title for such men, I *would* have let you thump Curtis."

"I didn't hire hit men. Gooey thinks he owes me. He has made an effort to pay his debt for years, even though I keep telling he owes me nothing. He sends me stuff all the damned time. How about that expensive watch you wear when you suit up in your fancy steaming duds? I've not heard you complain about getting that from him."

"I never knew he was Mafia!" Patty wailed. "You said he was an old shipmate. You did not mention his civilian occupation. Oh, I'll never wear that watch again!"

"You'll wear it, even if I have to strap it on you." I teased.

Patty flipped upright and spread-eagle me with her tiny body, grabbed me by the ears, pushed my head tightly into the pillow, then locked me with her big, gray eyes. "You do and I will smite *you*, you big lug!"

The wrestling match got right interesting. What we did to each other had nothing to do with smiting, quite the contrary. When we separated into two pieces, more or less, I hugged her so tightly she gasp. "If we continue to stop-gap our arguments like today, maybe I won't send you home in the morning."

Patty nipped my ear so sharply that I yelped. "You better keep me full-time! Otherwise, you have two choices. Dead and deceased!"

I was working an appropriate response when the animals started banging and scratching the door. That told me the downstairs phone was ringing, so I flipped the switch beside the bed and answered it. Patty lay her head next to my receiving ear so she could listen to the conversation too.

"Clay -- you won't believe what just happened!"

"Let's see, Bob . . . the city council is not going to ride us out of town on a rail ?"

"Get serious! Your lawyer just called. He said his church group is going to release a letter to the media on Monday. The contents of that letter will stun you to your knees!"

If he'd called a few ticks earlier, he would have caught me on my knees, more or less.

"Let me take another stab at guessing, Bob. They discovered one of my ancestors cast the golden calves that riled Moses so bad and another was head cuddling partner of Jezebel?"

"They are going to *endorse* you for congress! All six churches! Can you believe that?"

"Not real easy, I can't. I didn't expect even one of them to endorse me. I only wanted them to see I didn't have horns, a tail, cloven hooves, and the like."

"What are we talking about, Clay?" Bob asked, cautiously.

"I addressed them this afternoon. The whole bunch of them, six congregations piled into one church."

"You **WHAAAT**?"

"I just told you. I made my lawyer, who doubles as deacon of six churches tied head-toe in doctrine, muster the congregations of the churches. I let them poke at me and ask questions for over two hours. I didn't see any reason to bother you about it, seeing that you were so busy with Patty's interview"

Bob gave a lengthy groan, mumbled something about 'nut house here I come,' and clicked off. I think I heard the gurgle of a bottle being sucked on just before he hung up.

"I didn't think he'd exactly love what I done, Patty. There is only about one hundred-fifty of them total. Not many votes one way or the other."

Patty stroked my cheek with her soft, tiny hand. "The Rule of Seven, which sales people live by, is a theory that each person to whom a sales presentation is made will provide positive or negative information concerning either the sales person or the product to seven other people. I would be very surprised if your efforts do not produce five or six hundred votes!

No doubt about it . . . Patty was so smart it made my head hurt. She knew everything!

"Now, dearest, I will tell you of my day.

"The interview went well. That surprised me, Clay. She is known for asking sneaky questions and for being mean to persons for whom she has a dislike, such as republicans. She was pleasant throughout the entire interview. She did know certain things about me that I would not have thought she would have known.

"For example, she knew I carried straight A grades from first grade through college, except for a series of B's in the seventh grade. She asked why I received B's in something as simple as Home Economics, but never in difficult subjects. I explained my mother was a wonderful cook and I did not agree with the teacher as to the proper preparation of certain dishes.

"She attempted to argue me into agreeing abortion is a woman's right. Not bloody likely, Buccaneer – as you say. We then discussed a variety of woman's issues, one of which I knew nothing about. That subject was the 'glass ceiling,' with which I have no experience. We also discussed why a woman might want a job, even when she did not need one. I agreed some women do, but maintained many married women work only because it is necessary for the financial wellbeing of their family. We talked about the possibility of you being elected to congress. We ended the interview by me agreeing to appear on her program after I experience Washington for a while, if you are elected."

CHAPTER ELEVEN

GOOD MAN DOWN

Missus Post flagged me down as I turned from the brush-bordered county road into our lane. "I hear nothing but raves about your campaign, Clay. I always knew you'd go places, even though you were a terrible child, but I never so much as guessed it would be to congress!" Missus Post exclaimed, flapping at her sweaty face with the hem of her apron.

"I'm not there yet, Missus Post."

"You listen to me, Henry Clay Berkeley! You *will* be elected!"

"I hope you're right, Missus Post. You usually are."

"You bet I am! Oh, Patty went to her mother's to get a pattern for a dress she's making. She asked me to meet the school bus and keep Joe-Joe until she returns. I was waiting for the bus when I seen your truck coming. Now, you tell me, Clay, *what* am I going to do with that slab of peach cobbler I cut for Joe-Joe?"

"You could give it to me, like you did when I was going to school." I grinned, remembering the days Missus Post intercepted me when I got off the school bus and topped me off with Kool Aid in warm weather and hot cocoa when cold, coupled with a piece of cake, pie or cookies. Stopping at Missus Post's for my after-school snack was a ritual from the first grade until I left school to join the Navy.

"Oh, I have enough for both, but I'll have to bake tomorrow. My pie safe doesn't have more than three or four cakes and maybe two pies left. I baked the cobbler this morning for Mister Post. That man surely does love his sweets." Missus Post's motto was simple: feed one or twenty on an hour's notice.

I grabbed Joe-Joe as he descended from the kindergarten bus, threw him into the air and kissed him. "We have to go home, Joe-Joe. Missus Post says she's tired of you gobbling her goodies every day. Your freeloading days are over, Kid."

"Henry Clay Berkeley! You stop telling that boy stories."

"Daddy fibbed. I can telled when."

"Of course you can, Joe-Joe. He was a big fibber and teaser when he was a boy too. Scared the liver and lights out of me with some trick a dozen times! " Missus Post exclaimed, taking Joe-Joe out of my arms and giving him a big kiss. "Now both of you come in the house."

"How'd he teased you, Missus Post?"

"First, eat your cobbler and show me your school work and I'll tell you some of the mean things that devil did when he was growing up."

After we finished a bowl of cobbler with fresh cream, Joe-Joe exhibited his day's art work, slowly, one at a time, with the pride of El Greco. Missus Post had no children of her own, so she had an extremely high guess factor, or she'd relied on her experience with me. She accurately named each animal as Joe-Joe unwrinkled them across the table. His cow looked like a jumbled haystack with grape vines growing on it. So did his cat, his bulldog, his truck and his house. Then, he spread one I recognized.

"That's a good ship, Joe-Joe."

"Your ship, Daddy. See the gun? See the steering wheel?"

"That is a really good job, but that's not a steering wheel.

Remember what I told you it was when we visited the bridge when you rode the ship from Naples to Gaeta?"

Joe-Joe looked hard at the picture, then cried, "A helmet!"

"Pretty close, Son. It's called a 'helm.' Remember the machine next to it where you adjust the speed of the ship by changing the number of turns on the screw's shaft?"

"Lee helm!"

I hugged him. "You'll make a fine sailor someday, if that's what you want. Go on, Missus Post -- tell him my sins, then we have to go."

"Well, once your daddy caught my geese and tied bows made of feed sacking around their necks. Weren't they a sight! Then, one Fourth of July, your daddy and his friend painted red, white and blue stripes on the sides of my pigs with watercolors. He had my chickens so nervous from him zooming his bicycle up and down the lane that they wouldn't hardly lay eggs. I whipped him once when he rode his bike right through a flock of Rhode Island Red pullets I'd raised from biddies. He teased my buck sheep and like to wore my poor bull plumb out riding him from the time he was nine or ten.

"The worst was the Halloween when he was in the fifth grade. Him and two of his friends covered the inside of my picket fence with green cardboard. Why, I thought some fool boys had stolen several panels of fence as a Halloween prank! That green card-board looked just like grass. They got me good until I realized I should be seeing the color of the gravel on the lane, not the green of the yard grass if the fence was actually missing. Oh, he was a terror, your daddy was!"

Joe-Joe laughed and giggled, glancing sideways at me all the time Missus Post was telling him her tales. When she finished, I scooped him out of his seat. "Come on, Joe-Joe. You've learned enough meanness for one day. Let's go home before you learn stuff I'd better not catch you doing."

"He will, Clay. He will." Missus Post said, as she followed us out the door and onto the porch. "The sins of the father are vested unto the third and fourth generations."

Joe-Joe dived out of the truck, dashed through our gate, made a couple of passes around the front yard, then ran back to me.

"Where's my dog, Daddy?" he questioned, when Jarhead failed to meet him.

'Maybe your mother took him with her.

"Mommy is mean!"

"Joseph! I better not ever hear you say your mommy is mean, not ever! Your mommy is nice. Jarhead likes to ride in cars, so my guess is she took him. Go see Blue Suit."

Joe-Joe scooted up the porch steps, screeched to a halt for a moment, then turned and yelled, "Daddy, Blue Suit is crying!"

"Open the door and see what he wants!"

Joe-Joe barely cracked the front door before Blue Suit dived the length of the porch, zinged between my legs, streaked across the yard, cleared the picket fence and hit the ground running so fast he was flat against the grass. He was still yowling when he passed from view in the cherry trees at the head of the orchard.

I grabbed Joe-Joe by the shoulders, "Son, I want you to go to Missus Posts' house right now. You stay there until mommy or me comes to get you. You hear?"

Tears welled up in Joe-Joe's eyes, "Is something bad, Daddy?"

"I hope not, Son. Now go!"

I watched Joe-Joe enter Missus Post's yard, then turned and ran up the hill, trying to follow the course Blue Suit had steered through the orchard. I didn't know what the hell was going on, but Blue Suit feared the outdoors and something had to have happened to entice him into an area he considered a deep, dark wilderness. I cleared the orchard and made several passes around the overgrown, hillside field once used as a tobacco patch, but I didn't see my cat anywhere. I was about to clear the top of the ridge when I heard him yowling as if in pain, somewhere to the right of the old Indian burial ground.

I'd heard people say a shock caused their heart to stop, but I never believed it. I believed it then, when I seen Blue Suit yowling, licking Jarhead's flat nose and pawing Jarhead's face with his front paws. Jarhead was covered with blood!

I pulled the whimpering cat away from Jarhead's body and knelt beside my dog. I dropped my hand to stroke Jarhead's blood-covered flank and thought I felt a slight movement. He looked in such bad shape I couldn't believe he was still breathing, so I held my cheek against his flat nose. I was overjoyed to feel a weak, warm breath.

I inspected Jarhead as best I could without moving him. His left front leg was ripped apart. Gouges covered his neck and back. Blood, grayish ooze and mangled flesh completely filled his right eye cavity. The right side of his rubbery lip was torn and hanging loose. I started to pick him up, then realized the deep gouge across his back might have broken it. I needed something rigid on which to carry Jarhead to my truck. I needed it now!

I tore down the hill, heading for the barn when I seen Patty's little Lynx pull into the parking area. "Patty!" I screamed. "Jarhead's hurt! Tell the veterinarian we've got an emergency and need him right now. Hurry!"

"Hurt? How?"

"Go, Woman. Get the damned veterinarian., then bring a couple of clean sheets. Run!"

I didn't know about pressure points in dog bodies, but I searched with a coolness I didn't feel until I found a couple of places that seemed to slow the trickle of blood from Jarhead's almost totally severed leg. I locked my fingers around the upper stump of his leg. I feared the slight trickle of blood meant he'd already lost most of it. I prayed whatever had caused the wound had, somehow, clogged the blood vessels as I had seen happen in Vietnam.

"Jarhead, you never listened to me hardly at all. I want you to listen now. I want you to hang on. You crazy dog! You attacked me in bed every morning until Patty moved in and you drove me and folks in two counties nuts with your silly antics, but you'd better not die! Come on, Boy, I'll let you eat Missus Post's flower beds, mess with every gyp in the county and chase my cattle! Anything you want to do. Hang on, Boy!"

Patty came charging into the brush and briers before I could warn her of the terrible scene she would see. She threw a hand over her eyes and burst into tears. "Oh, my God! Oh, my God!"

"Try to get a piece of sheet over that mess in his eye socket. Don't worry about the eye ball! Clean some of the blood off his back too, if you can."

"Oh, I can!" Patty dropped to her knees, still sobbing.

Then, wonder of wonders! Jarhead curled his tongue up and licked feebly at the heel of Patty's hand, once or twice, before his tongue sagged to the ground beneath his jaw.

"Oh, he licked me! He's going to live!"

I looped a strip of sheet around Jarhead's leg with my free hand, then knotted it into a crude tourniquet with my teeth. That evolution was difficult, particularly with Blue Suit meowing and trying to help by pushing on all three of us.

"Patty-honey -- let me take over. You run out on the ridge and yell at the veterinarian., when you see him. Get that cat out of here too."

Patty legged it up the ridge with a squirming, reluctant Blue Suit in her arms.

"Poor old dog. You hang in there and I'll make you a nice liner for your basket out of that animal's skin. You track him down when you get better and I'll shoot the bastard, Jarhead.

"You hear me? Hang in there, Buddy. You don't want Patty and Joe-Joe to cry do you?

"You and me have been beer drinking buddies for years. You don't want me to cry, do you?" I begged as I worked to stop slight trickles of blood. Me cry? Master Chiefs don't cry. Hell, I was crying so hard I could barely see!

The many times I awarded Jarhead punishment of three days dried dog food and water and restricted him to the house passed through my mind as I worked. I recalled the times he'd tore hell out of Missus Post's yard, tried his best to impregnate every gyp he could get his paws on, led Blue Suit from the straight and narrow, dogs he'd whipped up on, pleasures he'd had putting to flight dogs and cats foolish enough to pick on Blue Suit, bulldog-snake duels and how he would knock a beer out of my hand with his paw and lap it from the floor if I failed to pour some in his bowl. Oh, he'd had his days! I wanted him to have many, many more days. It didn't appear like he was going to get them.

Patty, the veterinarian and his female striker came tearing around the blackberry thicket, much to my relief. The veterinarian gave Jarhead a quick inspection, then instructed his striker to slip a padded board affair beneath him. "We can do nothing here. I'll have to transport him to my hospital." he said, catching one end of the board and lifting.

"Need help carrying him, Doc?"

"We've got it. Let's go, Nancy!"

'We'll be right behind you. Come on, Patty."

Doctor Hormick's clean, brightly painted office with pictures of playful animals on the walls would normally have been a cheerful room. It now seemed a cold, sullen place filled with fear. I cuddled the still sobbing Patty in my arms and tried to stifle my own tears.

"Will he live, Clay?" Patty asked, in a shaky voice.

"I don't know, Kitten. He bled a lot and he's not real young. I suspect he's at least ten, maybe twelve."

"Dogs live longer than that."

"Yeah, they do. Some live more than twenty years old. We had a farm dog, a German Shepherd, that went to his reward when I was a kid. Dad said he was eighteen when he was killed by a bull!"

"Jarhead must live -- or Blue Suit will die too!"

"I don't know what Blue Suit will do, but he went off-plumb today. He somehow knew Jarhead was hurt and showed me where he was on the hill. They've steamed together a long time, maybe their entire life. Jeff might have gotten them at the same time when they were young."

One of my men died in Vietnam, having left his animals at a boarding kennel that threatened to put them in a pound after his death. The kennel had no interest in finding them a home. I paid boarding fees for a while, then instructed the kennel to ship the animals to my farm in care of Mister Pollard to await my return from Vietnam.

Blue Suit caused few problems, but the free booting, brawling, gyp loving Jarhead frequently caused me to curse my soft, sentimental heart for taking them in. I rarely gave thought to the companionship and laughter they provided me when I lived alone before I married Patty.

"Dearest, do you believe animals go to heaven? Do you think we will see our pets there?"

"Well . . . it would hardly be the wonderful place the Good Book says it is unless folks join up with their pets."

Patty started to say something, then gave a heaving sob and tried to slink inside my chest when the veterinarian came into the waiting room, pulling bloody gloves from his hands, then wiping his face with a towel.

"I wish I could tell you folks you dog is going to be okay, but I won't know his prognosis for quite a while.

"Damn anybody who would shoot a dog just to hurt him!"

"*Shoot* him? He was torn up by a panther, a bear or something."

"Why . . . I thought you knew, Mister Berkeley! It wasn't any sort of wild animal. An animal, yes, but not a *wild* one. A human animal shot him several times, probably with small caliber projectiles. Were I a pathologist, I'd say the first round knocked his leg from under him, or maybe the one across his eye was the round that put him into shock.

"For the amount of damage, I'd say the majority of shots were nothing more than fun and games. Fellow that cruel might have tried to see how many times he could burn him, just to watch him flinch. A man who would do such a thing should be horse whipped in public until the flesh is torn from his back, and then tied in a sack and thrown into the Hemlock River! I recommend you contact the sheriff and ask her to survey the area. What she might find could identify the shooter, but that is not too likely.

"I don't believe in keeping things from pet owners, so I'll tell you what I can about his condition. I don't give him much chance right now, but I wouldn't bet he won't live. He's a pretty tough dog, considering the number of old scars I found. If I can get him out of shock, he might make it. At best though, he will lose his right eye and the bottom two-thirds of his left front leg.

"You should decide as soon as possible whether you want a one-legged, one-eyed dog. It'll be awkward for him if he lives. He won't realize his eye is gone, but the missing leg will cause him stress until he becomes accustomed to walking with only three. If you don't want him, I can put him to sleep without --"

Patty leaped from my arms, poked an index finger sharply into the veterinarian's breastbone and let go with all three barrels of her main turret. "Oh, you fool! Of course, we want him! I will carry him in my arms for the rest of his life, if I must. You try to put my dog to sleep and I will -- I will . . . Oh, Clay-honey, thump him! Thump him big!"

It wasn't at all difficult to get the veterinarian back into his examination room and out of Patty's sight. I then went to work on the very angry woman who had cast off her moorings and thrown both ends of her hawser into the water.

"Doctor Hormick doesn't know how we feel about Jarhead. He's probably seen lots of folks who didn't want to pay big medical bills to keep a crippled animal around. Don't be mad at him, honey. He's just doing his job."

"He wants to kill my dog and you refuse to thump him. Bugger the bosun!" Patty cried, as she alternately fought my arms and tried to bury herself inside them. She was really mad! I could tell by her using 'Bugger the bosun' instead of her milder, 'Oh, damn-in-hell' expletive.'

"He was just giving us an option, honey. He doesn't want to kill Jarhead. He wouldn't be in this business if he didn't love animals. Let me save the thumping for the hunters who trespassed on our property and shot Jarhead. They ain't seen thumping until I finish with them."

"That mean, awful Curtis shot Jarhead!" It is my fault too!" Patty yelled, as she activated her entire saltwater wash down system.

"Curtis probably hasn't shot a gun since boot camp. Anyway, mean as he is, he wouldn't shoot a dog."

"He did too shoot Jarhead. Curtis was acting crazy! Oh, I should have told you."

"I don't see why you should have told me that. Curtis has always been off-center."

"Clay-honey – he is really crazy now! Joan told his mother he has been drinking heavily and carrying on since the night he wrote the retraction letter. He uttered threats against you too, a lot of threats. Bad threats! Aunt Molly called Mommy after Joan told her how he was acting. She was very worried about what her son might do. Mommy called me to warn you. And I did not do so. I feared you would thump Curtis. Oh, damn-in-hell!"

"I still don't see anything new. Curtis has threatened me for years. Don't worry about it, Kitten." I told her, petting the top of her wavy-curly head. "He didn't do it."

"He shot and tortured my dog! I caused it and you will not listen!"

"Honey, he couldn't hit a bear in the as . . . er, stern with a banjo."

"He can too shoot! Really good too! He was in trouble for killing animals when he was a teen. Daddy once whipped him for shooting his chickens. He even killed one of my pretty cats! I don't know what sort of guns he now has, but he once had a twenty-two Bee, a thirty-thirty and a twelve gauge shotgun -- a double barrel.

"Listen, Clay, he said he was going to get even with you. Joan said he said that a number of times, once even when he was sleeping drunk. What better way to hurt you than hurting someone you love? He is twisted and mean. Oh, what to do?"

"What I am going to do is run over to the sheriff's office and get Gunny to investigate the scene. I hope it isn't Curtis because I don't want to go to prison for killing him!"

"Leave Curtis alone! Let Elizabeth arrest him. Please don't harm him, Clay-honey. I could not stand you being in jail!"

"We're probably beating a dead horse anyway. Come on, let's go."

"You go, dearest. I am staying with Jarhead. He may need me."

Gunny came crashing through the briers to where I'd been staying out of his way while he inspected the area. He held out a massive hand partially filled with projectiles. "Here they are, all I could find. Found them buried in the dirt a ways from where Jarhead was found. I believe I know about where they were fired from, so let's walk to the top of that ridge and see if I'm right."

"You know, Gunny, I heard gunfire when I was at Missus Post's house, but I didn't pay attention. Someone is always hunting around here, posted land, or not."

We circled the ridge, moving slowly and carefully over the ground towards the point Gunny suspected of being the firing position. I knew about moving indirectly towards a position, but I didn't know about looking for evidence, so I stayed behind him and kept my mouth shut.

"Damn the bad luck!"

"What's wrong, Gunny?"

"Look at the top of the ridge! Nothing but rock outcrop. Nothing smaller than a crawler tractor would leave tracks. I believe this is the right area though."

We prowled the entire top of the ridge, but found nothing, not even an empty shell case.

"Nothing here to find, Clay. Let's cut down the ridge on a course that looks like the logical path a man would take to the road and see if we can find where he parked his car."

The berm of the road proved too dry to show car tracks.

"Gunny, how are we going to catch this bastard?"

"If we don't, Shipmate, it won't be for lack of effort on my part. Me and old Jarhead slopped up a lot of beer at Moe's. He'd been my best steaming buddy instead of you if he could have swapped sea stories. Not a very bright dog, but he was a good guy."

"Is, Gunny. Is."

"Is?"

"Don't make him dead."

"Yeah, sorry. I keep trying to treat this like a murder case. Old Barney Fife -- that's me."

"You'll catch him, Gunny. If anybody can, you will."

"We got a good chance with these projectiles. All we need to identify the shooter is the rifle. I'll know when they come back from the lab in Charleston. I'd bet they are twenty-two projectiles, but not regular twenty-two projectiles. I had to really dig to find them, so I would guess they are some sort of enhanced round, like a twenty-two hornet, maybe."

"*Hornet*? Hell, Gunny! Patty said something about Curtis owning a twenty-two Bee. Is that the same gun?"

"Yep. Folks call them 'Bee's' because the shell boxes have

a picture of a hornet on them. How did Patty know that?"

"She knew what sort of guns Curtis had when she was growing up. She's not a hunter,. She doesn't hunt, but she knows guns. Her daddy taught her to shoot really well. She almost broke a Frog's piggy bank at a shooting gallery in Toulon. She won five bottles of Champagne with a dozen or so shots by clipping the string the bottles hung from. She really got that Frog's attention! He wouldn't accept her money when we went back the next night. I still don't understand how she hit anything with those rusty, worn-out guns. I didn't do so very well."

"How many did you win, Clay?" Gunny chuckled.

"None. And that only cost me about two thousand francs."

"You must have had an off night. I've seen you shoot."

"Yeah. Maybe. But Patty is a regulation Annie Oakley."

"Then you better not piss her off, Shipmate!"

"You ever see a ninety-eight pound tactical nuke, Gunny?"

"No. Why?"

"Because that is what Patty is right now. And she doesn't much care whose battlefield she explodes on. I've never seen her so mad! That said, I'd better get back to the hospital before she decides to cut down on the veterinarian, then go after Curtis."

"She really believes Curtis done it, huh?"

"She really does, Shipmate. Anything bad happens to us out of the ordinary, the first person who pops into her pretty head is Curtis. She hates him so that she prays for forgiveness."

Patty was in the same chair where I left her, sniffing and wiping her eyes with a white hanky. I bent over and kissed her. Her lips quivered, but it wasn't from my kiss.

"Heard anything more about Jarhead?"

"No, dearest. I have seen him often, but he remains unconscious. The veterinarian is beginning to look worried."

"Aw, honey, you're imagining things. Jarhead's lasted this long. That's a good sign, considering how weak he must be from loss of blood.

"Kitten, Gunny found some spent projectiles. He's fairly certain they are twenty-two hornets, which he says are also known as Bee's. Gunny says he can make a case, if he can find the gun that fired them."

"Curtis has it!"

"I told him that, but how can Gunny get his hands on it legal-like? If he doesn't do it right, it won't stand up in court. You know that."

"But he has it! I've seen him shooting it. Oh, maybe a year or two before we married."

Even a dumb hillbilly can have a spark of inspiration.

"Where did you see him shoot it, Patty?"

"Why, he and a neighbor were shooting at kitchen matches tucked beneath the bark of one of the shag bark hickory trees behind Daddy's machinery shed. You know, the type match lit by striking the head against a rough texture? They flare up nicely when struck by a bullet. I do not remember the gun Robert used, but Curtis bragged and bragged about the accuracy and power of his twenty-two Bee."

"Is Robert still around?"

"Yes, he is. Robert Stanley. You met him at our wedding."

I laughed like a lunatic, then kissed her firmly. "You're the prize of the earth, Kitten. Wait until I tell Gunny!"

"Tell him what?" Patty questioned, as she trotted after me as I long-legged it down the passageway toward a telephone.

"That you just solved his case, if it was Curtis and if the projectiles are twenty-two hornets."

Gunny almost wet himself when I told him about Robert. Getting in touch with Robert wouldn't be a problem, considering he and his father owned the State Farm Agency about two blocks

153

from the courthouse. We agreed to meet at Moe's in a couple of hours, providing I could spring Patty away from Jarhead.

The toughest thing I ever did, except look at my Mother and Father in their coffins and at Patty laying tiny on the hospital bed after her operation, was walking into the room and seeing Jarhead. He had so many tubes and drains stuck in him he looked more like a gigantic hedgehog than a regulation bulldog. He wore more bandages than the last surviving participant of an LA gang war. I reached down and touched his flat nose. It was more than warm. It was as hot as a steam line! His breathing seemed steady, except for an occasional lengthy pause that scared sheer hell out of me.

Law or no law -- somebody was going to end looking like the aftermath of a full-dressed KKK member at a Black Panthers rally when I finished with him. All I needed was to know who and how I could do grievous bodily harm without turning into a brig rat myself. That he hurt Jarhead was enough to make me want to kill. That, added to him causing great mental anguish to Patty, made me ponder cruel and inhuman punishments before I killed him.

"Say, Doctor, how are you going to make him stay put when he wakes up. Jarhead is a move-around dog."

"I don't expect him to fully regain conscious for a while. When he does, I'll keep him floating and happy until . . . well, whatever happens."

"You do expect him to wake up, don't you?"

"Well . . . probably."

"Doc are you telling us he might not wake up -- ever?"

"I really can't tell yet, but the shock he suffered might be enough to keep him under after the anesthetic wears off, like a human in a coma. As the saying goes,. 'Time will tell.'"

"Patty, you haven't eaten since breakfast. I told Gunny I'd meet him at Moe's. We can get a plate from his steam line, or eat elsewhere if you want."

"I intend to stay with Jarhead! I am quite surprised that

you do not."

"Honey, we can't do any more for him. He doesn't know we're here."

"Oh, but he does! I can tell."

"I doubt that, Kitten. I didn't know anything at all after they started working on me in a mobile hospital. I only know I woke up in the hospital in San Diego, thousands of miles from where I was wounded."

"You're different!"

"Did you know I was with you in the Santa Cruz hospital?"

Patty had suffered a miscarriage with complications when we were stationed in Santa Cruz, Spain. The miscarriage revealed internal problems such that she could never again become pregnant, which led to our adopting Joe-Joe.

"I knew you were there . . . I think."

"You may both be right, Missus Berkeley. Your dog might sense a presence, but I don't believe it would make any difference to him. Anyway, you'll have to leave in a few minutes. My insurance will not permit you to remain in the hospital after hours. The woman who watches the animals at night is competent. She knows to call me. You shouldn't worry so much about your dog."

Patty got a real evil glint in her eye. "What would you do were I to chain myself to his cage, Doctor?" she asked, salt dripping from every word.

The veterinarian, gave me a wild, harassed look and threw his arms up in the air. "Good God, I don't know! I never had anything like that to happen."

"You need not worry, Doctor. I am not going to do that, but I most certainly would were I certain Jarhead knew I was present. So there!"

"Come, Clay-honey. We will get a beer and save the bottles. I may want to break them across a *certain* skull." she said, looking directly at the veterinarian.

CHAPTER TWELVE

FAITHFUL FRIENDS

Moe gimped from behind the bar and hugged Patty tightly. "I'm real sorry about your dog, honey. It's a damn shame, that's what it is. A real damn shame.

"Don't worry, Patty. Old Jarhead will be pesterin' hell out of your neighbors before long. He's too mean to die. If someone was to crack him one between the eyes with a sledgehammer, he'd bite the handle off and spit the pieces at the fellow what swung the hammer! Bring him in when he gets to walkin' and I'll pour him all the Rolling Rock he can drink." Moe invited as he slapped one beer and a small snifter glass of amber liquid on the bar.

"Patty, you don't want a beer. You want somethin' stronger. Take a slug of this fine brandy. It's from one of them bottles you got me during that winery tour we took in Andalusia. I kept a couple so I can pour a little tot now and again for folks I like. You notice, honey, I didn't give Boot Camp none."

"Oh, Moe, you are so sweet, but what I really want is something to eat."

"Drink it down, Girl! Steam line shut down after lunch. It'll take a while to call the hotel and have Missus Moore send over some vittles. A West Virginia beefsteak, some spuds, some soup beans and stuff. That'll do it."

There sure was a lot of hypocrisy going around. Moe had been shacked up with Missus Moore for eleventy-eleven years and still tried to hide it. Patty went off-center and took me smartly to task the one time I said something about them being shacked up. According to Patty, Missus Moore's inheritance lasted only so long as she remained a widow. Patty said they had lived together for years and years. She seemed to think they were too old to engage in sex. Yeah. Sure.

I walked out on the beach behind our house in Spain one evening to call them for supper only to see Moe patting her neat stern. It would not be gentlemanly to say where the gray-haired woman patted him, but that, coupled with their sneaky looks, told me they were into bone jumping in a big way, age or no age. I let Patty call it what she wanted. I called it shacking up, but not out loud.

I could understand Moe going after Missus Moore. For all her sixty odd years, she had the face and body of a trim forty year old just beginning to show her age. I didn't understand her attraction towards Moe though. He hid kindness beneath a demeanor as sour as a choke cherry and looked like an elderly mud turtle off his feed.

"Hey, Moe. Yu give Boot Camp uh few beers on us, but don't yu let him go hog wild at us a-buyin' th' suds." yelled my favorite barfly. "Sorry 'bout yur dog, Patty. Yu want us t' kill somebody fer yu?"

"I might, Mister Rawles. I will let you know." Patty said, exhibiting the first smile I'd seen flash since she first seen Jarhead laying in the weeds.

"Hit can't cause us no trouble with th' law. We'uns ain't a-goin' t' be here long nohows."

"Oh, hell! You old devils have been trying to kick off and go to the Big Beer Joint in the Sky for at least twenty years. You'll still be sucking up beer when they sew me in canvas, take the last stitch through my nose, and heave me over the side."

"Could be yu're right, Boot Camp, but thar ain't nary a-one uh our doctors thet'll 'cept beer is good fer uh man. Bunch of dopes! We'uns done outlived five-six sawbones!

"Say, Patty! Yur dog sucks up uh lot uh suds, so he oughta be stronger than sin on Sat'day night! Made outta whang leather he is, jus' like us old fellers."

"Boot Camp used t' carry him in here, afore he got yu. Thet dog would run t' th' cooler, paw th' damned thang open and knock hisself out uh beer like he knowed 'zactly what he were a-doin' He never knocked nothin' out but uh Rolling Rock neither. He'd whine an' cough an' slobber an' roll hit 'round 'til Moe popped hit an' poured hit into uh bowl. He'd suck hisself down uh couple of beers, then he'd find uh pair uh feet t' sleep on. He liked Moe's feet better'n any. Thet dog knowed who owned th' beer!

"Now, Patty, I don't 'spect th' vet. would 'low beer in his place an' dogs don't 'pear to 'preciate flowers an' sech, so we'uns 'll wait 'til he gets a-walkin' an' you tote him here. Whatsoever pleasures him, is his'n."

Patty's eyes were a little wet as she slid off the bar stool. She hugged and kissed every one of the nasty, old men -- right in front of God and everybody!

I liked and respected the old men who hung out in Moe's and I realized they liked me. Patty, though, owned their hearts as she had from the first day she'd entered Moe's. There was no doubt in my military mind that they *would* kill the person who caused her grief.

I waited until Patty downed most of her brandy before asking, "You seem to be bad down on our veterinarian, Kitten. Why?"

"Oh, I am just angry and frightened because of Jarhead and he makes me . . . Oh, I do not know! He acts as though he really does not care what happens to my dog. He acted the same when Daddy called him to treat animals. I just never liked him."

Strange how everything we owned was 'ours,' except

Jarhead and Blue Suit. They had, somehow, become 'my' since we married so far as Patty was concerned. Although I'd had the animals a good while before I met Patty, everybody now acted like Patty owned them outright. No one ever referred to 'Clay's dog.' It was always "Patty's dog.' I reasoned it made sense, in a way. Both animals took to Patty from the very first moment she met them. Blue Suit sniffed at her, then plopped twenty pounds of fat cat on her lap and lit off his sawmill. Jarhead looked at her like she was the Big Mighty Dog Factory in the Sky, then flopped his ugly head across her nice, white sneakers and slobbered all over them. Patty loved it!"

"Clay-honey, do you trust that veterinarian?"

"Mister Pollard used him for years. You just said your dad uses him. I don't think he would have lasted unless Dana Pollard and Charlie Patterson thought he was competent."

"Oh, that is true! Perhaps I think wrongly of him. He appears so . . . cold."

"I can understand that. Seeing sad stuff every day is probably like being in combat. You have to find a way to shut it out. I suspect that's why some medical folks act cold."

Either the circus had come to town and the elephants made their creep all at once, or Mister and Missus Gunny were about to grace our presence by trying to pass abreast through the door.

"Damnit! You two wreck my door casin', then you mash my stools. My floor is gettin' weak from the strain of you two beatin' feet on it. I'm gettin' damn tired of middle-aged folks comin' in here to lollygag and paw each other like teenagers. God, Elizabeth, you're the sheriff!"

Elizabeth wasn't prone to blushing, but her rich, creamy skin showed a slight tint. She slammed a near suitcase sized purse on the bar with a solid clunk, probably from the cannon she was carrying. "Be quiet, Moe! Set up a Budweiser and a Fall City before I haul you off to jail for insulting officers of the law."

Elizabeth locked Patty in arms the size of mile props and lifted her completely off the bar stool as she squeezed her against twin mountains. "If Delbert doesn't have the person who shot Jarhead locked up in three days, I'm going to fire him!"

"Why . . . you should not make such statements, Beth. Gunny will be everything possible to apprehend the shooter, who I believe is Curtis."

"I might even have to turn in my badge, Patty. I plan to shoot the bum, if I can't get enough proof to convict."

"*Beth!*"

"We're family. Same as. Delbert and Clay served together on and off since they went to sea on Noah's Ark. You're the little sister I never had. You think we're going to let anybody hurt you and not make them pay?"

It was embarrassing to see two grown women, one a regulation ex-schoolteacher and the other a full-scale sheriff, conducting salt water washdowns with Elizabeth leaking on top of Patty's head and Patty wetting down Elizabeth's upper mid-section. Gunny and I rolled our eyes at the ceiling. Patty and Elizabeth went in search of a booth away from unfeeling males.

Elizabeth always addressed Gunny as 'Delbert,' a name he thought was sissy. His wife either liked the name or used it to tease him. Her doing that tickled me until Gunny learned my first name was 'Henry,' after which Delbert didn't seen so funny. Thank goodness, Patty choose to address me as Clay.

"You going back to the hospital tonight?"

"Got chased out. I'm kinda glad too. I intended to send Patty home and stay with Jarhead, but I realized Patty wasn't going to go for that. She'd have worried and cried all night if she had stayed at the hospital. Better we both go home."

"How's Joe-Joe taking it?"

"He doesn't know. I sent him to Missus Post's before I followed Blue Suit up the hill. Patty called a while ago to tell her she'd get her mom to pick him up, but Missus Post wouldn't hear of that, so she's still got the little booger."

"Oh -- about those projectiles . . . Me and Mister Patterson dug around in that old hickory tree with wood chisels and found some. Not in the best shape, but I believe Charleston can test for a match. I sent them overnight mail, so I expect to hear something, maybe by tomorrow evening."

"I sorta hope they don't get a match, Gunny."

"Why in the hell would you want that? Some bastard shot your dog to rags and we want to put him away for a while. I hope it's Curtis. I never did like the creep."

"It's like this . . . I'd like to beat on him like a seaman hammering on a rusty pipe with a dull chipping hammer, but I can't. Patty won't let me for fear I'd get locked up. And she's right. Potential congressmen can't go around smiting folks. I'm caught in a loop, Gunny. I'm stuck worse than a hog in a rail fence."

"Not if the projectiles I found on the ridge matches those from the hickory. The statement Bob Stanley signed about an hour ago swears Curtis fired those into the tree. Curtis was shooting a twenty-two hornet. Robert was shooting a twenty-five caliber. He'll testify to that in court. Proof is not going to be a problem Once we can get a warrant for the gun on the basis of Robert's statement, it should be easy to get a conviction, if we do get a match. I hope the projectiles aren't too beat up to get a match! Some we found just beneath the shag bark and they look in pretty fair shape. Those that dug deep into the wood are in bad shape."

"What will he get if he did do it, Gunny? A fine? A month in jail? What?"

"That, I don't know. I read where a guy received five years probation and a big fine for throwing a lit firecracker to a sea gull in Florida."

"West Virginia is not Florida and, contrary to what we might think, Jarhead is just a dog. Folks shoot no-count hunting dogs all the damn time and nobody says zip."

"It'll piss me off if he doesn't get jail time. I'm hot to stick Curtis in the cell with a white trash, dope smoker who is in our keeping for the next year. He's so mean he slapped his eighty-one year old granny from bow to stern because she wouldn't give him her SSI check. He's a real jewel! The deputies have to club him three-four times a month just to keep him civil. He spends so much time in the Bad Boy Tank he's starting to think he's a mole that lost its fur. Giving him Curtis will make an early Christmas present -- a play toy to keep him from being lonely!

"It'll work out, Clay. If he doesn't get what we think he's got coming, you can sic our Mafia shipmate from *Mount McKinley* on him . . . like you done a couple of weeks ago."

"Now why in the hell would you think that, Gunny?"

"Stands to reason. You didn't do anything to make him mess his dress pants. I didn't. Angie would have whipped him sore. Book would have told everyone in town if he'd done it. Petty Officer Lew is transferred to Sigonella, Italy, four-five years ago. His wife wasn't here to sic her Sicilian relatives on him like she did to Curtis after you got fired from recruiting. Who's left?"

"It's damn funny that Patty accused me of the same thing. What did she tell you?"

"Nothing. I heard couple of city types were keeping a low profile in this area and checked it out. They didn't look to be doing anything wrong, so I left them alone. I later heard Curtis had a bad case of diarrhea, after which that stuff those screwy churches was spreading got squelched. It didn't take many brain cells to figure what happened. Elizabeth's mother heard from Missus Post about Curtis going off-plumb right after those two guys disappeared from this area. City boys in town. Curtis scared out of his skivvies. Adds up to Gooey, huh? "

"I'd have been better off if I'd whipped up on Curtis and took the heat from Patty."

"If you got it -- flaunt it! Ain't every fellow got their own private protection squad in their hip pocket. Maybe you can get Gooey to wipe out a few dope pushers for me. My dope problem around here would drop to zero if I could get rid of about six dope dealers.

"I caught one of the bastards over at Valley Head School about two months and a half ago with enough smoke weed to light off and launch the entire ninth grade. The dealer ain't real mobile yet. Those boys are bad to resist arrest. Happens ever time I catch one. Strange, that."

"I have to admit Gooey was handy, but I don't feel right about using somebody else to solve my problems. I was brought up to stomp my own snakes."

"Like you said, you can't do that no more. How's the race going? You must be making ground way the media is working overtime on you."

"Bob Criss said the polls on Friday showed me slightly ahead of my opponent. The guy is running so many ads his money supply is going dry. It's weird, but I have more money than I can use. I hope you don't have to lock me up with your granny basher for some sort of fraud."

"That's what Criss is for, isn't it?"

"So they tell me. Still, all that money rolling in worries me. That old man I told you about in Clarksburg, or maybe somebody else, probably has every wino in the state making thousand dollar contributions. I take a look at the list every so often and I never heard of *any* of those people! My opponent has likely been scamming Yankee Green Dollars for years, so I ought to be the hard up candidate, not him. I hope the Feds don't start looking at me."

"Clay, you don't actually believe all that money politicians throw around at election time comes from Joe Six-Pack, do you?"

"I know everybody is screwing the system, Gunny, but that doesn't make it right."

"Like a fellow running for Governor of Texas once said, 'When rape is inevitable, lay back and enjoy it.'"

"Look what it got him. Ann-baby beat him bad after that really bright statement."

"I sorta like that old gal. She might be a screaming liberal, but she's a tough, old bird in other ways. She cut the Texas death row population way down. Goes to prove that not all democrats are bad -- just the nutty ones and those in the media."

"Patty already clued me in on that. I no longer think drift factor and liberal are interchangeable words. I might shake hands with one now, selectively, of course."

"Elizabeth says the democrat committee is going stark raving bonkers. They can't understand how your polls remain fairly good with you telling the truth when it isn't always pleasant to hear."

"Elizabeth is a *democrat*? Great John Paul Jones! I've been consorting with the enemy!"

"That enemy is going to vote for you. So are many other democrats, I hear. It's the people down in the mud who believe the stuff they get from the government is free and will vote for the other guy.

"Say, I got in the deep, dark kimchee with Elizabeth the other night by telling her a joke. Do you know how to tell the difference between a skunk and a democrat road kill?"

"No, Gunny. Can't say that I do."

"No skid marks in front of the democrat!"

CHAPTER THIRTEEN

WAR AND ROSES

I watched the second hand creep to eight A.M., then dialed the veterinarian. I feared Patty would go off-center if I didn't have a situation report in hand by five minutes after the hospital opened.

"You folks should come in." the veterinarian advised in his cold, harsh voice.

My heart thumped. I looked across my shoulder into the kitchen to see if Patty was listening. She wasn't.

"Is he worse, Doctor?"

"Depends on what you call worse. His vital signs improved through the night, but he won't wake up. I could possibly wake him with a shot of stuff, but I'm reluctant to do that because of his condition. I've been thinking of things to try. This is slim, but it might help and can't hurt if a voice he knows talks to him. He probably won't hear it, but he might. I seen that work on a horse, but you have to understand it might not this time."

"What if it don't?"

"Depends on how much money you want to spend to keep him alive. Either way is okay with me, but don't you tell your wife

I said that. My chest still hurts where she jabbed me yesterday. I'd rather be stuck with a ball point pen than by your wife's finger. Damn, but she's strong for her size!"

"Yeah, she is. You probably know she's Charlie Patterson's daughter. She was something of a tomboy when growing up. She worked shoulder-to-shoulder with her dad on their farms. She ran heavy machinery, drove cattle trucks -- hell, you name it, she did it. Doctor, we'll be there in an hour."

I whipped into the kitchen where Patty was feeding Number One Son, told the kid to stay put, led her into the library and told her what the veterinarian said. Partly.

"Does it have to be a human voice, dearest?"

"What's on your mind?"

"Blue Suit! He has doctored Jarhead since . . . forever! Jarhead gets his skin torn in a fight – Blue Suit licks the wound until it is healed. Same when Jarhead runs afoul of a snake and gets bitten. Blue Suit has a magic tongue!"

"Why not? Bring Joe-Joe too. Two musketeers working on the third, so as to speak."

"Well, I do not know . . . I intended to explain Jarhead's situation last night, but he went to sleep while you were carrying him up the lane from Missus Post's. He never woke up when I put him into bed. What will he think when he sees Jarhead asleep with all those tubes sticking out of him? What should I tell him?"

"Get dressed. I'll tell him."

"Lovely!"

I snagged the kid and took him out on the shady side of the porch. I was still getting my ducks in a row when he asked, "Where's Jarhead?"

"Do you remember when we took a walk a while back and talked about what makes a person brave?"

"I'm brave, Daddy. You said."

"I know, but you have to be really brave today. If you cry,

166

it might hurt Jarhead. You have to talk to him like you do when you play trucks or something."

"We played Peter Pan!"

"Look, Joe-Joe. A real bad man hurt Jarhead and he can't play right now. He's got a bunch of boo-boos and the doctor put bandages on his boo-boos like mommy does when you get hurt. He's got a lot of tubes in his body so he'll get better. The problem is the sandman threw so much sand into his eyes that he can't wake up. We have to talk to him so he'll know we love him and want him to wake up. That job is going to take a lot of you being brave. That means you can't ask why he looks like he does. You can't cry either."

"Jarhead's got a bad boo-boo, Daddy?"

"Yes, he does. He looks terrible, but that's how folks look too, after a doctor works on them to make their boo-boo better. It will make Jarhead worse, if you cry. Do you understand why you must be very brave today?"

"OK, Daddy."

"Good. You can lead Blue Suit and make sure you tell him to be brave too. He can meow because he's not a person, but you tell him he can't cry. OK?"

Joe-Joe turned and slammed through the front door, giving the frosted glass pane yet another shock test. "I telled Blue Suit!"

Joe-Joe cheerfully pumped up Blue Suit's morale all the way to the hospital by explaining how he imagined Jarhead would look, but the blood drained from his face when he seen Jarhead laying unmoving in a cage. The only time I seen Joe-Joe's face that white was when he caught his fingers between a glass door and its casing at *Banco Santo Esperito* in Gaeta, Italy.

"Daddy! He's wrong!"

"Remember about being brave, Joe-Joe." I said, dropping my hand on his shoulder. "Go and sit by the cage and talk to Jarhead. You can let him smell your fingers, but don't pet him, or touch a boo-boo. You'll hurt him."

"Won't hurt!"

"If I remember right, you don't want anybody to touch your boo-boos. Not even to change a Band-Aid. Am I right?"

"Boo-boos hurt"

"And you'll hurt Jarhead's boo-boos if you touch his body. Just touch his nose a bit."

Joe-Joe put his slender hand through the wire and touched Jarhead lightly on the nose. "You got a big boo-boo. You can't played."

"He's sweet." whispered the fat, ruddy-faced female veterinarian striker.

"Hope he stays that way. Please watch him for a minute while I go and see what the doctor and my wife are doing."

Patty was nailed toe-to-toe with the veterinarian with her head cocked back at about a forty-five degree angle so she could lock eyes with him. Her lower lip was puffed out and her face wore a rose tine. Not a good sign, Buccaneer.

"Madam, you are the most stubborn woman I have had the misfortune to meet in all my years of practice!"

"I hope you did not intend that statement to shock me, Doctor Hormick. I have heard the same from my father many, many times. Now that you have determined my demeanor, why cannot my cat enter your hospital? Can you show health regulations where a perfectly clean cat is prohibited? A very gentlemanly animal too, I might add."

"Take that fat, feline monster wherever you want, Woman! Bring your farm animals too -- if you're certain it will help get that bulldog on his feet and out of my hospital!"

Patty laid her bright, broad-toothed smile on the veterinarian. "You are ever so nice for permitting Blue Suit to visit his best friend. Did you just hear Doctor Hormick, dearest? You must agree that he is an outstanding man."

"I agree with whatever you say."

The veterinarian gave me a look of sheer pity, whirled around and banged through the double doors into the examination room.

Patty scooped Blue Suit into her arms and said, "Thank you, dearest, for agreeing to let me speak with the doctor. One must employ reason with officious persons."

To say nothing of employing a head harder than the sides of a battle wagon and a will stronger than the Rock of Gibraltar!

"Mommy! Daddy! Jarhead licked my hand!" Joe-Joe yelled.

I looked at the attendant, who gave a little back and forth flip of her hand. *Maybe he did -- maybe he didn't.*

Blue Suit let out a loud yowl, braced both rear feet against Patty's breasts and sprung across the room. He leaped to the top of the cage with a stream of cat curses and clawed frantically at the wire.

"Can I let him inside, Doc?" I asked.

"Feel free, Mister Berkeley. I don't run the hospital. Your wife does."

I opened the cage door and held Blue Suit by his rib cage to prevent him from jumping on Jarhead's mangled body. He didn't even try. He crept to Jarhead's ugly head, touched him a few times with his soft paw, then started licking him about the face. If an animal's cries can indicate grief, we all heard it then.

Blue Suit would do a series of touching, meowing and licking, then look at us as if to ask, '*What the hell is going on here?*' He would then repeat his touching, meowing and licking with a little whimpering thrown in. Joe-Joe stood his ground, gently stroking the uninjured side of Jarhead's nose.

Patty heard it first. "He groaned! Oh, goody!"

I heard not a sound.

"He did it again!" Patty threw herself prone on the tile

floor, shoved her hand through the door, laid her fingers in front of his nostrils and commenced begging in a tearful, yet happy voice, "Oh, you beautiful, ugly bulldog. Wake up! We are all here, Jarhead. Do you want to see Joe-Joe and Blue Suit? I know it hurts, but you must wake up. Please!"

That time I heard it! The characteristic Jarhead gruff snort and muffled groan that could mean anything: happy, hungry, lust, pissed off, whatever.

"Look at me, Jarhead. I am right here." Patty pleaded

I stepped to the front of the cage just in time to see his remaining eye crack slowly open. He focused on Patty with his bloodshot eye and tried his best to slobber on her hand when he got her ranged in, but his tongue didn't have enough moisture to work up a decent Jarhead slobber.

Patty went bonkers. The rest of us maintained our reserved manner. We just danced around the place. Even the veterinarian knelt and patted Patty on her back.

"Oh, thank you, God!" Patty cried.

I thanked Him too.

The veterinarian lifted Jarhead from the cage and placed him on the operating table, then commenced to poke and prod at him Jarhead groaned. That caused a real mean look from Patty. Jarhead lifted his head slightly and let go with a weak mumble that probably indicated an extreme pissed off state.

The veterinarian finished his inspection, then filled a syringe an poked it through Jarhead's skin, which caused a much stronger mumbling groan."

"Doctor! What are you doing to my dog? He's awake now?"

"Madam, please trust me to exercise my profession."

"But you gave him a shot from the same bottle you injected last evening to ensure he would remain relaxed if he came awake during the night."

"Do you want him trying to crawl around in his state, Missus Berkeley?"

The gleam in Jarhead's one eye and his weak growl indicated he intended to chomp down on the stranger yelling at his beloved -- just as soon as he could get it all in one sea bag.

Blue Suit arched his back and hissed at the veterinarian.

"I am sorry for questioning you, Doctor." Patty murmured, in a subdued little voice.

Sure she was -- like a Tasmanian Devil is sorry.

Jarhead's entire body relaxed in a few minutes. He gave a groan and slowly closed his eyelid until only a thin slit of eyeball could be seen.

"Doctor! He is asleep again! He is not 'floating' as you said he would last evening."

It was the veterinarian who groaned that time. "Missus Berkeley -- have you used ever drugs?"

"Of course not. I detest drugs!"

"Permit me to rephrase. Did you receive drugs during an operation?"

"Why . . . yes. When I was in the naval hospital in Spain."

"How did you feel when the drug took effect?"

"I felt . . . Oh, sort of satisfied, I think."

"That is how your bulldog feels. He doesn't know what is going on around him, but he feels at peace and wants to doze."

"Oh."

"You may come twice a day to visit your dog. I would prefer early in the morning and in the late afternoon. Is nine and four o'clock okay?"

"Those hours are fine, Doctor." Patty said, sweetly.

The veterinarian displayed the first smile I'd seen that day. "You may bring your fat cat too, if you wish. I give him and your son the credit for pulling the dog out of his coma. You too, of course."

"Thank you, Doctor. I wondered how I would explain if Blue Suit were forbidden to visit."

"You explain things to a *cat*?"

"Certainly. Doesn't everybody?"

"I do not know, Missus Berkeley. I simply do not know. What I do know is your cat is grossly overweight."

"He is not overweight. His bulk is mostly hair."

"And he weighs . . . what?"

"Eighteen pounds, roughly converted from kilos -- when weighed in Italy, last March, I believe it was."

"Eighteen pounds. You consider that normal?"

"Blue Suit considers that normal! He does not over eat. Ever! The Italian veterinarian said he is an extremely healthy cat. He is too."

"But you give him little tidbits, don't you?"

"Well . . . yes. He likes an occasional treat."

"What sort of treats? Those for cats?"

"He does not care for cat junk foot. He likes sardines in oil, not mustard. He likes cheese with a strong odor and a bit of a Clark Bar, now and again. That is all he gets, except for cat food made of beef, pork, fish, shrimp and the like. Oh, I forgot pasta. He enjoys linguine."

"You should not give an animal candy and pasta! Both cause worms."

"Blue Suit does not have worms!"

"Says who?"

"Says an Italian veterinarian who graduated from A and M in Texas, which is in the United States!" Patty yelled, sticking it in and breaking it off.

"Er . . . I see. May I weigh your cat?"

"Certainly, provided you do not attempt to charge for an unsolicited examination."

The veterinarian gave Patty an evil look, picked up an instantly hostile Blue Suit and dumped him on a flat, stainless steel scale. Blue Suit, commenced dancing on the cold steel and let out a screech that probably made ex-doughboys within two blocks think the Huns were attacking.

"Ah! Twenty pounds, ten and one-half ounces." the veterinarian exclaimed, smugly. "Your cat is grossly overweight! What do you suppose he has been eating to have gained almost three pounds since his last weighing, Missus Berkeley? Clark bars and linguine, possibly?"

"Milk, maybe?" Patty said, helpfully.

"Milk? Do you now give more milk than before."

"Nooo, but Mister Pollard usually takes the animals when he goes to supervise the evening milking. He squirts milk to them directly from the cow's teats."

"Had you noticed when they returned, you would probably have seen their sides sticking out like swollen drums."

"Give me the diet, Doctor. You may charge us for that."

"Gladly, Madam. Gladly."

Patty gave me a wink and a bright smile, signifying one skirmish does not a battle lose. Little did that poor veterinarian know!

We stayed with Jarhead a while longer, probably to Doctor Hormick's dismay. He stood clear of Patty for the entire time. I suspect he realized he should let well enough alone. We were about to return home when Gunny called, wanting us to meet him and Elizabeth at Moe's. I was in the process of telling him we couldn't because of Joe-Joe and Blue Suit when Patty broke in to inform me she would drop them at her folks, go to church, the library, then meet us at Moe's.

Patty praised Doctor Hormick's medical expertise as we were taking our leave, but the poor devil had no idea of what he was in for when Patty reorganized her forces. Dislike between Patty and the veterinarian was as evident as forthcoming stormy weather at sea.

"Honey, I know why you're going to church, but why the library?" I asked as we were walking to the truck.

"Oh, just to browse a bit."

"Patty Lane?"

"I understand they have shelved some new books. Also, I want to see if they carry books on veterinarian practices and also health standards for animals, specifically, cats. Otherwise, I must stop by the book store to order those I need."

"Are you worried about our animals?"

"Not really. I just want to check the recommended weight for cats and dogs in relation to their bone mass. I might also read a bit about proper care of incapacitated animals, drugs, dosage, and the like. One can never know too much about the care of one's animals."

Doctor Hormick was the one who should have been cutting out for the church of his choice! He'd need all help available after Patty boned up on animal medicine.

"We nailed the bastard, Clay!" Gunny yelled, as I came through the door. "The projectiles were a match!"

"You got him in jail -- with the druggie? Can I go down and watch the great seduction?"

"No, Clay, not yet." Elizabeth said. "The county attorney won't be back until tomorrow, so we can't arrest him until he reviews the evidence. Gunny is just pulling your leg about putting Curtis with our favorite prisoner. I can't allow that, as much as I might want."

"Always someone around to throw a spoke through the

wheel." I grumbled.

"Sorry, Clay. I regret it too, but I don't make the law. That's why I'm going to arrest Curtis instead of Delbert. I don't need another resisting arrest complaint, which would certainly happen if Delbert made the arrest."

"So, Elizabeth -- you get him all comfy in a cell with all his little desires taken care of, how long before he goes to court?"

"A week. Maybe two. It depends on the judge. He'll make bail though."

"Too bad kangaroo courts and necktie parties are outlawed, Gunny. Damn the bad luck!"

"Yeah, Clay. Civilization has done fouled up justice."

"You two stop it and drink your beer!" Elizabeth ordered. "Where's Patty?"

"She's thanking God for saving Jarhead and studying on how to screw the veterinarian."

"**WHAAAT!**"

"I'll let her tell you what she intends. I hate to talk of bloodletting when I'm drinking."

"Patty still pissed at the Vet., huh?"

"You might say that, Gunny. Yeah, you *could* say that! Patty beat him to parade rest until he surrendered and let her take Blue Suit into the examining room. He tried to even his losses and went to work on her about our animals being overweight. He won that one, at least for now. Stand by for a ram! Patty went to get some veterinary books. Poor devil doesn't know the hell he's in for. He thinks he won."

Moe came from the store room and slapped a Fall City on the bar without me even asking. "How's Patty's dog, Clay."

"*Her* dog is going to be okay, we think. As okay as a one-eyes, three-legged dog can be."

"Jarhead will manage." Moe encouraged. "He might have

more of a stumble factor when he's drunk."

"Hey, Boot Camp, yu owe us some beer! Yu ain't bought us nary a-one in weeks. Yu done got right cheap since yu retired from the Navy. You hard up, or what?"

Patty came prancing through the door, kissed me, Elizabeth, Gunny, Moe, then each 'fly."

"You're in a good mood, Patty. You suspecting Clay might be able to perform tonight, for a change." Moe asked, setting her up a Budweiser.

Patty snapped. "He twice performed to my satisfaction just . . . Oh, darn you, Moe!"

Moe crackled. He loved to see Patty blush, but he enjoyed it even more when he managed to make her blurt something and then go Condition Red.

"Patty, I have a good news -- bad news thing to tell you. The good news is the projectiles match and we intend to arrest Curtis tomorrow." Elizabeth dropped her mine prop sized arm around Patty's shoulder, the weight almost bending her face to the bar. "I guess the bad news is it will hurt your family, him being a relative."

"I feel sorrow for Aunt Molly and Uncle Will. Joan too. The remainder of my family will probably cheer even though it will be embarrassing to have a relative incarcerated. I do wish, now, that I had let Clay thump him. I feel no sorry for Curtis! He brought shame upon himself. "

"You were right not to let Clay do that, Patty." Elizabeth said. "Curtis would have taken that opportunity to swear out an assault warrant, which would have finished Clay's campaign. Curtis would have loved that! I'm sure it kills him to see Clay pulling far ahead of him in civilian life as he did in the Navy."

"Speaking of campaigns, I stopped to see Bob on my way here and the man is not a happy kitty cat. He claims I haven't climbed on one stump since last week and that I have to get my as .

.. er, stern in gear tomorrow and do some grip and grins."

"Say, Clay, why don't I set it up so you can talk to all the law officers in the district?"

"I see no need to talk with the fuzz, Gunny. They *have* to vote for me. The incumbent is a bleeding heart, knee-jerk liberal who believes you nasty cops take advantage of downtrodden, socially blighted criminals who resented their daddy sleeping with their mommy."

CHAPTER FOURTEEN

SEARCH PARTY

Bob kept me turning and burning for the next three days, during which I crawled on enough stumps to supply a small paper mill for a week. I arrived back in Big Otter Friday afternoon barely early enough to visit Jarhead at the prescribed time. It was the first time I'd had a chance to visit him since he took a turn for the better. He now had a cast affair on his stump and some bandages were gone, but most of the drain tubes remained. He look terrible, something like a whale that attempted amorous advances to an aircraft carrier.

The veterinarian must have reduced Jarhead's intake of happy stuff because Jarhead lifted his head and gave me a little woof. He licked my hand as I patted his uninjured parts. His slobber supply appeared near normal.

Patty had one of my favorite meals waiting when I arrived home: pork chops fried crisp around the edges, mashed potatoes with white gravy, peas with tiny onions, fresh corn on the cob and a salad right out of her father's fall garden. She fussed over me while I ate supper, then fussed until she had me comfortable in my dad's old leather lounge chair with my shoes off, my feet up and a cup of hot coffee backed by a snifter of Spanish brandy to satisfy my weary soul. She even gave me a stogie!

"You look so tired and worn. Are you okay, Clay-honey?"

"I liked the sixteen-eighteen hour underway days in the Navy better, Kitten. I don't mind giving speeches to people, but taking to nincompoops wears my as . . . uh, wears me ragged."

"What nincompoops, dearest?"

"Oh, every crowd has a couple-three who want to argue about 'lose of' entitlements' because of budget reductions. I can't get them to understand that the money the government gives away originates with them. They can't understand we haven't got enough money to sustain what we now give, not unless we raise taxes a lot, let alone pay an increase. One young woman asked me why the government just doesn't print more money. I received a lot of blank looks when I explained paper money isn't worth zip by itself. The old time Romans must be laughing in their tombs watching us take the same path as they did."

Patty stood from where she had been folded at my feet with her beautifully shaped legs tucked beneath her. She stepped behind my chair and commenced kneading the muscles in my neck. "Poor baby. You will have to explain such for years and years."

"Yeah, if I get elected, or don't simply throw in the towel."

"Alpha: you will be elected.

"Bravo: you will be a wonderful congressman who will make people understand the need for whatever you endorse.

"Charlie: you would not quit now, not even if threatened with grievous bodily harm."

"I twisted around, pulled her head down and laid a big smooch on her. "Kitten, no one understands me better than you. You have it all in one sea bag."

"That is my duty, dearest. A wife must understand her husband and a husband must understand his wife if they are to properly support one another. Do you not think so?"

"Do frogs hang out on lily pads?"

"Clay-honey. If you were to remove your clothing and lay on the bed, I could give your tight muscles a good rub."

That sounded like a plan.

"Clay-honey?"

"Yes, Kitten."

"Did you enjoy your rub?"

"Do seals have flippers?"

"Everywhere?"

"Especially everywhere." I teased, knowing it would generate a big blush.

"Oh, I enjoyed everywhere too!"

"If you don't stop purring, I'm going to have to start feeding you cat food, honey."

"It is *your* fault. Who caresses my . . . er, places to make me tingle and want to do *That* with you. Imagine, an innocent little girl doing things like *That*"

"I suppose I enticed you into bed with the promise of a back rub? Huh, did I, huh?"

Patty smiled wickedly "One must do what one must do, dearest. I want to --"

"Not now! Wait a few minutes, Patty. You have me beat to parade rest right now."

"Not *That*! Listen. I must tell you something You will not like it."

"Strange how I usually don't when you start a conversation with that phrase."

"Uh, yes. Clay-honey, did you know Elizabeth does not yet have Curtis incarcerated?"

That question caused me to raise on one elbow and exercise at eye lock drill. "I didn't."

"Elizabeth received the warrant for his arrest, but then she experienced problems."

"Enlighten me, Patty"

"Curtis cannot be found! He was gone when she went to arrest him. Somebody must have informed him of his impending arrest. We suspect a member of the county attorney's staff whispered to someone employed at *Star-Journal* and they told Curtis.

"Regardless, he is gone. No one knows where. Both automobiles remain parked at his house. Gunny checked the airport and bus and train stations. If he departed the area, he hitch hiked."

"You little mouse! You didn't tell me when I phoned hone so I wouldn't be upset. Oh, what the hell. It wouldn't have done any good if I had known. One question. If he's still around, who'd hide him out?"

"I cannot think of anybody, dearest. Elizabeth and Gunny and her deputies have checked simply everywhere. No one has seen Curtis. Would you like a beer and a cigar, dearest?"

"It damned sure wouldn't hurt."

I lay there thinking, totally comfortable with a cold beer in one hand, a fine cigar in my mouth and the woman I loved against my side watching me with her big, gray eyes. Finally, I had an idea. Anybody can have them. Occasionally.

"Honey, if you were Curtis, where would you hide?"

"Why, I have no idea!"

"Think about it. You said he was in trouble when he was a kid. He must have hid out a few times, at least for a few hours. Where did he go? Do you know?"

"Not really, Uncle Will usually found him hiding somewhere on his farm. Daddy once found him a good ways from where he lived. That was, I believe, after he killed my petty cat."

"Where, honey?"

"Oh, in Daddy's timber tract on Spencer's Run Curtis camped there sometimes, so Daddy guessed that was where he would be."

"Do you think he might be there now?"

"Well . . . he might. He's grown now and would be much harder to locate if he were. Daddy's timber tract is over two hundred acres and it borders a state forest of . . . oh, I don't know -- many, many acres."

I gave that considerable thought, then put the beer on the nightstand. "You're the greatest, Kitten. I have the smartest wife in the entire world, the universe, even. What is your dad doing tomorrow, honey?"

"Why?"

"Oh, I thought we might take his hounds out for a run."

Patty's look told me she wasn't the least bit fooled, but she didn't make an issue of it. "I believe he would enjoy that very much."

"Good. I'll call him right now."

"Dearest, tell Daddy to take a rifle. You should take one too. The Marlin thirty-thirty would be ideal. There are wild animals in that area. Plus, one finds strange persons in the forests these days. You know, dearest -- marijuana growers, poachers . . . and some really evil people."

Sly little thing!

We were unable to locate any sign of Curtis in the timber tract, so Mister Patterson, a couple of his farm hands, Elizabeth, Gunny, two deputies and I re-grouped in a hollow at the edge of the state forest and planned our next search pattern with aid of an old Civilian Conservation Corps map.

I had not intended to end up with a posse, but I'd made the serious mistake of calling and asking Gunny if he wanted to ride shotgun. Gunny had made the grave mistake of telling Elizabeth. She picked right up on what we really intended to hunt and accompanied us in her capacity as sheriff, mainly, I think, to prevent a resisting arrest incident if we found Curtis.

Elizabeth climbed to the rim of the hollow and radioed the plane she'd strong-armed from the State Police. She said they weren't all that keen about loaning a plane and pilot. I suspect neither would have been forthcoming had they had known we were on the prowl for a dog shooter -- hard to tell with Elizabeth bearing down on them.

Elizabeth scrambled down through the brush and pointed a huge finger at a spot on the map. "Right here, on the far side of this hill, the pilot said there's either a jumble of camping stuff or trash on the ground, but she didn't go lower for fear of scaring off our fugitive, if he is nearby. There should not be trash in a state forest, so I suspect it is a bed roll and such stuff."

After a conference that would have made the White House staff proud, we separated into groups and entered the dense forest.

Elizabeth made certain she had total and complete control of Gunny and her deputies while Mister Patterson kept an eye on his farm hands. That left me to go my merry way alone, but only yards from the nearest searcher. None of my companions were aware of it, but I specifically chose my path of search because it looked the easiest route through the forest from Mister Patterson's timber tract. Curtis was one who always took the easier route.

The fall day was a barn burner and I was sweating like a hippy with a sock full of dope in a southern police station long before I gained the upper slope of a knob that supposedly led to a trail on the far side of the hill. I stopped beneath the wide branches of a tall, lonely spruce tree to catch my breath.

I was resting there, thinking how good I'd feel with Jarhead slack-tonguing and slobbering beside me, when I heard a slight noise on the far side of a greenbrier thicket to my left. I stepped behind the scaly trunk of the spruce and watched and listened, expecting a buck or a turkey gobbler to come stalking proudly into the clearing.

It was a different looking fellow from the usually fastidiously dressed Curtis who slinked around the thicket and into the clearing. Rivulets of sweat streaked his filthy, scratched face. The Salvation Army would have not accepted his clothing for donation to a wino. He was lugging a rifle in his off-hand.

I waited until he passed the spruce, then stepped quietly behind him with my father's lever-action thirty-thirty pointed directly between his shoulder blades. "Freeze, Curtis! I've got a locked and loaded rifle aimed right at your yellow backbone. I want you to bend down and lay that cannon on the ground. You better do it nice and slow too. I'd not mind shooting you."

Curtis hesitated so long I thought I'd get lucky Unfortunately for me, he bent slightly to the left and dropped his rifle in the white sandy soil by his foot.

Curtis never did have the backbone of a wooly worm, not unless he had an edge.

"Don't turn around! Walk straight for that log in front of you, climb over it, then sit with your back to me. Right now!"

"Are you going to hit me, or something?"

"Let's go with the 'something,' Curtis."

"I'll press charges. You have no authority!"

"Well, now you're quite wrong, Curtis. If I'd come by myself, I'd have had to conduct a citizen's arrest, which is as legal as a lashing in Singapore. But I had the misfortune to come with others, so I'll have to use the power vested in me by a person who likes you about as much as a dog likes snakes -- Elizabeth Thorton, our high sheriff. If she says I'm an acting deputy that's good enough for me. The judge too, I expect."

"Call her! You aren't allowed to lay a hand on me!"

"Don't get froggy on me! You'd better thank your guardian angel that I found you instead of Gunny. He'd have shot you deader than a crab above high tide.

"Now, Curtis, before we're rudely interrupted by somebody with a soft heart, I want you to lay forward on the ground, turn face up, then slide your left leg back across the log you're sitting on. Now!"

"No!"

I gave Curtis a little thump across his right shoulder with the barrel of my rifle, just to get his attention. That action received instant response as Curtis pitched forward with the grace of a helicopter falling from the sky, thereby accomplishing exactly what I wanted.

"Work yourself back towards me a little, Curtis. I want your thigh on the log -- about six inches above your knee."

I received near instant compliance. Amazing what a thump on a shin bone with a gun barrel will accomplish.

I lightly X'ed a spot just above his knee with the rifle barrel.

"Right there. You watch that spot, Curtis. Watch it real good now."

"Why?"

"That's roughly the location you tore Jarhead's leg off with your twenty-two. So, now that's where your leg is going to come apart when I blow it away with a thirty-thirty projectile."

"*Nooo*" Curtis screamed.

That wild scream blew my plan to scare Curtis all the way to hell and back, so I stepped back a bit, aimed the rifle and fired a round as close to his thigh as possible without hitting him. Bark and splinters flew in all directions.

"You didn't kill him, did you?" Elizabeth cried, lumbering through the thicket with Gunny under tow. I heard the remainder of the group threshing their way up the hill behind her.

"No. He sort of raised his rifle, so I fired a round into that log to get his attention, then he passed out. Lack of food and sleep, probably. Poor fellow."

Elizabeth seemed to buy my tale, but Gunny gave me a look that meant he knew a Santa Claus-Easter Bunny story when he heard one, to say nothing of Curtis' rifle laying on our side of the log.

Elizabeth showed a Colt forty-five beneath Curtis' chin and bent to inspect him. The forty-five looked like a derringer in her enormous hand. She rolled him on his side, then stood and ordered her tallest deputy to ready his handcuffs. She also informed her deputy he would serve as arresting officer of record because she didn't intend to spend a day in court.

When the deputy complied with her order, she flopped Curtis roughly on his back and slapped him across the face a couple of times with a hand that threatened to remove his head from his shoulders. Her attempt to bring him around probably put him under a while longer.

"Oh hell!" Elizabeth bitched. "You deputies tote him until he comes to. You don't have to be real gentle with him."

"Did he really resist arrest, Clay?" Gunny asked, hopefully.

"Not really. He just refused to do what I told him to do, sorta."

"That's resisting arrest as far as I 'm concerned. If the judge agrees that oughta get him maybe six months in the jug."

"Maybe you should add the fact that he turned my weak stomach when he fouled his pants."

"Yeah, it makes a body wonder why he did that."

It took a bit of old fashioned begging, but Elizabeth finally agreed to let me speak alone to the still woozy Curtis, who she had effortlessly heaved head-first on the rear seat of a patrol car after we half-carried him across the hills to our staging area in Mister Patterson's barn yard. She seemed in a good mood. I'd have hated to have seen her pissed!

"Curtis, You better damn well listen and abide with what I tell you.

"You've screwed with me and mine for the last time, Curtis. I'm not going to put up with it anymore. I don't know why you hate me, but it has been going on since we were kids and you couldn't let it go after we grew up. I thought you kept trying to get even with me for whatever you believed I'd done to you. I thought that even after you got me fired from recruiting. Now that you've shot Jarhead, I know it's something more. You're crazy, Curtis!

"Here it is, real simple.

"You've gotten dangerous to me and mine, Curtis. If you so much as speak to a member of my family, you're going to get a visit from my friends. They won't be just trying to scare you next time. They are going to put your ass away!

"I'd like to do it myself, Curtis, but blowing some goober away is considered conduct unbecoming for a potential lawmaker of the land. I can't even thump on you, so give serious thought to what I told you. Screw up and you're dead meat!"

"I'm moving from West Virginia before you kill me!"

"That's a damn good idea, Curtis. It could come to pass, if you stayed here, that I'd take one of your actions wrong when you really intended me good. If that were to happen, you'd soon be serving as cargo for a chunk of cement. I'd feel sorry if I made such a mistake, but that's the way it is. None of us are perfect.

"Have fun in jail, Curtis. They have a guy in there tougher than Mohammed Ali who likes boys. He'll love a handsome fellow like you. He might give you a lollypop!"

I'd barely re-joined the group standing near to the barn when Patty came wheeling into the Patterson's barnyard trailing a cloud of hot dust behind her. She lifted Joe-Joe out of her Lynx and set him running towards the house with a smart slap across his rump. Whatever stunt he pulled had been wrong.

When she'd finished hugging and kissing on everyone, she walked straight to the patrol car and stared at Curtis. I couldn't hear when she spoke, but I seen Curtis flinch before he said something in return.

"Daddy," she called. "Will you take Curtis behind the barn

and shoot him for me?"

Mister Patterson winked at Elizabeth, picked up his rifle from where he'd leaned it against a hog apple tree and sauntered to the patrol car. I decided to stand clear of this one.

"You have to tell me what you want, honey. Shooting can cover a lot of ground. Do you want him shot dead, or just shot up a little?"

"Oh, I do not want him dead. He has children. Just shoot him a little, Daddy. In both legs and one arm, please."

"You heard my daughter, Curtis." Mister Patterson said, raising his rifle.

Curtis went out again.

"That's it!" Elizabeth yelled. "George, you get in that car and get the prisoner the hell out of here. I'm sworn to uphold the law and preventing folks from terrifying prisoners falls in that category." She opened the car door and peered at Curtis. She made a face, turned away and said, "You'll want to open all the windows, George. He did it again!"

Mister Patterson seemed to think we were in need of liquid refreshment and dug up some pretty fine beer, brewed by one of his farm hands, which he served in Mason jars.

"Don't you feel bad, Patty, for leading Curtis down the prime rose path like that?" I teased.

"I do not!" Patty said, bravely sucking at her jar of home brew. "First, he shot my dog. Second, he had the gall to call me nasty names."

"What did he call you, honey?" Mister Patterson asked, softly, the very same question I had on my own lips.

"He said that I . . . Well, I'm not going to use *those* words! He said, in effect, that I was a fornicating female dog and a woman of the town who plied her trade."

"Should have shot the fool! Damn it, Sheriff. You hold to the letter of the law too close at times." Patty's daddy exclaimed, getting all red and looking like he wanted to kill. "Well, I might be an old man, but I'll whip him bloody with a trace chain when he gets out of jail!"

"Yeah, Pa, we have to keep things in their proper order, But I think he intends to get out of Dodge when he finishes his sentence. That's what he just told me."

"Oh, I hope he goes as far as China!" Patty cried. "Clay-honey. I must go and see Joan."

"Boy are you getting mean! I'd have sworn you'd never rub something in to anybody. Well, I guess that's fair. Joan did you a lot of dirt.

"Don't you dare think that of me, Henry Clay Berkeley! I am going to see if she needs anything. I feel sorry for her. She will be feeling quite low when she learns of Curtis' arrest."

CHAPTER FIFTEEN

WILDCAT

"I let you off all day on Sundays -- most Saturdays too, then you come in on Monday looking like a tired bloodhound. What do you do all day Sunday? Throw rocks at old ladies, climb trees and swing on vines." Bob greeted when I walked tiredly into headquarters.

"I didn't do anything yesterday, except go to church and hang around the house. Fact is, Bob, I spent most of the afternoon and evening in bed . . . resting."

"Hah! What about Saturday? Are you trying to set up as a bounty hunter if this election doesn't work out for you?"

"Say **Whaaat**?"

"I don't know what you did yesterday to get so frazzled, but you sure didn't read any newspapers like a good, little candidate. Here, look at this editorial in the Sunday *Star-Journal*."

JOHN WAYNE RIDES THE RANGE

Henry Clay Berkeley (a few might know him as the fire-breathing, scripture and history quoting, republican candidate for the U.S. House of Representatives) took the law into his own hands last Saturday by mounting armed search for the man he accuses of shooting his dog. He located his prey in Hemlock River State Forest and marched him to jail at the point of a gun. His self-appointed, one-man posse seems quite extreme, considering the accused is guilty, at most, of a misdemeanor and the evidence is largely circumstantial.

Mr. Berkeley apparently believes local law officials incompetent of arresting even the alleged shooter of a mere animal. This is consistent with his reputation for violence against those who disagree with him. His condemnation of the stable underpinnings of our society is equally well known.

The days of individual eye-for-an-eye justice is long past. Necktie parties, whippings by the KKK and mob justice are, thankfully, dim pages in our history. Mr. Berkeley seems to yearn for the return to those days of yore.

The individual Mr. Berkeley apprehended under archaic authority of 'Citizen's Arrest,' appeared ill-used when led into jail. One wonders what the violent Mr. Berkeley might have done to cause such disorientation in a human being.

John Wayne passed years ago. It is time Mr. Berkeley, and men of such ilk, realize John Wayne's portrayal of violent, single-handed justice was nothing more than fabrication. The time to lay to rest the legend of individual, white hat justice and John Wayne's tall in the saddle image is long past due.

Some will cheer the macho efforts of Mr. Berkeley and the number of citizens supporting his campaign will increase slightly from the handful of supporters he now enjoys. Fortunately, those desiring a stable environment for their children realize there is no need for such action by a private citizen and the exploits of Mr. Berkeley will be condemned.

We believe strongly the John Wayne attitude of Mr. Berkeley does much to prove his total unsuitability for the esteemed office to which he aspires.

I crumpled the newspaper and heaved it into the trash can.

"That's your total comment, Clay?"

"I reserve comment for the lying ass who wrote it." I said, struggling into my suit jacket.

"You are going where?"

"I can't read a fellow from The Book without seeing him." I said, heading for the door.

"Clay, you go over there, you'll be playing right into their hands! Oh, hell -- I know you won't listen. I'm calling Patty!" He yelled, dialing the telephone, connected, then begged Patty to get her stern to headquarters before I transformed my campaign into flotsam and jetsam. He slammed the receiver into its hook, breathing like he just ran a four-minute mile.

I wondered if the man's health was good.

"Clay, you're looking at this all wrong. You've received darned good publicity! Every hard nosed hillbilly in West Virginia is toasting you in that booze they make with twigs and ants floating in it. You're a damned hero to them!" he said, retrieving the crumpled newspaper from the trash can and smoothing it out.

"That may be, Bob, but that article is flat out bull from the git-go! Stinky-boy Burton had his lie-making machinery all ahead full for this one."

"You know him?"

"Since the first grade. He was a stone ass then and he's a stone ass now! Not just my opinion either. How'd you think he got the name Stinky-boy? It wasn't from body exhaust. He was a Mark One - Mod Zero stinker to everyone, except teachers. He took suction on them like a mine pump. He'd sneak around and catch us in mischief, then tattle. What he tattled was rarely the exact truth. The little prig got his ass clobbered pretty darned often by somebody he'd ratted on, but it didn't break him of sucking eggs. This garbage he wrote is typical.

"Bob, I wasn't alone. Sheriff Thorton was in charge of the search party and there were other people involved. Yeah, I found him, but I didn't arrest Curtis and I didn't march him to jail. One of the deputies made the arrest and transported him to jail. You notice Stinky didn't mention the name of the man we captured. I can tell you why. It's because the guy we arrested is a card-carrying member of the media who works on his newspaper!

"Curtis Longly, Patty's first cousin, wrote that church manifesto against me. And he is the clod who shot Jarhead. You call the sheriff and ask about the evidence being circumstantial. It's as concrete as it gets, unless you have two-three witnesses and a photo."

"I tried to call the sheriff, Clay. This editorial was the first I knew of your John Wayne caper, so I thought I best smooth the waters with the local law. I didn't know she was directly involved in the arrest. She wasn't in her office. The deputy who took my call said she was headed to the *Star-Journal*. He sounded rather excited. Now I understand why."

"Stinky better start praying Saint Peter sends his soul to heaven, because Elizabeth will send his lard-assed body straight to hell! She's likely to forget she's the sheriff and a retired Army major and beat him into a state of ill-health. If she doesn't, I don't want to be in the same town when Gunny gets his hands on him. I might even get to tag him myself, if Patty will let me. Some things light off Patty like a twelve hundred pound boiler. Things like this, for example."

"Come on! Patty is the kindest, sweetest woman I know."

"Her ancestors were mountain women who fought Indians to parade rest right alongside their husband. You see Patty mad and you'll know why Indians got the hell out of Dodge!

"Want to hear a good one? As recent as last Saturday,

Patty ordered her daddy to put a few rounds in Curtis' hide -- like in both legs and one arm! She'd likely done it herself, but I guess that's what she thinks daddies are for."

Bob buried his head in the palms of his hands.

A shower of gravel slapping the side of the building and a squeal of brakes tipped me off. I could almost smell the tires smoking. "Your animal handler has arrived, Bob." I told him, about two seconds before Patty came steaming through the door.

Patty bent and kissed me then slapped both hands on her hips and eye locked me. "If you intend to thump Mister Burton again, I think you should tell me what he did this time."

"I sincerely hope 'again' refers to their school fights." Bob commented.

"Oh, I did not know Clay thumped him in school!" Patty squealed, clapping her hands.

Patty's comment caused Bob to shake a whole handful of anti-acid pills from his rapidly dwindling supply and chuck them down with a slug of coffee.

"Did you thump him in school too, Clay-honey?"

"Yep, every time he ratted on me."

"And you were spanked for doing that, both in school and at home?"

"Like the sun coming up and the sun going down."

"I detested tattletales when I taught school. It was difficult for me to treat tattletales fairly."

Bob let out a moan like a sick calf, fished a bottle of Jim Beam from a desk drawer and tried his best to choke on it. The man had obviously led a sheltered life.

"Patty, I can't stand another session of pulling information from Clay. Explain their most recent fight. Surely not since Stin . . . er, Mister Burton started publishing *Star-Journal*."

"Why . . . yes, it must have been over a year after his father died. I am fairly certain of that because Mommy, Daddy and I attended his funeral when I was a junior in college and --"

"Stop! Don't you do it to me too. Forget the background. When did Clay fight him?"

"He wrote an editorial that Clay considered demeaning to the Navy. It contained falsehoods concerning how sailors were treated unfairly and how Navy justice was not justice at all. Mister Burton wrote that after his relative was thrown out of the Navy. There is absolutely no doubt that officer got exactly what he deserved. He caused a ship to run aground!"

"So Clay took offense and challenged the freedom of the press by beating him up?"

"Not at all! Clay tried diligently to speak with Mister Burton, but he refused to see him. He had previously refused to meet with Clay's captain too.

"One evening after Clay had actually given up trying to speak with him, we were in the Holiday Inn lounge when Mister Burton and five men from his newspaper arrived. Clay attempted to employ that opportunity to explain why the editorial was incorrect. Mister Burton yelled terribly at Clay and called him names, mostly about Clay's having fought in Vietnam. He no doubt felt secure with those men accompanying him, otherwise, he would not have dared talk to Clay in such a manner!"

"So Clay slugged him?"

"No, but when Mister Burton finished yelling, he gave Clay a rather sharp push away from his table."

"Ah, now we're getting somewhere. That's when Clay hit him?"

"No, he didn't hit him then."

"Tell me, Patty -- do both of your families come from a long line of people who wrote the fine print for insurance policies?"

"No! Why do you ask?"

"Because I feel like Hitler after his meeting with Franco in the Brenner Pass. He said he'd rather have his teeth drilled without gas than talk to Franco again. Getting information out of either of you makes me appreciate Hitler's experience!"

"What didn't I tell you, Bob?"

"You *didn't* tell me when Clay hit him! That's *what* you didn't tell me!"

"Oh. Well, Clay only struck him once."

"When, for God's sake?"

"I greatly admired Clay's restraint that night, but I believe he was wrong. He should have thumped Mister Burton much earlier, considering the names he called him."

"When? When? When?"

"Why, directly after Mister Burton spit on Clay's khaki shirt"

"ARGUUUH!"

"Oh, you want to know *When*, as a date or time? Well, I was then Clay's steady, but we were not yet engaged. It must have May -- or maybe June six years ago. What Clay did to was lovely! It cost over fifty dollars to replace the glassware Mister Burton broke during his flight across the table. I enjoyed it so much I tried to chip in on the bill for damages incurred."

"You *admire* violence?"

"Of course not! But there are times --"

"Back to the original subject. Clay knocked him over at least one table. I understand that. I now understand that happened years ago. Now, tell me. Did that one blow end the fight?"

"Yes, it did, but it would not have ended had Clay been alone."

"And why was that?"

"The newspaper employees stood as if they intended to do Clay harm, so Gunny, Elizabeth and I stood too. That ended the fracas. There were more of them present than there were of us, but they wanted no part of Gunny, Elizabeth and Clay together. Gunny and Elizabeth, in particular, intimidated them. Me too, to a lesser extent."

"What did they believe you were going to do, Patty?"

"Just because I am tiny does not mean I am helpless! I had access to a perfectly stout crystal decanter. I also had my pistol, if any of them chose to brandish a weapon. Elizabeth had a handgun too, of course. She was then chief deputy sheriff and was required to carry one."

"A pistol!" Bob groaned. "She carried a pistol!"

"You consider that odd? Why? Many women carry a weapon. I've carried mine since I was fourteen."

"Your parents *approved* of that?"

"They certainly did! Daddy gave it to me for my birthday. Mother discussed various situations during which I might need to use it. If we ever have a daughter we will teach her as my parents taught me.

"A gun is a useful tool, not only for self-protection. I once killed a strange acting fox that was found to have rabies, an egg stealing skunk, and a weasel that was trying to get into the hen house. I've killed an untold number of snakes and grain eating rats too."

Bob made a gurgling noise and took another long pull out of his jug. He looked quite ill, so I told him he should go to the hotel and lie down. I wondered about Patty's comment about teaching firearms to a future daughter. Patty's miscarriage ended the possibility of her ever conceiving. Damned strange statement.

"I'd be afraid to go to the morgue if I were *dead*! You Beverly Hillbillies might decide to shoot up a few enemies. Tell me, Patty -- do you have a gun with you right now?"

"I certainly do! There are a few unsavory people even in Big Otter. I always carry it, except in Europe. They do not like guns in Europe. I found that strange."

"I suppose you're armed too, Clay? Oh, never mind! I'm sure you are. Every right thinking mountaineer packs a rod."

"I'm clean, Bob. I only carry when outside this area and Patty is not with me. She's the better shot."

"Does Joe-Joe carry a little heat too, Patty. What does Jarhead and Blue Suit use – tommy guns?" Bob asked, sarcastically.

"I realize you think you are funny, Bob, but animals do not require weapons, other than those they naturally possess. I believe our animals would do considerable damage to a person unfortunate enough to attack a member of our family!

"Joe-Joe has only a toy rifle. One that shoots cork balls. We purchased that rifle in Italy when he turned three. We want him comfortable with the feel of a gun before he receives his first real rifle, which will be the single-shot twenty-two Clay used when he became old enough -- at seven or eight, I suppose."

"Wife! Bulldog! Cat! Little boy! You didn't waste time adding firepower to your clan, Clay. Keep them in training all the time, I suppose?"

"Clay rarely has spare time and will have less if he goes to congress. I will teach Joe-Joe the proper use of a weapon if Clay is unavailable. He must learn. Our world is becoming more danger-ous with each passing year. One cannot be too young to under-stand the use of a gun."

That caused another increase in the profits of Jim Beam.

"Better let me have a snort of that store-bought'n stump juice, Bob."

"You don't drink hard stuff, do you?"

"Not often, but I feel a bit faint. I never knew Patty was packing a gun when we were dating. When I think of what I contemplated doing to her, but didn't -- and the times she got mad because I wouldn't. Oh, boy!"

"They're never going to believe this in Washington!"

Bob reluctantly let Patty read the editorial. I suspect he was reluctant to let her do so for fear she'd shoot up the newspaper.

Patty lifted safety valves. "Bugger the bosun! This is nothing but pure balderdash! I can certainly understand why you wanted to thump him, Clay-honey. I would let you go right now, but Elizabeth will lay a course correction on him. I hope she beats the fool unmercifully!"

"Elizabeth is at his office right now, so you'll find out real soon, Kitten."

"Kitten? You call her *Kitten?*" Bob questioned. You oughta call her W*ildcat!* God, I'll never understand hillbillies. They *all* believe in bloodthirsty retribution!

"How'd I get into this mess? I'll tell you how I got into this mess. A rich, old hillbilly catches me after a bad run of the ponies and offers to cross my palms with silver if I get you elected. I take the job, then learn I have a hardheaded nut on my hands. Do I worry? I do not worry because I believe his wife is a sweet, levelheaded woman who keeps him under tight control. Now I learn I have two violent nuts on my hands. Nuts who carry guns and beat up on folks they don't like.

"When they get bored, they team up with relatives and run the ridges with a female sheriff and her demented ex-Marine husband, both bigger than giants. Hey! They have a great time chasing a man through the woods -- hoping they can get off a couple of bullets so their gun barrels don't get rusty and they'll have something to talk about on Saturday night. When that doesn't work out, the sweet, little wife asks her daddy to shoot the man to flinders!

"Oh, God -- I'm in *trouble!*"

"You sound quite tipsy, Bob, Clay and I must visit Jarhead, then we are going to Moe's. We want to discover what transpired between Elizabeth and Mister Burton. I think you should go to your hotel and take a nap as Clay suggested. I really do!"

"Oh, no! I'm not getting more than a dozen feet from either

of you. One of you might go after that publisher and shoot the place up. I ask only one thing. Will you ensure people understand that I'm not a member of the Berkeley-Patterson-Thorton Clan, so I don't get involved in feuds? Feuding looks terrible bad on a resume."

"I'm all for Moe's and checking in with Elizabeth and Gunny, Kitten, but the veterinarian might give us some guff for coming to his hospital so late in the morning." I observed, figuring to shut Bob up by ignoring him.

"I do not use vulgar language, Clay-honey -- you know that. However, if he does, I can think of two words I would enjoy saying to that nasty man. The second word would be *you*!"

I admired the upper leg Patty inadvertently exhibited as she lowered herself beside the cage, tucked her legs neatly beneath her cute stern and petted Jarhead's half-bandaged head. I caught the veterinarian eyeballing her legs. Dirty old man!

Jarhead slobbered on us in his usual manner. He seemed fit and ready to crawl out of his cage and check the place out for stray gyps.

"He looks pretty strong, Doctor. When can we take him home?"

"I originally believed he would be here much longer, but he's healing nicely. The eye cavity has nearly stopped draining. His leg, what's left of it, is scabbing over. I'll let him try walking on three legs in three-four days. If he manages without damage, I see no reason why he cannot then leave, provided you return him every three days so I can monitor the healing process."

"Oh, wonderful!" Patty cried, kissing Jarhead on his wet nose. "Blue Suit and Joe-Joe will be so happy."

"Jarhead too, I expect, Kitten."

"*Kitten!*" Bob mumbled.

"Did you say something?" The veterinarian asked Bob.

"Why would I say anything? It is impossible to communicate with Bonnie and Clyde. I get lightheaded when I try."

"Er . . . if you're referring to the Berkeley's, I've noticed that, Sir. Yes, Sir, I really have noticed that!"

Patty kissed Jarhead again, climbed to her feet and delicately dusted her stern. "We must go, dearest, if we are to catch Beth and Gunny at Moe's during their lunch hour.

"Oh, Doctor Hormick! Have you had an opportunity to read and *understand* the paper I provided you from the veterinarian college? I found the weight tables quite interesting."

"I do not intend to debate veterinary medicine with a layperson, Missus Berkeley!" The veterinarian yelled, fumbling tobacco into his pipe and spilling a good portion of the contents of his leather pouch on the deck in the process.

Lots of nervous folks around, lately

"I will bring Blue Suit in for a routine checkup after Jarhead is released, even though you do not know much about the proper weight for cats." Patty said, sweetly.

"Madam, I respectfully request you take that damned fat cat and shove him . . . er, take him to Doctor Furman in Furnace Valley. I *never* liked Furman!"

Patty won another one . . . sort of.

Gunny and Elizabeth were head-to-head at the bar, laughing and giggling, with Moe on the opposite side of the bar glaring at them. Before we could even get the greetings out of the way, Moe threw his bar towel into the deep sink and stomped towards the beer cooler. "Lord, there's the other two! What'd you people think this place is, a stagin' ground for martial orgies."

"Naw, we think it's what it is, a cheap, slop chute. Better ask Bob what he wants before you pop a third one, Moe. He's not a beer drinker. You two satisfied looking Thorton's want anything?" I queried.

"Don't know about Elizabeth, but I personally never drink on duty." Gunny said, draining his beer.

Elizabeth laid a friendly little slap across his shoulders that'd shattered the backbone of a camel. "I should fire you for lying, Delbert -- if not for drinking during duty hours. Yes, thank you, Clay, I'll have my club soda freshened. One of us must remain sober."

"I'll have whatever is strongest, Mister Mosley, Less the local product." Bob slurred, now that the effect of the Jim Beam had kicked in.

"You look bad beat down, Mister Criss. Clay give you his old address book of sluts, which he ain't used since Patty started fixing his problem, which he gets once a quarter?" Moe said, getting back at me for casting slurs on his bar.

Patty blushed, but didn't say anything. Unless Moe broadsided her, she knew better than prod a bull with a pitchfork."

"I'm failing rapidly, Mister Mosley. Very rapidly, I fear." Bob said, sucking Maker's Mark like a legionnaire sucking water after a long, dry spell in the desert.

"You catching something, Mister Criss?"

"Nothing, except insanity. Berkeley's are stark raving nuts! They carry loaded guns, they argue and fight and insult people. They shouldn't be allowed loose!"

"You just now figurin' that out? We knowed it since they went to work on each other a few years ago. You think they're confusin' now, you oughta seen 'em when they were tryin' to mate. Neither of them acted like they had any sense a-tall.

"Them regulars down the bar, we call 'em barflies, had a pool as to when Patty was a-goin' to smack Clay over the head with a bottle. She got hotter than a sawmill boiler ever time one of his women got mentioned. Clay, though, he was too busy chasin' skirts and drinkin' beer with Gunny to understand Patty lusted after him like a cat after fresh milk. Man, he treated Patty like a little kid girl and that really boiled her water. I figured she'd shoot him a-fore they ever got around to any real serious lovin'."

"You knew she carried a gun back then, Moe?" I asked, wondering if I should cool Patty's face with a fire hose."

"Why, hell yes! Didn't you?"

"Afraid I didn't, Moe. It's a wonder I didn't get shot."

"Clay-honey! Few women shoot men they intend to marry."

"Them, Kitten, is the worst kind."

"You hear that? He called her 'Kitten.' Kittens don't jump into bar fights swinging decanters at people." Bob slurred. "I say they're both nuts!"

"Oh, Bob! Should we go to a booth, Beth?"

"Let's, Patty. Things are weird here today."

"They've been more than weird for me since I took this job." Bob proclaimed, solemnly. "Let me have a double this time, Mister Mosley."

The barflies, sensing a kindred soul who looked like he might be flush with Yankee Green Dollars, snapped Bob off his stool and guided him to their lair at the distant end of the bar where they seated him beside a retired WAC. That suited me. The man was flat nervous!

"Well, Gunny -- now that we've got rid of the wives and riffraff, Elizabeth looks in a right good mood. What'd she do, throw Stinky out of his third floor window?"

"Elizabeth ain't much on scuttlebutting, but she swears they had a nice talk. You believe that?"

"Not bloody likely, Buccaneer!"

"She says he was apologetic about leaving her and the other folks out of the picture. Said he'd run a piece tomorrow explaining he'd been given the wrong dope."

"Gunny, you tell me -- why would a guy who owns and publishes a newspaper back down without Elizabeth threatening to dismember him?"

"I can't, Clay. He was for her last election, but only because she's a democrat. He's not big on women running anything."

"There's nothing in the editorial she can take Stinky to court for. I don't understand what she could have said to make Stinky see the light. She say anything about me, Gunny?"

"Yeah, she did. She liked that editorial so far as you're concerned. She thinks your walk in the woods will get you a lot of votes. John Wayne is big in these hills. What lit her boiler off was Stinky making like her office wasn't able to catch Curtis."

"So, Shipmate, it looks like old Stinky tried to get wise, but stepped on it and mashed the pink part instead."

"I'd say that. I'd also say he's some kind of pissed at having to bite the bullet on that editorial too. I don't know him well, but I learned to hate his sleazy ass what with his lying editorials about the military. You think he'll try to get even some way, Clay?"

"I don't read that paper, but I hear he's already wrote that I'm everything bad, except maybe a rapist. He can't do more than write more junk that calls me names. He doesn't have the balls to try anything physical.

"Elizabeth, now . . . I don't know, Gunny. I don't know what hammer she used, but you can bet she had one. My guess is he'll support somebody else for sheriff next election."

"He started doing that last primary election, only his candidate was a real loser. Turned out old Bill Smyth was selling more than gas in that ratty, little service station he owns."

"Dope?"

"He ain't near smart enough to get away with that! He was making a little book and running punch boards. He was selling heavy porno too."

"Sounds like a real solid citizen, just the type for sheriff."

"Old Bill got off with a fine and a suspended sentence. His relatives still ain't real happy I arrested him. I think one of the bastards shot at me when I was looking for a still over on Hinkle's Run. Somebody shot at me!

"It was the damnedest thing, Clay. There I was chasing his ass through a dark woods when I tripped over a grapevine, went crashing down this steep gully and landed smack-dab on a still I'd spent days looking for! It was hid so well that I likely would never found it if that sucker hadn't shot at me. He done the community a real service that night. Probably saved a few men their life, or at least their eyesight."

"How so?"

"The fools were condensing the steam from the cooker through old car radiators! That's the reason I was looking for it -- cases of poisoning springing up all over. One guy across state line nearly went blind from drinking that stuff. I don't mess with people who run a little 'shine to put food on the table, but I'm not putting up with folks who make junk that can kill.

"What happened, I suspect, was they made a few bucks running 'shine the regular way, then got greedy and wanted to speed things up, so they used old radiators instead of a copper condenser coil. Radiators will condense a lot more steam than a coil. Quicker too, but it injects the residue from the coolant into the run of moonshine. My understanding is that drinking it is the same as drinking straight wood alcohol."

"You caught them?"

"Damn straight I caught them. All except the one who shot at me. I never found out if he was one of the moonshiners."

"It's a wonder they didn't wipe you slick and hide your body in an abandon coal mine."

"I gave them no chance! Me dropping in on them like that -- and I do mean dropping, gave me a whole new opportunity to engage in a little old-fashioned hip-to-thigh justice without being accused of police brutality."

"I don't expect four moonshiners stressed you too bad. You took on five in Palma one night."

"That was tough, them being Royal Marines. I didn't get help from you either. That little one knocked you directly South with about two good licks."

"That Royal was six-two and two-hundred plus pounds!"

"That's what I said. He was a little fellow."

"Clay-honey!" Patty called. I told Missus Post I would pick up Joe-Joe by two o'clock."

"Clay, you want me to drop the drunk you put off on the barflies at the hotel? It's on my way."

"Naw, Gunny he's making merry with the 'flies and it looks like he might be making a run on the WAC – or maybe the WAC is making runs on him. He won't feel so merry when he looks in his wallet tomorrow morning."

"Got that straight. The 'flies will drain his coin purse like the coroner drains a corpse."

We picked up our rug rat, had an early supper, chucked his worn-out carcass into the rack, then watched the news. I still wasn't popular with the media set, which reminded me of something. "How'd Elizabeth influence Stinky to back water, Kitten?" I asked Patty, who was curled on the floor in front my of chair, giving Blue Suit his daily brushing.

"She knew about his cocaine."

"His **Whaaat**?"

"Cocaine. He is not selling. He is just using."

"*Stinky*? Really? She *blackmailed* Stinky for *cocaine*?"

"She did not blackmail him, dearest. Elizabeth would not stoop to such tactics."

"Then I don't understand."

"She intended to speak to him about transporting that drug into her area since she learned of it. Today was the first opportunity."

"That's blackmail, anyway you look at it."

"It is not! She simply told him she would not like to arrest a person of his community standing for something so stupid as bringing cocaine into her area of responsibility. She did, however, promise she would arrest him immediately if she learned of a future purchase. "

"Looks like old Stinky understood exactly why she was there."

"One could say that."

"Is Stinky going to cash out and go to the Big Newsroom in the Sky?" I asked, hopefully.

"Elizabeth thinks not. He does not appear a big user. He swore he first tried cocaine at a convention in Charleston last spring."

"How'd she know about, it if he isn't selling?"

"Stinky could not be a great thinker to openly purchase a drug when he is so widely recognizable. His picture is displayed on the editorial page of the Star-Journal every day and that newspaper is sold throughout West Virginia. Consequently, the Charleston police recognized him on the video of a stakeout they were conducting. The amount he purchased was minuscule, so they did not arrest him. They were more interested in obtaining additional evidence on the dealer. They notified Elizabeth in the event he later started selling drugs, as so often happens."

"I wouldn't have tagged Stinky-boy as a drug user. He is such a priss."

"Elizabeth says those who use drugs would surprise you."

"Not much surprises me these days."

"Then, dearest, let me surprise you." Patty pitched Blue Suit on the couch, crawled on my lap and whispered in my ear, "I have this long-standing desire to make love with John Wayne!"

CHAPTER SIXTEEN

POLE AXED

The campaign heated to where I wished I'd never involved myself with politics. I, a talking sort of fellow, spouted so many words a literary entrepreneur could have taped, edited, then marketed a quick study course titled: *Spoken Hillbilly,* providing there was a market for such a thing. There might well be. A major British university, Oxford, I believe, once sent professors to West Virginia to study the idiom and dig out unclear and lost meaning of words used in Shakespeare and Chaucer, which isolated hillbillies were reputed to use in day-to-day conversation.

After a hard week on the road, with as many as six speeches in one day, I came crawling home at zero-dark-thirty-Thursday evening, kissed Patty, nodded over supper, then crashed and burned. I hit the road again Friday, gave two speeches in two towns that morning, made a local speech Friday afternoon, and followed that with another speech at a VFW post Friday night. Even Patty was dragging stern by the time we hit our pit about midnight.

Bob wanted me stumping Saturday too, but I nixed that like a big dog, even after he chastised me mightily about our poll numbers not moving either up or down, which he called 'stagnant.'

My opponent sold two-three blocks of coal for advertising money, although most polls showed me anywhere from three to twenty-four points behind him and none had me above him by more than a point or two. The widespread polls confused sheer hell out of Bob. I finally took pity on the ever-growing wrinkle factory and cut him in on The Big Picture, something I'd been trying to do since we started campaigning.

"Bob, it's like that Washington buzz thing. You just don't get it!"

"West Virginia folks respond to honesty. Oh, they might not like it, but most have enough sense to know when a person has laid The Word upon them. They admire a person with gonads big enough to lay it flat out. Will they vote for me? Hell if I know! Probably not, if they think the other guy is going to give them a freebee in their government check, but they will admire the man who tells them the truth and will probably consider voting for him. Today, they decide they will vote for him -- tomorrow, they will forgot what he said and say they will vote for the other fellow. Hence, polling numbers all over the place."

"Ruined! That's what the poll spread tell me. Ruined!" Bob wailed, frantically uncorking his jug -- Maker's Mark, this time.

"Polls aren't zip to me until Monday morning. I'm outta here! I'm meeting Patty and springing Jarhead out of sick bay. He's coming off the binnacle list today. The veterinarian kept him additional days because of something he wanted to keep an eye on. You need to take a break too. Go hang with the 'flies and listen to them reminisce about World War Two. Maybe if you tell the biggest lie that WAC you've been making goggle eyes with will grant you her favors."

I made a full-power run out the door before Bob could get the bottleneck out of his mouth. I could hear his cussing and screaming how I was a lazy, unfeeling bum who didn't respect his elders as I hot footed it down Magnolia Avenue. The man must have had some plantation owning ancestors!

Patty snuggled tightly against me as Joe-Joe dashed through the double-glass doors of the hospital with a bang, laying a little terror on the poor veterinarian who was likely already in Panic State One over Patty's imminent arrival.

I initially thought some great disaster had come upon the local animal population, then realized I knew every person packed in the fair-sized waiting room.

"Go get your dog, Patty." Missus Post ordered, having usurped the leadership normally held by Gunny in any sort of gathering. Patty blinked back tears and bounced happily towards the examining room.

"We'uns done brung Jarhead uh whole six-pack uh cold Rolling Rock, Boot Camp, but thet damned vet. says he can't have no beer in here! How's Jarhead 'sposed to celebrate a-gettin' sprung from this hole without nary uh beer?" complained my favorite 'fly.

His lecture on the health benefits of beer drown beneath the wave of hand clapping and cheering that flowed across the room. Jarhead sort of wobbled and scrambled through the wide open doors trying to maintain his balance on three legs, a feat he had not yet fully mastered. He wavered back and forth in front of Missus Post, looking up at her as if he expected to get pounced on for something he had done to her yard. When the expected chewing out was not forthcoming, he apparently said to hell with it and wobbled over to Moe, bent his remaining front leg until his wide chest touched the floor. He then laid his mangled head across Moe's worn slippers and sighed.

"Where's uh damn bowl? Somebody git uh bowl! Screw the damn Vet! Jarhead's gittin' uh beer!"

Jarhead wasn't recognized for much in the way of accomplishment, but he won wide admiration when he overcame his afflictions in just days. He didn't seem to miss his eye, but I noticed the occasional cocking of his head so he could lock onto targets. He learned to rocket along at a pretty good clip with a weird, stern swinging gait, but his steering a 'Steady as you go' course was a shaky. He was prone to slew off to port. Gunny got taken to task by Patty when he suggested we rename Jarhead 'Pegleg' or 'Tripod.'

The final week of the campaign was, in a word, frantic -- a real flail-ex, to use an old Navy term for an evolution ill-conceived, confusing or poorly executed. Bob kept me hard at it. I barely crawled off one stump before I was on another. Although the best I received from any poll was three points ahead, my worthy opponent went stark, raving bonkers. He called me everything from a high-school dropout to a booze hound to a womanizer of the first water. Bob heard on the political flack circuit my opponent's campaign workers had contacted my old girlfriends to see he could dig up dirt.

Either my lady friends felt sorry for me, forgot they knew me, didn't want to remember me, didn't want to admit they knew me -- or, maybe, still liked me. Regardless, none contributed the slightest amount of dirt my opponent could use against me. He then dug up and promulgated the bit about my grandfather being a long-haul bootlegger. Bob said my opponent screwed up badly with that tactic because the church folks, who had promised to vote for me, wouldn't back out, and I had gained the votes of the bootleggers and the stump juice distillers and their mass of relatives. He figured I gained votes of stump juice drinkers too.

There didn't seem to be one single member of the media, less Paul Rankin, who could report even the shortest reference to my campaign without using words such as: religious right, right-wing, strident, inexperienced, unfocused, schemer, negative, wealthy.

The media mice started standing mid, day and eve watches to scribble anti-Berkeley editorials. They blamed the republicans for everything from Montezuma's Revenge to the War of Eighteen-Twelve. They somehow made me directly responsible! One made a veiled hint that one of my ancestors provided support to Simon Girty during the French-Indian War. That could have been true. None of my ancestors were in the running for sainthood – a few were flat out low down when it came to wine, women and song . . .

and money!

Election day dawned cold and wet, but the rain slacked to a gray, foggy mist by seven o'clock. My morale was gray too, particularly after a survey of the previous day's polls reported I was down an average of twelve points. Stinky-boy's *Star-Journal* gleefully broadcast that their own Daily Pulse showed me down in excess of twenty-eight points.

Patty and I arrived at the polling place just after seven o'clock in the morning to cast our ballots, thinking we'd be about the only folks there, other than election officials and a few dedicated folks who wanted to vote before going to work. We were greatly surprised!

People waiting to vote spilled from the double door entrance of Pearl S. Buck High School, onto the outside walkway and down the sidewalk. There were dozens of them, some clapping and cheering when Patty and I walked down the street from where we'd parked. I also heard jeers followed by what sounded like cries of pain.

We received offers to proceed to the head of the line, but refused and fell into line with the rest of the damp folks. Patty immediately commenced chatting with everyone within speaking distance about everything from what the wide black band on wooly worms might mean for winter weather to the cost of coffee at the Kroger store. The big turnout if repeated across the congressional district was serious bad news. My opponent had a strong, years-old base of supporters who would likely brave the weather to vote. Mine were not likely to do so.

I pondered the possibility I had let the country pass me by during the years I'd spent in the Navy. I thought the country had reached its nether point when assorted asses were trying to burn it down during the Vietnam War. That and the happenings in the current era made me wonder if we weren't plunging towards the bottom of the heap at a terrific rate. Questions I'd received throughout my campaign, and had heard asked of other candidates on radio and TV, made me wonder about the level of knowledge of the American citizen.

We stopped in our headquarters after voting. Bob was not to be found. I figured he'd hit the bar circuit the night before and was laying in a ditch somewhere, if he had not crawled into a woods and strung himself from a tree. I tried to boost the morale of our campaign workers, but it was difficult to shore up their confidence when I had none.

Patty and I returned home. She tried her best to cheer me up, but her best efforts fell short .I gaffed her off and even turned down an advance she whipped on me around mid-afternoon! I moped around the house thinking of how I had let my supporters down until around seven in the evening when we headed out to attend the election returns bash at headquarters.

It is fact that free food and drink will bring out a host of people, but I suspected there would be no more than a hundred folks at our headquarters. There was no doubt in my military mind that the turnout would be similar to the funeral of some real popular fellow such as a banker, lawyer or child molester.

We, or maybe only I, received the Mother of All Surprises when I followed Patty through the door of our headquarters! Balloons and confetti of all colors floated across a room packed bulkhead to bulkhead with cheering, clapping, whistling people. Bob whispered something to Patty -- probably yelled it, really, to overcome the extremely high noise level. She turned and laid a lip lock on me that would have burned the eyebrows off the statue of David.

"Clay-honey, oh, you pessimist, you . . . Oh, you are so far ahead in the returns your opponent can never catch up. You won! Big time!" Patty screamed, dancing madly around me. "I have been trying to tell you all day that you would win, but you would not listen. Oh Goodness. Splice the Mainbrace!"

Splicing the mainbrace on sailing ships must have been a terribly arduous job because captains authorized an issue of uncut rum upon completion of that evolution. Consequently, the term evolved over the years to serving out any sort of alcohol to celebrate a major occurrence Patty's 'Splice the Mainbrace' wasn't outwardly possible because no booze was available. We had only soft drinks. Still, flasks would appear and be shared, so a limited splicing of the mainbrace would happen.

Gunny's massive hand snapped me flat off the floor and heaved me half-way across the room into the mob of folks wanting to shake my hand, slap me on the back and, in some cases, kiss me, which I didn't think Patty would care for even in her wild state. Folks were loudly demanding a speech. I could barely hear my own words, let alone hear what any one person speaking to me was saying.

Then it got dark.

CHAPTER SEVENTEEN

BINNACLE LIST

I'd have enjoyed the floating feeling of whiteness had it not been for gremlins sticking red-hot pokers in my right hip, stomach and shoulder. I repeatedly tried to chase them off, but the little buggers kept returning with a vengeance. The more the floating sensation faded, the hotter they heated their pokers. The overall effect caused me to think I'd been in this place before, but I couldn't recall when or why. I was studying on that when the whiteness started turning into a dim, foggy gray and I started hearing voices.

"Get his wife and that monster out of here!"

Something soft slipped across my forehead, down my cheeks, disappeared for a tick, then slipped into my left hand and squeezed.

"*Clay*! *Clay-honey*! Dearest, talk to me!"

I tried, but I didn't hear my own voice.

"Gunny! *Do something*! Oh, I am going to die too!"

I heard muffled sobs and a rich, heavy voice making soothing sounds, but I couldn't grasp the conversation. Nor did I understand the gruff, menacing words followed closely by a frightened squeal.

"I will not have you threatening me! I can do no more!"

"What you will do is find your ass in your own hospital if he don't make it! You other folks! You muster up the best quack you have, or I'm going to pull this doctor's arms off, real slow, one at a time -- until you do!"

That conversation ended with a scream and a cry to call the police.

"He *is* the police! I'll call Doctor Ryan. I really think I should!" cried a female voice.

Gremlins, sobbing, curses, squeals and other assorted happenings made me pretty sure that were I had landed was not a place I wanted to be. Somebody was in sick bay -- and that somebody was me! My intent was, I think, to question this revelation, but three or four of the damned gremlins gave me a series of sharp jabs in my starboard side. It got white and quiet again until I heard another series of conversations.

"Damn it, Whitt I told you once I told you forty times, I'm on call twenty-four hours a day. God, Whitt, that's a puncture wound in his stomach! He's probably bleeding inside and you stitched it up! Get your skinny ass down to the operating room and make ready to open him up!

"Nurse, get these people the hell out of here!"

"We're staying. Get cracking and get Clay done right. If he don't show better signs real damned quick, getting sued ain't going to be one of your problems!" growled a gruff voice that sounded familiar.

"Stand aside, Missus Berkeley and let me work!" ordered the strong voice that had ate old Whitt's stern to parade rest.

I couldn't see her, but I felt her there, petting my face, gripping my hand and dripping tears like a quiet, spring rain.

"She can stand anywhere she damn well pleases!"

"Sheriff, if you don't get your husband the hell out of my face, I'm going to stick him with a needle that'll put him out for a week! This man might be bleeding to death!"

The questions I was about to ask turned into the least of my worries when a gremlin, who had been setting wedges in my pelvic area for what seemed hours, swung his maul from near vertical and sunk one wedge all the way to my tail bone. That encouraged a multitude of gremlins to start sticking things in me from knee to neck. I heard a series of orders over my wailing, felt a sharp prick in my left arm and returned to my white place.

I experienced the strangest dreams . . . over and over.

I dreamed my mother and father and a host of other people were standing by my bed. It was particularly strange because my parents looked young – like in their marriage picture that hung in the library of my old farm house. The host of other folks, dressed in long out of date attire, just stood there sorta inspecting me. I felt that I should know who they were, but didn't. I dreamed my Dad and Mom spoke to me at length, but could recall little of what they had said. What I did later recall involved me being needed where I was. Strange. Odd. Weird. Whatever . . .

A clanking rattle, followed by a flash of light across my eyelids woke me. I tried to wipe my eyes, but my arm wouldn't move. Experimentation revealed that nothing wanted to move on my starboard side. Then a gremlin pinned my right arm to the mat with either a spear or a pitchfork. Another little prick let me have a good one in the vicinity of my upper, right leg with a sharp ax. I let out a war whoop they probably heard in Elkins.

"Don't move! Stop trying! Keep back, Missus Berkeley, until Doctor Ryan gets here."

"You stop hurting him and I will!"

I tried again to open my eyes, but my eyelids seemed stuck. Somebody solved that problem by swabbing something cold and damp across each eyelid. I cracked them open a mite and seen sunlight lacing through the blinds, outlining Patty with streams of light.

"Hey Kitten." I croaked.

Patty gave a little moan, made a downward half-bend from the waist like she was going to bury her face into my chest, pulled back suddenly, then placed a light, angel kiss on my lips."

"Stand aside!" ordered a man whose authoritarian voice I'd heard before. His voice was louder than Gunny's, but he was only a five-zip-nothing tall runt with wisps of white hair on his head.

The doctor poked at me, which caused a gremlin of the second string to jab at me a bit, but nothing like they had done before. The first string guys were probably all worn out and off duty. I drifted off again. I felt much more aware when I next woke up and seen Patty sitting beside the bed. I had questions in my mind.

"Kitten, why am I here?"

'Oh, dearest!" Patty cried, followed by an outbreak of sobbing, which she choked off with difficulty.

"Well?" I questioned, trying to lay my best master chief look on her as was needed when she tried to evade answering me. It didn't work this time.

She kept gaffing me off, but I kept bugging and pinging on her each time I woke up until she began to tell me what was going on. She might have said dozen words before the doctor came popping through the hatch.

"You're alert. That's good.

"She can't tell you exactly what happened, Mister Berkeley, and neither can I. I'm like the fellow who said all he knew was what he read in the newspapers. All I know is what I received from Gunny Thorton who, had I not once been a naval surgeon attached to the Fleet Marines, would have intimidated me like he did Doctor Whitt. I can't fault Gunny. He saved your life by insisting my staff call me. Enough about that. Doctor Whitt is no longer with us.

"You were shot. The good is the projectile hit your hip, but didn't shatter and fill your intestines with shrapnel. The bad was the projectile cracked your hip and drove bone splinters into a couple of your intestines. The round then proceeded upward, broke your right collarbone and took a huge gouge out of your shoulder, which damaged your ball joint socket. There is disagreement as to the caliber of the projectile.

"Gunny believes it must have been a powerful weapon that fired it. I, and other doctors, believe it was a small caliber projectile. We collected the residue and Gunny sent them to Charleston for analysis, but the tiny pieces found in the shoulder area were useless for analysis. The caliber is not important. What is important in that one projectile did a lot of damage.

"Doctor Whitt's suture concealed a penetrating wound, instead of a deep flesh wound as he believed. You were full of blood when I opened your cavity! We got that cleaned up and the intestines sutured, then certain blood vessels ruptured. You'll have to participate in a lot of blood drives to repay the Red Cross Blood Bank!

"If that wasn't enough, you developed pneumonia.

"Prognosis? You could well have a slight limp after the hip bone knits. How long? I don't know, Mister Berkeley. I expect recovery of your right arm too, but it might remain stiff and difficult to raise higher than shoulder level. I wouldn't count on doing any hunting with a long gun. You were very lucky, Mister Berkeley. Gunny told me, as I had already surmised from the scars on your face and body, that you were lucky before. The Man Upstairs, or his trusted agent, has truly looked out for you!"

God always reminds us of His many blessings, although we often do not appreciate them. We choose, rather, to think Good Things happen to us because of our own efforts. I was acutely aware of His blessings the second day after I fully rejoined the world, what with Patty's neat stern nestled on the side of the bed between my left arm and my rib cage and Gunny and Elizabeth filling about a quarter of the room on the other side of my bed. Talk about a warm, comfortable feeling!

That feeling continued with a number of people, including

the barflies, visiting every day. Gunny had already told me Patty spent the entire period I'd been there either in the chair beside my bed, or when totally exhausted, curled on the adjacent bed. He said he'd intended to lash himself firmly to the room too, but hit a severe obstruction when he tried to do so. Elizabeth sided with the hospital authorities and dragged him off. Missus Post wasn't having any truck with hospital authorities and spent the first three nights in or near my room, right along with Patty's mother and father.

"OK, Gunny -- it's now time to fish, or cut bait! I've tried to get Patty to tell me what happened. All she'll tell me is I got shot, got pneumonia and that she's in love with Doctor Ryan for fixing me up. You said some nut walked up and tried to do a Robert Kennedy on me. But no one, including you, seems to want to tell me who done it. Now, if you're all afraid I'll crawl out of bed and hunt the bastard down, you can forget that. I'm in no shape to do much of anything and I am not ashamed of that fact. Now, who *done* it?

"We're not really sure, Clay. You see --"

"Let me guess who Patty thinks done it. Curtis!"

"I have believed that from the beginning, dearest. Oh, I cannot explain. You try, Gunny. Please." Patty begged.

"Santa Claus done it because I've not been a good little boy, huh?" I said, tired of being gaffed off, for what reason I knew not. It was also a great source of mystery why Patty couldn't explain. Explaining was something she did very well -- too well, really.

"Easy, Clay. Hold on to your as . . . er, hat. The investigation report I turned in says Stinky-boy did it!"

"WHAAAT?"

"Clay, you might remember that folks were packed really tight in that room. I wasn't further than a dozen or so people away from you and I didn't even hear a shot. The noise in that room was terrible and far too loud to hear much of anything. I smelled powder after you fell, but I was so busy trying to check you out that I didn't see anyone leave the room. I likely couldn't have anyway what with the crowd of folks packed together. The shooter had to have elbowed his way out of the room. There was no way he could have walked or ran through the mob of people. Strange that nobody seen a damned thing and I don't believe anyone is covering up. Place was so crowded that even folks right near the shooting didn't hear or see anything. Everybody questioned was good about trying to help. Most of them were really mad too."

"Well, then -- how he hell do you know it was Stinky?"

"The evidence says he done it, but I'm not all that sure. Stinky, if he done it, went home, sniffed himself a little more nose candy, put maybe the same gun, a forty-four, in his word locker and blew the top of his skull slam off. Something ain't right, Clay. No one who knows him believes Stinky had the nerve to even think about doing something like that."

"Then who?"

"Curtis, I'm certain, but I'll never prove that."

"I can't see it, Gunny. If he'd have been there, I'd have smelled him, or something. I didn't."

"No one seen him there, but a town Mountie seen him crossing the street and climbing into his car on Ohio Avenue, one street over from your headquarters, in roughly the time you got shot. He didn't think anything about it at the time, but later remembered Curtis looked in one hell of a hurry and was holding his raincoat like he was keeping something from banging against his leg. Like a gun, maybe?"

"Then why did Stinky kill himself? It makes no sense, does it?"

"Maybe it does. Maybe it does."

"According to the gal who cleans the area where Stinky's office is located, he fired Curtis that evening -- put a rocket right up his as . . . er, stern. She says they were arguing, cussing and blaming each other because exit polls were showing you'd be elected. Curtis blamed Stinky for allowing that to happen. Apparently Curtis had some dirt on you he wanted to use in the newspaper and Stinky never let him do that, probably for fear of you beating the shi . . . er, the stuffing out of him. The cleaning lady won't swear to it, but thinks she heard noises, like somebody getting hit. She got the hell out of Dodge when she heard that.

"My thought train tells me Stinky was so het up he laid into Curtis, or Curtis laid into him. Probably Curtis laid into him. Curtis is lots bigger than Stinky. I figure Curtis knocked him stern west, then set him up to look like he killed you, which I believe Curtis planned on doing since we chucked him into jail.

"That tracks too. Mister Patterson said his brother-in-law was worried silly about something Curtis blurted after he bailed out of jail. I questioned Will Longly, but Curtis is his son and he wouldn't admit to hearing anything. Yeah, Shipmate, I believe Curtis seen his chance, gundecked Stinky's suicide, then beat feet over and shot you. It could have happened the other way around too. I like that he shot you first, then shot Stinky. Otherwise, how could he be so certain you'd be there directly after he shot Stinky? Or, taking it a step farther, how could he even know he could get close to you before somebody discovered Stinky's body?"

"Pretty far-fetched, isn't it? The whole damned theory, I mean."

"Not so far-fetched. Stinky died right around the time you were shot. He could have been killed before or after you were shot, so says the coroner.

"When I started looking into Stinky's demise, I heard lots of rumors about hissy fits between him and Curtis. Several folks have heard something or seen something, but not one of them had anything concrete -- just scuttlebutt, mostly.

"I made a point to run into the sports editor when he was in his cups and I plied him mightily with liquor. Vodka and orange juice, really. He flat has no use for Curtis. Said he knew him well and claimed to have complained when Stinky hired him. According to him, Curtis started swinging his little hatchet at everybody almost as soon as he was hired. The editors banded together and tried to talk Stinky into getting rid of Curtis, but couldn't get him to agree.

"Curtis kept doing his thing and the hard feelings and bad working atmosphere started working its way through the chain-of-command. Morale got worse and worse and people quit, good people according to the sports editor. The Jarhead episode and that John Wayne editorial brought it to a head, so this guy and two other heavies marched into Stinky's office and demanded Stinky knock off the vendetta against you and fire Curtis before they didn't have any employees left, including them!

"Seems the newspaper was having other problems too. They lost hells of advertising starting sometime last summer. Companies that had advertised in that paper since it was founded canceled their advertising with no notice and wouldn't discuss the reason they did it. The paper wasn't going broke, but it was running on the edge of no profit. I heard that and remembered what you told me about that old man who talked you into running for congress said about watching for a newspaper to start having problems. I guess he meant it.

"Anyway, Stinky agreed with his executives and he did tone down the stuff against you a bit. He backed down on firing Curtis, but he called him into his office and demoted him from a field reporter to a Snuffy type desk job. That, coupled with other failed shots the staff had taken to get rid of Curtis made them think he had some sort of hold over Stinky.

"Curtis got meaner and meaner and the Staff kept pinging on Stinky until he again agreed to fire Curtis. The sports editor thinks Stinky called Curtis into his office a few of days before he died and smacked him with a two-week notice. He isn't certain about that, but Curtis did sign on to a job in Oregon shortly after he thinks it happened. Curtis did tell you he was getting out of West Virginia before you killed him, which could have been the reason for the Oregon job and not the firing.

"If all that is fact, Curtis started hating Stinky and wanted to get even with him. He already hated you. The Jarhead shooting got him pitched into jail, which was likely the biggest em-harassment he ever experienced, considering the ego he has. The way I figure Curtis is he believed it was somehow all your fault. Finding some way to get even with you was probably a real big item in his mind from the day you grabbed him in the woods. Think about this . . .

"Curtis' stuff was way down in shi . . .er, mud, and you were making headway at running for congress. Then Stinky lands on him with both feet. Probably tells him to do his worst, but he's history on the paper. Now Curtis has another fellow to get even with. Since Stinky was known to run open at the mouth about what he'd like to do to you when he was drinking, Curtis seen a way to get even with you both.

"Clay, I grilled Curtis like he was a lump of meat. Curtis did nothing, except grin at me the whole time. Boy, did I want to bash that slick grin clean through the back of his head! I itched to turn his weird purple eyes black! But, doom to me, Elizabeth was there the whole time I was working on him"

"I would have said you were way off course a few weeks ago, Gunny, but after the Jarhead shooting and the stuff Patty said about him shooting animals just for giggles, I'm not so sure. Maybe he does have the balls to shoot a human. Speaking of which, when is he going to trial for shooting Jarhead?"

"Clay, there's one question you never asked?"

"Which is?"

"You never asked how long you've been on the binnacle list. You poured blood when Doc Ryan opened your belly! They pumped blood into your carcass like pumping gas into a car. He cleaned and stitched for four-five hours and worked on you a few more times over the next couple-three days. Then the pneumonia kicked in. Clay, you liked to di, di . . . er, sorry, Patty. Anyway, except for some short periods when you woke up for a tick, you were out of this world for eighteen days! You wasn't really here, Shipmate, but the world still turned.

"Curtis went to court eleven days after you were shot. He cried to the judge about moving to Oregon because he was threatened with death by several people, including you. Did I say cried? Yeah, he cried, like a sissy kid. His bawling impressed the judge who likely believed that you, or maybe me, or maybe Mister

Patterson, would waste him. If it is any consolation, he chewed on Curtis for a good, long while, which got him crying even more. I mean he flat laid it on Curtis! Far as I know that Judge Sparks has never been in the military, but he surely does know some nasty things to say to a man!

"He never actually mentioned Curtis shooting you, but I could tell he thought just like me, Elizabeth and the country attorney. When the judge wound down, he told Curtis he originally intended to sentence him to a month in jail, five hundred dollars and a hundred hours of community service at the Humane Society and, get this, *six months* in the jug for resisting arrest! But since Curtis has a job offer out of state, he'd cut that down. He fined Curtis one thousand dollars, provided he left West Virginia within seventy-two hours. Curtis jumped near slick the sorry bastard did. Sorry, Patty. I didn't mean to cuss in front of you."

"He *is* a sorry bastard, Gunny! He is worse than even that. Oh, I can think of much stronger words to describe *him*." Patty exclaimed, sheer hate pouring out of his voice.

"Patty, I don't want the slightest argument or discussion, but you know I'm going to have to take care of him once and for all. I don't yet know how, but I have to do it, Patty, You or Joe-Joe might be next if I don't put him away, somehow."

"That will not be necessary, dearest. We believe someone already did!"

"Let me tell him, Patty." Gunny interjected. " I know stuff you don't."

"Me and Mister Patterson had a talk with Curtis before he left for Eugene, Oregon. We told him if we ever laid eyes on him, even close to West Virginia, he'd end up deep in an abandoned mine shaft. We made no bones about it. Told him straight out that so long as either of us was alive, he wouldn't be in that condition if he even spoke to a member of the Berkeley or Patterson family ever again.

"He hauled stern out of here and I figured we'd seen the last of him. Then, I received a call from the Eugene Police Department. The sergeant said Curtis' wife reported him missing when he didn't return from work after his fifth day on the job. Curtis' personal stuff was mostly still unpacked in his office. His car was found in the parking lot where he worked. No money was missing from his bank account and nothing had been charged on his credit card. No hotel rooms, no tickets, no nothing. The sergeant asked me to pad around to ensure Curtis wasn't back in West Virginia.

"There isn't much that goes on around here that I don't know about, but I nosed around anyway. No one heard anything from Curtis since he left, except when Joan called their folks to tell them they arrived safely in Eugene. Clay, I'm certainly not going to tell the Eugene Police, but I believe Gooey had him hit!"

"Oh, come on Gunny! I was just jacking my jaws when I told Curtis that. Anyway, I've been out cold since the shooting, mostly."

"I know you didn't have anything to do with it, but Gooey flew in on his jet and tracked me down the day after you were shot. Clay, he was some kind of mad when I told him how bad off you were. He said it was a good thing the man who shot you was already dead or he'd damned well get that way -- and soon.

"Gooey hung around the area until the doctor decided you would likely make it, then flew off, still mad as hell. He came back four days later and hit me right between my running lights. Bang! He said he knew for certain who really shot you and he didn't need the kind of proof I did to take care of him. I was pretty sure who he was talking about, but I played dumb. I did, though, tell him what you said about stomping your own snakes.

"Gooey said to tell you that he'd studied on what happened and how you was limited in what you could do about it. He laughed and said, 'Remember how we used to give bad gear the Float Test when we aboard *Mount Mac*? Gunny, I have declared that fellow bad gear!'

"So, Clay, you tell me. Do you think Curtis is still among the living?"

"I don't know, Gunny. You know how guys like Gooey are

-- paying debts is an honor thing. I sure hope he didn't do something to Curtis. I'd blame myself."

"For *what*? Because a high-grade gambler thinks he owes you to the point you can't make a move without him knowing about it? There is no way this could be your fault."

I had trouble sleeping after Gunny left and Patty, against my firm orders to go home, changed into her nightgown in the bathroom, kissed me goodnight like I was a child, then curled beneath the covers of the adjacent bed. I thought of my fights with Curtis during our years in school, some of which I won and some the older, physically stronger Curtis won. At best I could remember we had our first scrap the first week of the first grade when he slapped me across the face because I beat him to the merry-go-round.

Curtis was a mean little kid! Sit on a sharp tack, Curtis put it on your chair. Spill ink all over hell and half of Georgia when you tilted the bottle, Curtis had loosened the top. Get slammed in the back of the head with a pebble-filled spit ball, Curtis had launched it from a strong rubber band. Find yourself flat on your stern with your tailbone sticking plumb out the top of your skull, Curtis had pulled the chair from beneath you as you sat down.

Curtis graduated high school and entered the University of Louisville. He intended to get a degree in journalism, but was, as the English say, 'Sent Down' in his freshman year, for something so terrible his mother and father would not even tell Patty's parents. He joined the Navy after that, more than a year before I did.

Our paths next crossed when I reported on temporary duty to help write a new course at Radioman School at Naval Training Center San Diego and Curtis was attached to the Public Affairs Office at Naval Air Station North Island as a first class petty officer. I was so glad to see a homeboy that I give our past differences no thought. Curtis wasn't at all friendly and stared hatefully at my new CPO uniform. I then realized I'd joined the Navy as a seaman recruit when Curtis was a seaman waiting to take the examination for third class petty officer, and he was angry because I had advanced above him to the esteemed rank of chief petty officer.

That was the last conversation I attempted until we ended up assigned to Naval Recruiting District, Big Otter, West Virginia. Curtis was then a chief petty officer and I was a master chief petty officer, two grades senior and in a rank held by less than one percent of the total force. Curtis spent a percentage of his time trying to put me into positions of embarrassment. I rarely had a week when I didn't hear of Curtis laying bad mouth on me.

His scheming ultimately backfired in a huge way. He, unknowingly, did me an enormous favor by arranging an interview with the editor of a college newspaper. The interview cost me a perfectly good part-time mistress of some months standing, but gained me the best woman in the world as my wife, something Curtis surely did not intend to happen. The fact that Patty Lane Patterson was the first cousin of Curtis probably hurt him even more. Strangely enough, I never understood why Curtis hated me. I never hated him, not until he really got my attention when he shot Jarhead and caused Patty untold mental anguish.

Curtis wasn't the type of guy who would be conspicuous by his absence, but he did care for his wife and children. Contrary to what Patty and others believed about him, there had to have been some good in his mean, twisted soul. I thought of praying for him, but realized I'd have a hard time convincing the Lord I hadn't shifted into hypocrite mode, particularly when I had been studying on smiting him myself. I decided to pray for him anyway and hope the Lord would understand.

I lay in bed a few more days, after which I was allowed to run the passageways, roam the small hospital and generally hell about the premises, provided I done that in a wheelchair. The doctor would not even consider turning me loose on crutches, for fear Gunny and I would cut out to a slop chute. He had already accused Gunny of sneaking me an occasional beer. Gunny? Sneak beer?

I pushed and prodded on Patty to return home at night as

soon as I was deemed somewhat mobile. She protested mightily, but complied after I told her I would have Gunny physically heave her out of the hospital if she didn't leave on her own power by six o'clock every evening. She really needed to go home. She was worn out!

I was sitting in the hospital's minuscule garden, smoking one of the cigars Mister Patterson had slipped me, enjoying the clean mountain air and the warm, early December sunshine when a tap on my left shoulder like to scared the liver and lights out of me.

"It doesn't look like I'll get to see how you hicks bury their dead. Do you stick them inside hollow trees, or do you cover them with rocks so bears and stuff can't get at them?"

I made nice and done my grip and grin, then I pounced on him. "Gooey, you walking chancre sore! You flat got my attention this time by sticking your nose in my affairs, something you've done for years. I want it stopped!

"Yeah, I did ask for your help a couple-three months ago, but not this time." I looked around to ensure the area was free of big-eared folks, then continued. "You having Curtis Longly wasted was a real low thing. We had it handled locally. We didn't need or want outside help, you afterbirth of an Air Force gang bang! I swear I'll --"

"Hey, don't jump my frame! I didn't put him down. He's around. He's just not here."

"Everybody knows he's not *here,* Gooey, including the Eugene Police and maybe even the FBI. If he's anywhere else, his wife doesn't know about it. Yeah, she's something of a witch, but she doesn't deserve to go out of her mind with worry over that fool. So, where is he?"

"I'm not telling you, Clay. You'd blab it across the country to stop people worrying. You couldn't stand to see people hurting when I worked for you and I doubt you've changed.

"Let's just say he's in good health, working in his profession and making a few bucks. He was given a ride in a nice

Lear jet to a place a long, long way off. And, Clay, his wife does know he's okay. His mom and dad know too. I'll send his wife and kids to him if she wants to go and will keep her mouth shut as to their location. So far she's indicated no interest in joining Curtis."

"Where is he, Gooey?" I asked, giving him my meanest master chief look.

"You are never going to know and you can stop glaring at me. Don't go looking for him, Clay! You have little chance of finding him. If you did, we'd just move him and we have a lot of places to stash him, other than in real deep water.

"Look! He wasn't drafted, he sorta volunteered. He fears you, Gunny or Patty's dad intend to kill him. I don't know if he has always been paranoid, but he sure is now! He's so paranoid he claims to have seen your father-in-law watching him at rest stops on his way to Oregon! He really did volunteer to go away, not that I didn't influence his belief that he was close to becoming a dead man and I was the one who'd kill him if you died. I pretty much knew by that time that you were going to be okay, but I had fears too. I feared you would go hunting for Curtis as soon as you were mobile. You would have, you know. Now, you can't!"

"I don't know as if I believe you, Gooey. You told Gunny you were going to turn him into fish food, or some such. Now you tell me you *employed* him?"

"I didn't employ him myself. Guys owe me favors, see. He *is* employed and is living in a not too shabby villa in a far country. He's bad goods and a piss poor human, but he's not half bad at his profession. The guys he works for like his work. You can stop worrying about him. He's not going any place. He has no passport and no means of getting one where he is."

"Gooey, I listened to you tell stories on the quiet mid watches in our old ship and I know how you folks operate. At least I know something about how generations before you operated, if you were telling the truth. So, why didn't you turn him into lobster chow, like you said?"

"You want him chilled? Consider him cold!"

"I don't want him dead, dammit! I want him alive. If anybody wastes him, it will be me! I just want to know why you backed down on what you told Gunny."

"I realized on my way back to Jersey that you'd be really angry if I had the scum who shot you taken out. You're way too soft-heated. So soft-heated you hurt yourself sometimes. You've got big balls, but you're too nice by half!

"Look, Clay. You must know I think a lot of you. You're the first man I really respected. And there is a damn good reason why.

"My Dad was deported the year I was born, but you knew that. What you don't know is I was able to see him, for maybe a week or two each year. He wasn't the most interested of fathers. My Mother is not the Italian mama-Mia type, not by a long shot! Oh, she gave me everything I wanted and a lot I didn't, but that was it. She moved in her own circle, leaving me with a Frog governess most of the time.

"I was a lonely kid, Clay, living in a Manhattan high rise with no kids anywhere near me. I attended a private school until eighteen. I didn't like any of my classmates. Mainly because they had some idea of who I was and had little to do with me. They were a stuck up bunch! Now days some of them come looking for a loan or influence, acting like we were best buddies. I sometimes help them just to make them feel bad at having to accept help from a greasy Italian they believe is a gangster. Yeah, that's what some called me, a greasy Italian. I kicked their asses, but that didn't stop my hurt It hurt because I am neither greasy nor swarthy.

"The draft started breathing on me when I graduated from that sissy school, so I joined the Navy to keep out of the Army. Well, not really. Mother said she could get it fixed so I wouldn't be drafted. I wanted to serve though. I wanted to go *anywhere*! I knew what my Father had planned for me in my life. I didn't want that, but you don't tell my kind of people no.

"I finished Radioman School and received orders to *Mount*

McKinley. I was pretty impressed and tickled when an instructor told me she was a command ship with a lot of history and that General MacArthur embarked in her during the Inchon landing in the Korean War.

"I caught up with *Mount Mac* in Rhodes, Greece and was assigned to your watch section. I was happy aboard her from the first. I lived on my seaman's pay, so I'd fit in with the guys. My shipmates never learned my Mother put a thousand dollars in my account every quarter! My shipmates nicknamed me 'Gooey' within a week. I'd never had a nickname before. Boy, but I was proud of that. I fit in! Even Gunny, the boss of the Marine Communications Detachment, treated me okay and he was senior to all of us, including you.

"You treated me like all the rest and that was firm, but with respect. I know I caused you grief with the crazy stunts I pulled ashore. The chief chewed your ass every time I did something, but you never once mentioned what the chief said to you. You simply nailed me to the cross for what I had done wrong ashore -- and that was the end of it.

"You stood up for me at Captain's Mast, toe-to-toe with our sundowner captain. And you were only a second class petty officer. Old Barksdale wanted a piece of me really bad. He was thinking court martial. Later, a guy in the personnel office whispered to us that the CO lowered your evaluation marks in leadership and supervisory ability and he did it because you stood up for me. Yeah, the watch section knew, Clay. Probably the entire com-communications department knew. Do you *really* think I'm going to let anybody do you harm. Think again, Clay. Think again!"

"Gooey, how many times do I have to tell you that you owe me **NOTHING** repeat **NOTHING**? You were innocent and I was able to make the captain understand that. That's all that happened and it was my duty to do it. Stop thinking you owe me!"

"I do owe you! Not one single petty officer, chief, or officer would have dared stand up to that mean bastard of a captain. They'd have let him heave me out of the Navy with a bad conduct discharge, for something I didn't even do. You spoke up. That's the way you're made. Now, if you will shut up and stop trying to give me rudder orders, I'll tell you things you *don't* know.

"A guy had a good conversation with Curtis during the long flight to wherever, sort of a one-way conversation. My guy asked the questions. Curtis answered. That sort of conversation.

"Curtis is bad gear -- real bad gear. He's paranoid. He was born mean too, we believe.

"Curtis was kicked out of college, supposedly for causing problems with other students. What he really did was rape a girl. He hurt the girl bad. He beat her while he was raping her. What saved him was an uncle who was a judge. The girl didn't have an uncle judge and she didn't come from a real good family, so she was a victim all the way around. She didn't even get the satisfaction of seeing him sent to the Big House. Curtis still doesn't seem to believe he did anything wrong. He wanted a piece of her and took what he wanted.

"I'm pretty sure you don't know why he hates you so bad and I doubt your wife does either. He's not really hated you for all that long. He disliked you for a very long time, but he didn't hate you. Not until you married his cousin. Then he started hating you. You see, Clay, he's been in love, maybe infatuation is a better word, with her since she was a young girl, first cousin or no first cousin. And he still is!

"I met Perky Patty here in the hospital while you were in Ga-Ga Land. She'd be a Rolls Royce if she were an automobile! She's pure gold! I'm more than rich and one hell of a lot better looking than you, but I never had a girl like her, not after three marriages. I admired and envied you when I was a kid in the Navy and I admire and envy you now. I really do!

"Your opinion of me is important, so I swung by today to clear the air after Gunny told me you was angry about what you thought I had done to Curtis. Well, I have to fly to London and meet some people related to the Queen Bee, so I'd better get underway. Take it easy, Big Guy. Keep a tight lip. I will see you again!"

Gooey turned at the hatch and smiled his movie star smile. "Perky Patty wasn't real friendly when we met, but she warmed up after she discovered I'm not a killer like she seemed to believe. You need to take care of yourself and get off the binnacle list -- or Patty will be steaming with me after she shifts her occupational specialty from wife to widow!"

I dreaded telling Patty that Curtis held a long-standing love for her, but that had to happen. If I didn't she would suspect I was hiding something from her and pester me until I spilled my guts. How she always knew when I tried to hide something from her was a mystery. I knew she was too bright by half, but it seemed something else, like maybe she could read minds.

I was certain Patty would not derive joy from that knowledge and I was correct. She was deeply shocked and dismayed and burst into tears.

"I do not believe that, Clay! Even if I heard it directly from Curtis' mouth, I would not believe it. Curtis treated me terribly all my life. Oh, you would not believe the nasty things he did. Sometimes he struck me and sometimes he tried to touch me. He last physically attacked me when I was sixteen. He dragged me behind the cattle pen fence and attempted to touch me in places no man, except you, ever touched.

"Well, Sir, it was Curtis who screamed that time. And he had reason. I was making a sincere effort to pin him against the fence with a pitchfork when Daddy appeared and put a stop to my efforts. I was the size I am now, but Daddy turned me over his knee and gave me a good, sound spanking when he seen the tine holes in the wood where I had stabbed at Curtis and missed! I was afraid to tell Daddy what Curtis had tried. Daddy would have killed him!

"His evil acts were just that. Evil! None of his actions involved love. I believe he did beat and sexually assault that girl Gooey told you about. No, I refuse to believe he is either infatuated, or in love with me. It is impossible! He was nearly a teen when I was born! I've disliked him all of my life and now,

234

since Jarhead and you, I *hate* him! Do not mention it to me again!"
Patty wailed

"All I know is what Gooey told me, Kitten. He didn't go
into detail about how they extracted information from Curtis.
Curtis is a twisted sort of fellow and might harbor hate-love feelings, particularly since he can't have you, you two being first
cousins. Just take it for what it's worth. Exactly nothing."

"I sincerely believe Curtis is insane, at least to some
degree." Patty grabbed me by the upper left arm and locked her
big, gray eyes with mine. "Clay-honey, I am afraid!"

I doubt Patty was afraid for herself. Her family helped
settle our part of West Virginia, arriving a couple of years after the
first settlers, Henry Clay Berkeley and his wife, Margaret Louise.
Patty had a lot of mountain woman in her. She feared little, if
anything.

CHAPTER EIGHTEEN

UNDERWAY

Doctor Ryan finally released me from the hospital so I could celebrate Christmas at home, but he was not totally satisfied with the way my hip was healing. My shoulder remained stuff, but not painful. I managed to talk him into letting me walk with crutches, but he cautioned me. No, what he did was threaten me! He said I need not worry about getting shot by another person if I fouled up the work he had done -- he would do the shooting himself.

I was not about to walk the passageways of the capitol on crutches, so I missed the briefings provided to freshmen members of congress. Patty found books in the library and cumshawed some information from Bob Criss and set forth mightily in an attempt to improve my knowledge of how congress worked. She actually volunteered for this immense task! I knew as much about congress as a duck-billed platypus knows about operating oil rigs in the North Sea.

Then, Mister Prissy New Englander appeared on my door-step, looking like he had just stepped from his final fitting at a London tailor. Had he sported a bowler hat, he could have walked the streets of The City and not one English banker would have thought him out of place.

"I am Jay Morgan Worthington, Congressman Berkeley. Sir, no one from your organization has contacted me and I must know your intentions." His Boston accent and cultured speech told me there was a sissy university in his past.

"What are you and what do you need to know? Maybe I can give you some assistance."

"I manage legislative affairs for Congressman Burnside. He asked I inform you of his regret for the things he said about you during the campaign. He is deeply appreciative that you did not do the same to him. He said what he did is his fault, but he was led astray by the media. He had no idea you are an honorable man who really does strive to provide straight talk, rather than spin. He, therefore, directed I extend all possible courtesy and assistance and stated he stands ready to assist in any manner. I intend to do that, but I urgently need to meet with the person who will replace me. We must commence turnover!"

"I've not hired anybody, like in not a single person. My doctor has not said if he will let me go to Washington when congress takes up. I might be missing in action, AWOL, even."

The look on Mister Worthington's face would have frozen a snake!

"Hey, I haven't been caulking off totally. I did try to hire my campaign manager to run things, but he said there's not enough money in it to keep him in funds to play the ponies. He's not interested in the power of the position. Power doesn't interest him. Ponies do

"So, Mister Worthington, my line is all payed out and I'm having problems hanging on to the bitter end. I may have to use my wife for a while, which will surely get me a bunch of nasty articles in newspapers. I guess all you can do is brief my wife and me."

"I traveled here thinking you had a staff . . . *someone* with whom I could coordinate. I had no idea of your present status. Sir, you are in terrible position if you intend to assume the office you just gained. You must have a staff!

"My solution is, Sir, you retain the present staff. We are in place and understand the workings of congress, all of government, really. I do believe the majority of the staff would remain, including the woman who runs your office in Big Otter. Please understand I did not come with the intention of applying for a position. I did not even realize one was available."

"I have an *office* in Big Otter?"

"Uh, no, you do not yet have an office in Big Otter. You could probably rent the one Congressman Burnside is vacating, but you will need a competent person to interface with constituents. The aide currently in that position is excellent."

"Well, now . . . Patty! Come in here. Please."

Patty came charging through the hatch. I then realized she had not known Mister Worthington was in the house and probably thought I'd fallen off my crutches. It would not have been the first time the sneaky things tripped me up.

I introduced the two of them, then briefed her on why he was here and what he wanted. Patty extended her hand and laid her broad-toothed smile on him. "Welcome to Berkeley's Knob, Mister Worthington. Was your trip satisfactory."

"The flight was satisfactory, Madam, but the drive from the airport was . . . well, it was terrible. Your roads are far too narrow and much too crooked. They frightened me.

"Wild, Wonderful, West Virginia may or may not be wonderful, but it certainly is wild. I actually saw a *bear* not distance from the highway. That started me worrying about mechanical failure. You may rest assured I would not have left the automobile to investigate the problem, not with a bear prowling about. I would have suffered exposure until a passing local assisted me!

"I do not wish to offend you, but you will learn, if we continue to associate, that I speak my mind. Always."

"Speaking one's mind is an excellent attribute, Mister Worthington. My husband is the same. Our roads *are* poor. Clay maintains the settlers who built the roads did not survey them.

They simply charted the path of a drunken blacksnake through the mountains!

"Black bears are not often harmful to humans unless they are with cubs or cornered. Our only really dangerous animal is the mountain lion. They have a reputation of being unstable and are known to attack people, although this has not happened in years, so far as I am aware.

"I have a question. Why would you, who supported a democrat, shift allegiance to a republican?"

"Congressional staff generally care little for whom they work. Yes, most belong to the same party as their employer, particularly the lower ranking aides who are most often appointed from among family." he explained, then actually made a joke! "I sometimes think congress exists solely to provide employment to unsavory relatives!

"There a number of persons, such as myself, whose profession is legislative affairs. We exist in both houses of congress and in the White House and other governing bodies. A particular political party is not generally a consideration. Some aides register as an independent, rather than by party affiliation.

"In answer to the other part of your question . . . I carefully followed your campaign, particularly when I realized you could very well win. I then submitted resumes, for which I received excellent responses. I am well known in the capitol and elsewhere in Washington. I invite you to inquire of this to your campaign manager. I have worked with Robert Criss on more than one occasion. He will speak highly of me.

"I did not consider retaining my position because I did not realize it would be available until now when I learned you are totally without assistance. I enjoy . . . no, I seek difficult tasks. Association with you would certainly be that. Mister and Missus Berkeley, I am applying to retain the position I now hold."

Patty disappeared while I continued talking to Mister Worthington, who remained stiff as a railroad tie. This appeared his normal demeanor. He sort of shuddered when I asked if he would like to sample West Virginia's stump juice, but seemed quite pleased when I offered a snifter of my nearly depleted supply of Spanish brandy. I suspect he would have fainted had I offered him a bottle of regular American beer. This was not a suds man! I could hardly wait to turn the barflies loose on him -- if we hired him.

Patty came bouncing back into the library and laid a warm, dazzling smile on Mister Worthington, then topped off his brandy. I suspected what she had done and stood by.

"Clay-honey, I just spoke with Mister Criss who stated he has known Mister Worthington for several years and would hire him in 'the blink of a frog's eye.' Bob said he is probably the most experienced legislative aide in Washington." Patty then run open for a good ten minutes concerning the stellar qualifications of Mister Worthington, who looked a mite dazed when she finished. Patty was big on using a lot of words.

"I have noticed something strange, Clay. Bob's speech was rather dull when he arrived in West Virginia, but he now speaks like a native, Why is that, dearest?"

"West Virginia has rubbed off on him, Kitten. He is now competent in Spoken Hillbilly." Bob had not returned to Washington after the election, so I suspected something else had rubbed of on him . . . a retired WAC, vintage Korean War!

Patty fed Mister Worthington a fine supper of meat loaf baked with boiled eggs inside, creamed onions, mashed potatoes with homemade gravy and her usual dozen or so side dishes of vegetables and relishes. She topped that off with blackberry pie covered with thick, fresh cream, which Mister Worthington tasted very carefully before devouring it. Patty picked up on his action and set a second even larger slice in front of him. He did not refuse.

"Congressman Berkeley, I am in dire need of assistance." he said, after we three were again seated in front of the library fireplace with his second snifter of brandy.

Uh, Oh, here it comes.

"Lay it on me, Mister Worthington, but call me Clay."

"This is a very large house, very old, very odd, yet very comfortable. There appears to be considerable land surrounding the house, many acres, I would surmise. You have employees, do you not?"

"Sort of. More like family than hired help. One is a lady who comes twice a week to help Patty. She is not a maid. She helped my mother with the housework after I was born and she kept house for me before I married. We have a farm manager who was here before I was born. He has three, sometimes four, hired hands. One of the three is newly hired and isn't much to brag about just yet, but he needed work and he fills the billet. Is there a reason for you asking?"

"Yes, there is. I do not intend to drive that terrible, wild animal infested road to the airport. Would you be so kind as to have one of your employees drive me there?"

I mustered in at the hospital the last Thursday of the year like a good, little boy, for my weekly check-up. Doctor Ryan did his usual doctor-type poking and prodding before telling me I could likely start walking without crutches in two-three weeks.

He was not impressed when I informed him the State of the Nation was in jeopardy if I failed to attend the opening session of congress. He informed me if I went to Washington before he gave permission it would not be safe to return to Big Otter. After chewing on me for wanting to cruise around without crutches, he smiled and said my wife and I could probably resume 'Marital Congress' without pain or injury to my hip. That was certainly fine with me, but he was way late. Patty and I had already managed that quite well. Patty was hard in the right places, soft in the right places -- and limber in the right places.

Still on the binnacle list and forbidden to leave Big Otter under penalty of death presented a problem. Someone had to find us a place to live in Washington. That someone turned out to be

Patty who had never rented or purchased a house, or been to Washington, except for her high school graduation trip. I sent her off into the Wilds of Washington, fearing she would not be able to successfully accomplish her mission. I should have known that concern was in error.

Patty came steaming through the hatch, brushing snow from her collar and shoulders, grinning like a possum in a poke berry patch. She hugged and kissed me, then flopped down in a chair that would have held two people her size and extended her feet to the fireplace.

"Oh, that feels so good! It is cold outside. Washington was equally cold, but not nearly so snowy and windy. Clay-honey, a beer would go nicely. Please."

It was not a problem to reach the small reefer from my arm chair and get us a beer, so I did. Patty took a healthy swallow and thumped the beer down on the end table. "You will probably receive a call from that fool you and Daddy call a lawyer, if he has not already telephoned!"

I requested elaboration of that statement.

"I took option on a house. A nice house too. Mister Worthington found it. It belongs to a senator who lost his re-election bid. It is located in Virginia, but well within driving distance of the capitol. It is in a safe neighborhood and has a large, fenced yard for Joe-Joe and our animals. It cost only four hundred and ninety thousand dollars."

Patty extended a rather harsh look when I spewed beer all over the front of the fireplace, causing the fire to sputter. "Well I did! And it is quite a good deal too. Listen.

"Mister Worthington explained a tax advantage of which I was not aware. If I knew of it, I never gave it thought even though I prepared Daddy's taxes since I was fifteen. I had no reason to investigate it. Daddy owes no money on real estate. Oh, it is such a good deal!

"We borrow the money from a bank here, or in

Washington, probably here, since we have a hefty deposit in our bank. We then make payments and sell the house at a good profit in two years, or whenever we relocate back to West Virginia.

"Don't look so mean, Clay! Mister Worthington knows about such things and assured me the house has increased in price since the senator purchased it. Mister Worthington, the real estate agent and a banker with whom I spoke expects the house to again increase several thousand dollars within the next two years. The banker is eager to finance the house if we decide not to finance it with our bank.

"Clay-dearest, there are advantages to buying this house. One is we will almost certainly make a profit when we sell. Two is that the first seven years of house payments are almost totally consumed by interest, which we can write off from our income taxes! The income tax refund will nearly equal the house payments for the first seven years. Yes, we have sufficient money to purchase the house outright, without a loan, but we would get no tax refund."

I was doing a complete inventory of my sea bag when she gave me a quizzical look and asked, "Dearest, how many years has it been since you *really* inspected your financial situation, particularly the taxes you have been paying, other than on your Navy salary. Your business taxes, I mean?"

"Uh . . . would you believe like, maybe, never?"

"Bugger the bosun! How did you *ever* survive without me? Really, Clay!

"To be fair, I accept partial blame because I did not follow through on managing our finances as I told you I would. I told you that one night in Santa Cruz when you explained, somewhat, our holdings and our financial condition. I did not follow through. I was too interested in chasing you around the Mediterranean and paid little attention to the documents Mister Pollard sent us. You obviously did not do so either, but then you would not recognize a balance sheet or a lengthy tax form if you found one in your pocket. We are both fools!"

"Uh, why so, honey?"

"That *stupid* lawyer we have is 'why so.' And Daddy has the same idiot! Clay, he has not properly computed your business taxes for at least six years -- probably a lot longer. Really! It appears he simply copied the figures from year to year, adjusted them slightly and submitted them to IRS.

"I am certain Mister Pollard kept careful records of expenditures and losses because he and I briefly reviewed his running books before we left for Spain. He was very good at explaining them too. I believe every penny expended and every profit and every loss is recorded in his records. I suspect the lawyer did nothing with those figures. The ones he submitted are totally incorrect!

Great John Paul Jones! Save all sailors at sea!

"How many thousands of dollars do we owe?"

"Nothing! And that is what we will recoup. Nothing!"

"Patty, I'm not going to light your boiler by saying I'm stupid, but I don't understand."

"Clay, listen. You lived on your Navy salary while single and we have lived on that amount since we married, except for the few weeks when I had a salary too. That was what we filed as our joint return. I prepared those returns since we married and those returns are correct.

"The taxes on our property and the profit we derived from said property are filed differently. They are filed as a privately owned company.-- Berkeley's Knob Farms, just as your grandfather set it up. The lawyer computed and submitted all the required tax documents for Berkeley's Knob Farms and those are the faulty ones.

"He understands little about taxes, or is so lazy he gun-decked the documents. You overpaid your taxes because of his actions. I have no idea of the amount, but it is a lot!"

I was concerned about what Patty was telling me, but it tickled me to hear her use the nautical term, 'gundecked,' for falsifying a document, or covering something up. Her use of that term, for the first time so far as I remembered, was yet more proof that I had corrupted her in more ways than one in only six years.

"You could file amended returns. For how many years I do not know, but that would certainly get attention of IRS. I intend to investigate this. We do not want to get into trouble and maybe heavily fined.

"Clay, your legal documents are in my car. Boxes of them. I fired the lawyer!"

That statement caused a ship-wide inventory of all my storerooms.

"OK, Patty, you fired our lawyer, he stays fired. How did you learn all this?"

"I suspected you would faint when I told you the price of the house, so I stopped by the lawyer's office to determine if it is feasible to buy the house for Berkeley's Knob Farms, rather than buying it ourselves . . . and would doing so also be a tax advantage. It appears it would not.

"Anyway, I needed to review recent tax documents to obtain a baseline income level to present to the bank. All I knew much about was your Navy retainer and what I remembered from the day books when I went over them with Mister Pollard. I had no idea at all of the total income from our farms, interest earnings and coal and gas royalties and the like.

"The lawyer acted as if he did not understand what I wanted and got somewhat huffy, so I demanded he give me the past returns, thinking I could figure it myself. That was when I noticed the figures from year to year were the same, or nearly the same. I then started reviewing the returns since we married and found he did not compute any of the losses that I could recall, such as the three cows killed by lightening year before last and the stand of timber that burned the year after we went to Spain. The cost of the fence around the Sycamore Run farm was not listed as a business expense and neither was the John Deere tractor we purchased two years ago. There must be dozens of other losses I do not remember that were not reported. His idea of depreciation on our farm equipment is a joke too.

"Clay, I found no major difference in the reported figures for the past six years. What he did was deliberate! The figures could not possibly be that close year to year.

"I will see an accountant tomorrow and instruct him to audit the entire estate from the time your parent's will was probated until now. Lord knows what he will find! Please think about this while I shower and change my clothing.

I had barely absorbed any of the tax cluster-seduction when Patty returned to the library carrying a stack of pamphlets and brochures. "We need a new automobile, Clay-dearest. Rather, we need new transportation."

"If you want it, get it. Buy it for the farm so we can write it off on taxes like you just told me, Smarty Pants."

"Yes, I believe we can write it off and we should. What would you like?"

"I've got Dad's old Power Wagon. That's all I need."

"You intend to drive that ancient truck around Washington? As a congressman? Really?"

"You've seen the traffic on the Beltway. I'd drive a Sherman tank if I had one!"

"Once again our thoughts coincide! That is precisely the reason I do not want to take the Lynx. It is too frail what with so many accidents in the Washington area. The specifications of various vehicles are contained in these brochures, but what I would like is a crew cab, Ford F-250 pick-up, with four-wheel drive and wide, heavy, lug tires!"

"Uh, You don't want a monster truck. Why not a Cadillac, Lincoln, or another big car"

"Large cars are little stronger than my Lynx. Clay, they no longer manufacture sturdy vehicles such as the Power Wagon and

Daddy's 1958 Ford pick-up. Either of those vehicles would damage a train. I want a big truck. I want one of those tough F-250's!"

"Kitten, I don't care what you buy, but you have to get something where you can reach the foot controls and still see out of the windshield. That means you have to get a small vehicle, or one that adjusts the seats, the steering wheel and so forth."

"Oh, really, Clay! I can drive anything! I've operated tractors and a small bulldozer and lots of farm machinery when I was growing up. I drove Daddy's International cattle truck all over. I once drove it from Elkins Stockyard with a load of calves. It has a manual clutch and a floor gear shift and, I believe, ten forward gears, counting bulldog. No, maybe it has fourteen forward gears -- I just can't remember. That truck is huge. It has a twenty-four foot bed!"

We departed Berkeley's Knob en route Northern Virginia on a cold, snowy February morning. We comprised a small convoy on US 50 East with Patty leading in her new, red F-250. I rode shotgun in the seat beside her with my gimpy leg cocked to the door side. Mister Pollard and our newest farm hand, Ben Niles, followed in my Power Wagon, towing a farm pick-up they would use to return home. Joe-Joe, Jarhead and Blue Suit would follow when we were settled.

My sweet, super-intelligent, pixie wife laid another Patty Lane shocker on me just as we crossed Cheat River.

"Clay-dearest, I do not believe we will like living in Washington and we will certainly miss West Virginia. Washington appears a nasty city! I have studied the means whereby one obtains nomination for governor of West Virginia. Listen . . ."

The End

ABOUT THE AUTHOR

. Author was raised on a hillside farm in West Virginia. He had his first paid job at the age of seven, riding ancient horses engaged in pulling hay shocks from meadow to stacking point He worked on his parents' farm and for neighbors until he enlisted in the Navy at seventeen.

He was double-hatted in his last Navy billet as Command Master Chief of the United States Sixth Fleet and Assistant Communications Readiness Officer. He shipped as Radio Electronics Officer in the United States Merchant Marine after retiring from the Navy.

He is married to the former Agueda Caceres Perez of Madrid, Spain.

www.ingramcontent.com/pod-product-compliance
Lightning Source LLC
Chambersburg PA
CBHW071130200626
46817CB00018B/2606

* 9 780692 262160 *